Fate of the Stolen

TJ RITOSSA

Fulton Books, Inc.
Meadville, PA

Published by Fulton Books 2021

ISBN 978-1-63710-344-9 (paperback)
ISBN 978-1-63710-345-6 (digital)

Printed in the United States of America

Chapter 1

As the rain fell from the sky and pelted the ground in anger, James thought to himself, this was the kind of night that he should be by the fire with a beer in his hand, not outside with a crying baby. He looked down at the baby he was holding and tried not to feel the warmth that came from something living, a human being. He knew what he had to do. It really did not matter if he wanted to or not. He did not have the choice of disobeying the boss's orders. If he did disobey, then he would die. It was that simple. He would probably be shot in both legs and left outside for the wolves or bears to finish him up. Damn, he hated wolves. He shuddered even thinking about the big gray wolves that he had seen coming dangerously close to the cabin. Their black eyes staring into the dark, waiting for the right moment to make their move and try to steal the food or even an attempt at surrounding an unsuspecting guard. This was not the way he wanted to die.

He pulled out his gun, just in case he saw a flicker of movement, a big animal with hungry eyes coming toward him. The baby was screaming full force now, loud enough to wake the dead. He stole a quick glance at this tiny baby. That was a mistake. The guilt came flooding back when he saw a light little tuft of blond hair and large blue eyes attached to this little body that couldn't weigh more than the boot he was wearing. He started running faster. The sooner he did this job, the better. After all, it was just a baby. Not even really a baby yet, not even an hour old. She didn't even know what life was. She would soon be dead, and then she wouldn't be cold and hungry anymore.

There, James thought to himself, *I am doing this baby girl a favor, ending her suffering.*

He felt much better now about the whole thing. His big burly hand went up to his unshaven face, and he wiped the raindrops off his wet forehead. He ran up the side of the mountain to the entrance of the cave he had passed the other day when he was gathering wood for the fire. This storm was something else! The wind was picking up, howling like a pack of wolves. Was it the wind or the wolves he was hearing? He shivered more from fear than from the cold raindrops soaking him to the bone. He grabbed a bunch of leaves with his free hand and placed the crying baby on top of them. There was nothing else he could do for this baby now. This was out of his hands. If God wanted this baby alive, then the baby would live.

James chuckled to himself. He wasn't actually killing this baby. He was just laying the baby down in the woods. James crinkled up his nose. Who was he trying to kid. This little bundle of joy was a goner. The baby was as good as dead. Not even a tiny bone from her body will be left to find in a few days. The animals will feast on this soft, helpless morsel. So actually, he told himself that he was helping the animals that lived up here in the Colorado mountains. Hell, they needed to eat too. James thought to himself that he really was a caring guy, more or less.

He heard noises to the left in the bushes. He looked over quickly. He really didn't want to know if there was an animal there or not. Lightning lit up the sky above, and the thunder sounded like it was very close. Too close for comfort. James hated being outside in the woods at night. Especially up here by the mountains. So he took that as a sign from above and started to run back to the warmth and safety of the cabin. As he ran down the flooded dirt path, he glanced back at the face of the cave where he left the baby; he thought he saw something at the entrance of the cave, something big. Lightning lit up the sky like fireworks. James stopped in his tracks for a brief second. Did he see something big come out of the trees? He wiped his eyes. Was his mind playing tricks on him? It was probably a branch that fell from the nearby tree; after all, it was starting to storm fiercely, and the wind was howling. A small twinge of guilt ran through his mind again, but he pushed it out as quick as it came. After all, the baby had stopped crying, which meant the baby was already gone, probably a small evening snack for the pack of wolves that lived up in this Colorado forest. Nothing he could do now. He had done his job and now deserved the reward waiting back for him at the cabin. His mind drifted to the new redhead that they had just brought in today. That young, curvy body, probably not even seventeen years old! She had big green eyes that told of her innocence. He ran full speed ahead with an evil smile lighting up his bearded face. The baby girl completely erased from his thoughts.

The rain and cold assaulted the newborn baby as she lay on the leaves in front of the cave. The baby's crying echoed through the Colorado forest. As the moon escaped from under a cloud, the area in front of the cave showed rapid movement. A pack of gray wolves came out of the wooded area to investigate the loud, wailing noise. They had picked up this new scent and were curious enough to come out in the pelting rain to investigate. As the female wolf leaned over the moving, tiny baby, she instantly felt a connection with this helpless creature. The baby lifted her little hand to hold on to the wolf. The wolf could smell the birth scent still lingering on this little being. Her motherly instincts were kicking in. She had just given birth to a litter of four pups last week. She put her wet nose down to pick up the scent of the baby again and started to pull the leaf pile into the cave, knowing the baby would not survive long in the cold and rain. As soon as the baby was inside the cave, the female wolf wrapped her warm body around the little alien critter. The baby stopped crying when she felt the warm, comfortable fur form around her tiny frame wrapping her up like a big fluffy blanket. She instantly closed her eyes and laid her tiny hand on the back of the wolf. The female wolf looked up at the rest of the pack and made it clear that this little hairless animal was now part of the family. The wolf pups snuggled in close to drink milk, taking advantage of their momma laying down. Even though the noise was foreign coming from this little animal, they all felt the connection with her. The need to protect her overcame them all. The wolf pack settled inside the cave for the night, keeping their eyes on the tiny new addition to their pack.

As James walked quickly down the trail and into the warmth of the cabin, he glanced like he always did at the two guards at the front of the door. He gave them a nod. They were out here in the middle of the forest, miles from any civilization and off the beaten trails, but you could never be too careful. The last thing they needed was the police getting suspicious and blowing their cover. The cabin was quiet for the most part, but he could hear a few of the guys playing poker in the other room by the fire. As tempting as it was to pass through and try to win some money, he had a bigger goal. He was, after all, the right-hand man.

Niko had brought him into this business five years ago. He remembered the exact day that Niko called him and asked him how he felt about making over five hundred thousand a year. He was curious but reluctant. James and Niko had done a few other jobs together, and most of them were involving guns and drugs. Smuggling. Niko was a smart businessman. He had the brains and the ability to find jobs that would bring in a lot of money. Niko was one bad dude. The kind of guy you want on your side, not against you. From the stories he had heard, there were not too many guys left alive that had crossed Niko. Niko had the uncanny ability to stay out of jail. James had been lucky so far; he had a few close calls but no jail time.

He remembered the quick second he was going to tell Niko that he wasn't interested, but shit, that was a good amount of money! And money made his life so much easier. So James told Niko to talk. Niko went on to say that it was human trafficking. That was surprising, even to James. James had heard about more operations popping up, but he wasn't crazy about kidnapping. Niko said that this market he was interested in was growing quickly. Especially the market for young girls. This need of young girls was a billion-dollar market, and he was not going to miss out. James remembered how Niko sat him down and told him his plan, grabbing the girls without getting caught, how to find the right victim and how they sell them off to the highest bidder. He told him that there was a network, a system, They looked for girls that were not supervised or girls that took the same path home every day. Or runaways were an easy mark. But Niko did not prefer runaways.

The market that Niko was working in would cater to men that were willing to pay big bucks for girls that were not drug users or prostitutes. There was a need for a certain type. They wanted them young, sometimes even as young as twelve or thirteen. Most of all they wanted them innocent. Niko did not like to grab girls that were really young if he did not have to. He tried not to let his disgust for these rich men affect the business relationship with them. He would kidnap the very young girls, or sometimes boys, only if there was an elite client that requested it. But the amount of pay would be double any ordinary sale. The clients that they were dealing with wanted girls that were pretty and innocent. As James thought back to that conversation, he started to get excited thinking about the first time he did a job for Niko in this operation. He grabbed the teenage girl with the long blond hair and icy-blue eyes. This particular girl, Jesse, had walked this street on her way home almost every day. Niko had seen her one day and had James stalk her for weeks. He remembered the thrill he felt when his van pulled up to the quiet street. She came right up to the van when he asked her if she had seen a little white poodle that belonged to his kids. He showed her a picture as he opened the door and stepped out. She looked at the picture of the little fluff ball and told him she had not seen any dog on her way home. She had smiled and commented that the puppy was so cute! James didn't hesitate one second, taking advantage of her distraction with the picture. She couldn't have weighed more than one hundred pounds when he lifted her up and threw her in the van. The screams and the crying lasted about two seconds before he tied her up and forced the needle in her arm. She was out in the blink of an eye. James had never felt a rush like that. This beautiful, innocent girl was at his mercy. He had felt so powerful! That feeling of power was what kept him in this business for so long. He had the power over this girl's life. It was almost as if he could feel the energy surge through his veins, like a drug. There was nothing like it.

"Hey, Niko!" James yelled as he walked up the stairs, wiping those thoughts away reluctantly. "Where the hell are you?" Niko appeared out of one of the locked doors, looking agitated as he asked James about the baby. "I took care of the baby," replied James. "She is probably sitting in the stomach of a family of gray wolves that I saw up there earlier."

Niko noticed the small smile that appeared on James's face as he reported the outcome of that poor baby. He knew James was a tough guy all around, but his only worry with hiring him in this business was how he seemed to enjoy the job of taking these girls and bringing them here, to their base camp. Enjoyed it way too much. Niko did not enjoy kidnapping these young girls and uprooting their whole lives. Turning these young and beautiful girls into sex slaves for these overly rich men that were usually equally overweight and assholes. Niko did it for the money. He was a businessman. He saw a need, and he fulfilled that need and got paid a pretty penny for doing it quickly and without getting caught. He had made a name for himself because he was smart and levelheaded. James was not levelheaded. He would have to keep an eye on him so he didn't mess up this nice little business he had going on here. His thoughts quickly disappeared as he heard the girl Jesse crying again. He remembered why he was so agitated.

Jesse, the girl they picked up in California, was a stunner! A tiny blonde fireball! They had watched her for about two weeks, the way she walked to class and her habits. Niko thought about the day he and James grabbed her. He knew right away she would make them double the amount of money of most of the other girls. She was a little older, maybe eighteen, but she looked about fifteen. Her long blond hair and her very trim figure, with beautiful blue eyes and a perfect smile. Yes! She was definitely worth the two weeks they spent on her. Niko liked to take trips to other states and see if there were any good prospects. It kept the law enforcement guessing. This girl was definitely a great find. And the fight she put up. She had spunk! James loved the fight, but Niko did not. Niko preferred getting the job done with no issues.

There were no problems bringing Jesse into Colorado, but the issues showed up soon after. She was a smart one. She knew right away when James came out of the van when he had asked if she saw a lost dog that something wasn't right. She had smiled and looked at the picture but then had caught on quickly. She saw the inside of the van and instantly tried to run to her car, but she was about two seconds too slow. James grabbed her, and she had tried to bite him and kick him, making James curse out loud. But in the end, he himself had been ready in the van with the shot of Propofol, which he administered as soon as James had thrown her in the back, picking her up in one big move.

His thoughts turned to the night they brought her in the cabin. That was about six months ago. He wanted to give her a day before getting her all pretty and cleaned up and taking the pictures they needed to put her on the sale page. He remembered thinking how he was going to market this one only to his best customers. He was practically drooling with the thought of the money she would make them. She was beyond beautiful! He even let himself fantasize for a moment that maybe he could be the one to break her in. He was tempted, but he did not want to get in the habit of using the girls he brought in. That was a bad business practice. And that went double for James. The market was for innocent girls, or at least mostly innocent. I mean, you could never be sure about any of these girls in this day and age. But either way, a girl that has that kind of fighting spirit is a special find for his customers. Some of them loved the added excitement of a little resistance and breaking the girls in. It would be sad that Jesse's spirit would be gone forever once she was sold. It would be broken soon after she was bought. It always was. But that was the name of this game, and Niko knew he had earned himself a very reputable spot in the trafficking world. He wasn't necessarily happy about breaking up families, or about ruining the life of some young girl, but hey, bad things happen every day in every part of this world. If he hadn't jumped into this type of business, then someone else surely would have. Why shouldn't he at least make some very good money off it?

The crying was louder now coming from Jesse, pulling him right out of his thoughts about what a find she was. Yeah, some find, that was until he brought her back to the cabin and she told him she was ten weeks pregnant. He did not believe a word she said. She was lying to try to gain pity for herself and possibly her freedom. He did not believe her until about three days later when she started to throw up every morning. What a mess! He sent one of his guys over to the local store, which was about fifty miles away, to buy a pregnancy test. The damn test came out positive. His fury started to rise again just like it did that day he found out. He slapped her across the face and told her she was no use to him now that he would have to kill her. She begged for her life and the life of her unborn baby. The look of pure fear on Jesse's face when James pulled out his knife and wanted to cut the baby out right there and be done with it.

Niko had stopped him, and after much thought, he decided to let her keep the baby, for now. She was still worth a lot of money to him, and if she could regain her shape after the baby was born, he would still make loads of cash from selling her. Maybe he would even sell the baby, he had thought. But he had decided against that, too much trouble dealing with a baby. This whole plan was going to be risky. He could not risk bringing her anywhere for an abortion. They usually did not hold on to a girl any longer than necessary, at the most a month. Keeping a girl captive was just too risky. Too risky and too much trouble. Niko was taking a huge chance on keeping this little blonde beauty here through her pregnancy, but he had a feeling it would pay off in the end. He could use the baby to help keep her in line. She would listen to him and not cause any trouble if she thought that her baby would be safe in the end. So they kept her in her room and made sure she had good food and some exercise. Jesse was off limits to everyone but Niko and James. And even James was kept out of the room most of the time because he scared Jesse.

Niko grabbed James and pulled him into the room where Jesse was kept. She was curled up in a ball and crying her eyes out. She looked pale and tiny, even more so now since she had just delivered a baby a few hours ago. Jesse looked up at them with her big blue eyes, and in a voice that was barely audible, she said, "Where is my baby girl? Please bring her to me, I promise I will do whatever you want if you just let me hold her!" She struggled to stand up, but Niko pushed her back down.

"Listen, girl, you need to rest and gain your strength back! You are not going to be any good to me looking the way you do now, forget about your baby!"

Jesse became hysterical with those words.

Niko backed up a few steps and knelt down by her, and in a strangely sweet voice, he said, "Listen, Jesse, we found your baby a good home. She is headed to a nice warm house with new parents that will take care of her and love her."

James stared at Niko like he was crazy, and when he opened his mouth to start to say something, Niko gave him a warning look that James knew he couldn't ignore, so he shut his mouth abruptly. Niko looked at Jesse, and he could tell that his lies had the effect he was hoping for. She was crying less, and she looked a little happier, more relaxed. Niko patted Jesse's head like she was a toddler and walked out the door, motioning for James to follow. As he looked back, he smiled at Jesse and said good night.

Jesse looked at Niko as he walked out with James. As the door slammed shut, she stood and walked weakly over to the bed. She looked down at the blood that had dropped on the blanket from her birth. Her birth to her beautiful little girl. She wiped her tears away and replaced them with a look of determination. Jesse knew what her future held and knew it was no place for a baby. She allowed herself one last memory of her sweet baby girl. The tiny hand that had reached out to touch her face before James had grabbed the baby and wrapped it in a blanket and stormed out the door. She had thought that they were going to kill the baby. Her baby! Her sweet little girl with a tuft of blond hair and big blue eyes. Her baby girl would never know her, but she would always be her mother. No matter what.

Jesse made a vow to herself and to God that she would escape no matter how long it took, and when she did, she would find her baby girl and explain everything to her. She would love her and be a good mom to her. Jesse started to close her eyes. She was exhausted. She felt happy. At least her baby was safe, that was the most important thing. Jesse knew she was a fighter, and she would fight. She would not stop until they were all dead, every last one of these monsters. Right now the important thing was that she gets her strength back. She drank the milk and ate the food that Niko had brought in for her. Part of her wanted to just waste away here and disappear, but the other part wanted to fight and escape. The last thought before she fell asleep was how she would find James and Niko and kill them both for the way that they ripped apart her life and took her baby from her. One day it would happen; she just needed to be patient. Be patient and play the game.

Chapter 2

Three years later

Alysse woke early, like she always did. She needed her alone time, just an hour or so by herself to get her mind and body ready for the adventure of living another day. She pulled her long fingers through her curly red hair and poured herself a cup of coffee, deciding on drinking it black today. She was feeling a little more tired than usual. She glanced in the mirror as she walked by. She stopped and stared. She did not recognize the face that stared back at her through the glass. She looked as pale as a ghost, and her little splashes of freckles seemed to jump out of her skin.

Coffee cup in hand, she quietly walked out on the balcony and took in the sight that was laid out before her. She took a deep breath of the fresh mountain air. Instantly she felt some of the weight lifted off her. Colorado was beautiful! Looking out from her balcony, she saw endless trees. Not just any trees, big beautiful trees that went on forever and ever. The trees in Colorado were the kind of trees that you dreamed about camping under on a moonlit night, she thought. The kind of trees that were teeming with all kinds of wildlife! This forest was the kind of place that fairy tales came true in!

Alysse took another exaggerated breath of fresh air. She had never seen anything so beautiful. And then you look beyond the forest and see the mountains. The mountains were breathtaking! So majestic sitting there like they were protecting the trees and everything that lived inside of the vast forest. The peaks of the mountains dusted with white. She took another deep breath and felt more alive than she had in a long time. This fresh mountain air was filling her soul.

Giving her hope. Alysse set down her coffee cup and stretched her arms out. It was amazing how a change of scenery could make your life worth living again. Alysse knew it wasn't the change of scenery that was slowly pulling her soul back to life; it was Michael. Michael was her rock. Her reason for trying to live. Michael had been right to force her to come on this little trip. And he did force her, practically dragging her through the airport. Making her leave her bed, the bed that had been her life for the last few months. But he had been right. Michael was always right. Of course, she would never tell him that! His ego was already crowding them out of their home back in Ohio. She smiled at the thought of him, and she realized that slowly, very slowly, she was smiling a little bit more every day.

She let herself think back on the last five years. She had married Michael almost six years ago today. It had definitely been love at first sight! Remembering how he had asked her out on their first date, and then it was history from there. They had decided to marry within the year. Foregoing a huge wedding so that they could be husband and wife as quickly as possible. Alysse thought back on their wedding vows: for better or for worse. It had been the best year of her life, and then it had quickly become the worst years of her life. They didn't think about having a baby during the first year. They were enjoying the married bliss! The honeymoon year was great, so great, in fact, that the memories brought that smile back to her face.

Michael was her person; she knew it from the moment she met him. He looked exactly the same now as he did back then. His tall athletic frame, with just enough muscles to make her heart beat a little faster each time he would take off his shirt. He had that clean, good-looking charm about him. He was so easy to talk to. They would have long conversations curled up in the hammock in the backyard of their house. They both knew that they were meant to be together. After the first year, they had decided that they couldn't wait to start a family. Michael wanted three sons, but she had reminded him that they would try until she had her daughter, even if they had to have a very large family. Alysse had always dreamed of a little red-haired baby that she could dress up in little flowery dresses and little matching hair bows! A little curly haired beauty that would grow up being loved every day of her life. Alysse remembered how she couldn't wait to be a mother. And she also couldn't wait to see Michael as a father. There had been no doubt in her mind that he would be a wonderful father.

That year they had tried almost every night but not really thinking about the outcome. Just enjoying their lovemaking. After nine months, Alysse had started to get moody and stressed around the time of her period, and she started praying every day that her period would not come. But it always did. And when it did, it would put her in a depression for the whole week. She would sulk and feel sorry for herself. She remembered thinking that it should not be this hard to get pregnant. They were both young and healthy, so why? Why? Halfway through the second year of trying to get pregnant, Alysse had been an emotional mess. Her only focus in life had been getting pregnant. She had bought every book there was on conceiving and tried every position and every ritual. Anything that might give them a baby. She didn't even see what this was doing to Michael. She was so self-absorbed in the whole process. Even Michael did not want to try anymore because of the pain he saw Alysse going through every month when the pregnancy test had turned out to be negative. Michael had tried to be the positive one, and he kept assuring Alysse that it would happen. They would have a baby. But it never did happen.

About the third year of trying, they had decided to start testing and see if there was a problem with either of them. Alysse remembered the day they had started the testing. She hadn't been able to eat or sleep. Her voice had been a whisper when she answered the doctor's questions to the best of her ability. The testing did not turn up anything that would keep them from conceiving a child, the doctor had said. He had told them that they were trying too hard, which was causing undue stress. The doctor had mentioned that stress could be the reason they were not having any luck. And he told them that stress was their enemy if they wanted to try and have a child. He told them to relax and just enjoy married life and not worry about making a baby.

Alysse remembers how she had broken down in tears, not knowing if they were tears of happiness or sadness. There wasn't a medical reason, so why couldn't they conceive? They would have to keep trying, and at the time she did not know if she could handle the upcoming months of finding out that a pregnancy did not occur again. The disappointment of knowing that her body was not growing a new life inside. Her only thought had been that her body was a wasteland; nothing could grow in it. Then one month later, everything changed.

It was April. Alysse remembers the day like she was living it at this moment. She had woken up feeling somehow different. Her stomach had been queasy, and she had no energy. At first her mind wouldn't let her think it could be a baby. Did she have the flu? Or was she finally pregnant? Her excitement had been overwhelming. Alysse recalled how she called Michael right away and told him the good news, but he had sounded so sad and exhausted. He didn't believe it could be a possibility. He had told her to just relax and wait for him to come home before taking the pregnancy test. Alysse knew he had been worried that the negative test would push her over the edge. Michael had known she was too fragile. And Michael had been right. She had been fragile.

Knowing that she had not been herself for a long time, they had not been the couple that they had been when they were married. It had only been a year, and all their joy and happiness had disappeared, replaced by lost hope and depression. Alysse had taken a deep breath and told Michael that she would wait. But that hadn't happened. she didn't wait. Within the hour, she had taken the test. She had left it sitting on the bathroom counter. Slowly she had walked into the bathroom but then walked back out. She remembers how she had spent the whole day walking in and out of the bathroom. She did that twenty times throughout the day.

By the time Michael had come home from work that day, Alysse was just sitting on the chair in the living room with her arms wrapped around herself, looking pale and exhausted. She was slowly rocking back and forth. Michael had naturally assumed the worse, that the test had been negative. He ran over and hugged her. Alysse had lifted her head and looked at Michael. Her eyes that used to sparkle with life now looked worn and void of everything but sadness. Standing up, she had taken his hand and slowly walked into the bathroom with him by her side. She remembers how she had pointed to the test sitting there on the countertop and had motioned for Michael to look at the result, because she just couldn't bear seeing the answer.

Alysse remembers it as if it were yesterday. Michael had picked up the pregnancy test and stared at it for what seemed like hours. All of a sudden, he ran over to her and picked her up and swung her around screaming, "We are pregnant!" At first Alysse had thought that he was reading it wrong, so she had grabbed it from his hands and started crying. After all this time, they were pregnant! They were pregnant! For the next two months Alysse had felt like she was walking on clouds. She had never been happier. They had never been happier. They finally were starting their family. The family that they had waited for. This miracle had occurred, and they were finally moving forward with their lives and putting the hopelessness behind. Alysse had told everyone that they were having a baby! She had even bought infant clothes online for a little girl.

And then, almost as if she was reliving that day again, a tear fell from her eye. The pain was still so real, so strong, going right through her body. The pain ripped through her memory like a knife. Alysse had lost the baby. Michael was devastated too, but he didn't dare show it around her. The days after the miscarriage, Alysse barely remembered anything. She was breathing, but she was not living. Her whole world had turned upside down. Michael assured her since they had gotten pregnant once that it would happen again. They had to be patient and positive. He told her over and over again that it would happen again. And by some miracle, it did! Four months later the whole ordeal repeated itself. They found out they were pregnant, and a month after finding out, Alysse miscarried again.

Alysse remembers screaming, "Why, God, why are you punishing me?" It was just too much. She couldn't function. She had not wanted to live anymore. The pain had been too deep. She did not want to leave her bed. She did not want to live with the pain that was there every day and every second of her life. Michael had worried because she wouldn't eat or go outside. Her mind was not as strong as Michael's. Her will to live started to disappear. Her body failed her. God failed her. There was nothing to look forward to, no baby. No family for them. Alysse knew she couldn't go through another pregnancy and another miscarriage. It would kill her.

That was over six months ago today. And it was one week ago that Michael had planned this trip to the Colorado mountains. Her initial response was that she would not go. She had no desire to leave their home, but he had pushed her and pushed her until she finally did not have the energy to fight him anymore. She had not left the house in months, and she barely ate during the time leading up to this trip. But Michael did not give up on her, and because of him, here she was in Colorado.

As Alysse took a deep breath and looked around at this beautiful little cottage overlooking the mountains, she silently thanked God for Michael. He had mentioned adoption, but she turned the idea down flat. She wanted their child. She wanted their little girl with the curly red hair and Michael's big heart. So she told him no. If she could not have their child, then she did not want any child. That was last week. But things were changing, Alysse was changing. By the grace of God and by Michael's love, she was slowly becoming alive again. She knew that she wanted to live now and that they would start the adoption process as soon as they returned home. She would be a mother to a baby that needed her, and Michael would be a father. Michael was right; they had each other, and they would adopt a baby that needed them. Alysse's one wish in life was to have a family to grow old with; it wouldn't matter to her if their child was adopted. She would give everything she had to that baby and love it like it was her own. The thought of them bringing a baby into their house filled her heart with joy. How could she have been so selfish? She would be the wife and mother that Michael deserved. He was everything to her.

Michael walked outside at the moment, his wavy brown hair all over the place. The stubble on his chin growing overnight, like it always did. Alysse remembered how she used to joke about their baby being part animal with all that hair that he grew overnight. His big brown eyes sparkled when he looked at her. He was so handsome, and as he walked over and put his arms around her, she looked up and smiled and told him that she loved him. His smile was so big it could have covered the whole state of Colorado, and Alysse realized she had been very selfish, stuck in her own pain and not even realizing what Michael was going through. She made a promise right there on that balcony that she would be happy no matter what happened because she had the love of her life with her. And together they could overcome anything that came their way. He leaned down and kissed her.

"I love you, Alysse, and everything will be fine."

"How about some breakfast," Alysse said, going into the kitchen.

Michael followed her in and started to open the refrigerator. Michael responded by pulling out some eggs and bacon. "Babe, eat well today because we are going on a hike to explore the forest and mountains. It's a beautiful day, and the fresh air will do us both some good."

Alysse wasn't sure that she was up for a hike, but she knew she wouldn't disappoint Michael. After they finished their breakfast and threw on some hiking clothes, they started out on the trail. The day was crisp for early May, but the fresh air went deep into her soul and made her feel like she was a brand-new person. The scenery was breathtaking, and Michael seemed to know every flower, animal, and insect they came across.

"I think you are making some of these names up!" Alysse laughed, skipping down the path. He had picked a very exotic-looking flower that was growing in a splotch of sunlight, just off the trail. The purple color of the flower clashed drastically with Alysse's red hair, as Michael placed it by her ear.

"You are beautiful, Alysse," Michael said. The look he gave her after putting it on the side of her head made her stop and give him a huge kiss right on his lips. Michael grabbed her hand and pulled her close. She felt the goose bumps that she used to feel when they were together. The goose bumps she used to feel whenever Michael had touched her. They had disappeared for years, but now they were back! This was going to be an unforgettable day, a new beginning for them. Alysse was feeling happy. That word had left her vocabulary and had stayed hidden for a long time. And today it was the word she wanted to use over and over again. Yes! There was something magical happening today. She could feel it deep inside her soul. Today was the new beginning of their lives, their marriage, and Alysse knew for certain that she was ready to fight for her life back. She was ready to show Michael that she was the woman that he married years ago. She was back!

After hiking about five miles, the trail started to go upward into the mountains. Alysse was feeling a little fatigued, the months of lying in bed and no physical activity was wearing on her. But she did not want to stop. Michael was smiling the whole hike he was so happy. Michael grabbed her hand and started pulling her over to a clearing next to a crystal clear stream. He put down his backpack and pulled out a blanket, which he laid on the ground. Alysse started giggling as she was lifted off her feet and thrown gently on the blanket. She was able to catch her breath. That was until Michael's kisses were all over her neck and face, and as they were kissing, he pulled out the small water bottles and some fruit and cheese he had snuck into the backpack this morning while Alysse was getting dressed.

"Michael, this is perfect, you always think of everything. Our own little picnic in the middle of the wild!" Alysse exclaimed. The spring breeze was a little chilly, but Alysse didn't want this moment in time to end. It felt like they were the only two people in the world, and all the past years of sadness seemed to disappear into thin air.

After their little feast in the forest, they sat and just talked. Alysse knew Michael had wanted to make love to her right there, but he held back, not wanting to push her until she was ready again. So instead, Michael cradled her in his arms. Her head lay against his strong chest. It was as if she could feel his strength passing into her frail body. Alysse stood up first.

"Michael, as beautiful as it is here, let's get moving and explore the rest of this trail."

She was feeling a little anxious. She felt like today was full of new surprises, and she wanted to experience everything she could up here in the magical mountains. As Alysse was grabbing the blanket by the two ends and walking toward Michael to complete the fold, she heard a slight rustle in the woods to the side of the stream.

"Michael, did you hear something?" Alysse whispered to him.

Michael looked at her and smiled. "It's the big bad wolf, and he is coming to steal the rest of the food," he teased. As Alysse relaxed a little, she saw something run by. It wasn't an animal. It looked like a child! A child with blond hair. She swore it was blond hair!

"Michael, it's a child!" Alysse screamed as she dropped the blanket and started running toward the area she had seen the child. He looked at her like she was crazy but started on the trail with her running ahead.

"Alysse, please, there are no people around. We have not seen a soul since we passed the couple along the trail hours ago."

Alysse hurried down the path and turned into the woods where she saw movement. She could hear Michael screaming for her to wait for him and to be careful. She felt like she was being guided by some higher power.

"There was a child, Michael, a little child! We have to help the poor little thing!" She instantly saw the worry in Michael's eyes. He didn't believe her. *He thinks that I am seeing what I want to see. Was he right?*

All of a sudden Alysse stopped in her tracks. There in front of her was a big gray wolf. She was beautiful and majestic. She was blocking the path, and Alysse realized she was not scared at all. She just stood there and stared at them. Not moving at all. It was almost like a statue. It was surreal! Michael came up behind Alysse and put his arms around her waist.

"Slowly walk back with me, Alysse. There could be more than one," Michael whispered in her ear.

Alysse knew this was not the animal she saw on the trail. The wolf just stared at the two of them and slowly turned around and headed into the woods. The wolf seemed to stop and look back at them, and she did this two times, almost as if to see if they were following her. Slowly Alysse started to back up, but as she did, she heard a sound—it was a human sound. Alysse quickly looked back at

Michael, and she knew from the look in his eyes that he had heard it too. She wasn't crazy!

They walked in the direction of the sound, and nothing could have prepared them for what they saw before them. The gray wolf was standing before them, and right next to him was a baby. It was a little naked baby with a head of dirty blond hair. Not really a baby, more like a toddler. It was hard to tell how old exactly, but she couldn't have been more than two or three years old.

"Michael!" Alysse screamed. "It's a baby girl!"

This didn't make sense, but none of that mattered. What mattered was that there was a helpless little baby girl holding onto a big gray wolf! Michael grabbed Alysse. He knew she was going to run right up and take the baby. The wolf seemed to hesitate for a second, not wanting to leave, but somehow knowing she should. Alysse tried talking to the little girl, but she wouldn't even look at them. The wolf seemed to stare at Michael and Alysse for a long time. The baby was making some kind of noise. Was it a cry? Was it a howl? The only thing Alysse could think of was this baby girl and how she needed to help her. She was so dirty, mud and dirt on her hands and legs.

She needs some clothes, Alysse thought. *I need to dress her and give her food.* This was not making sense. How could a little girl be here in front of them? How did she survive out here? Was her mother around? There were so many unanswered questions. The wolf backed up toward the trail. The baby started crying. Slowly the wolf turned around and stopped by the baby. Unbelievably, the baby grabbed onto the wolf, and the wolf licked the baby's hand and buried its nose into the baby's neck. Michael and Alysse stood there stunned. Alysse was the first to react. She started to slowly inch forward. There was no way she was leaving this baby with the wolf.

The wolf put her head up and looked at Alysse, but she did not back down. The wolf stared at her, but she did not feel fear at all. Alysse started talking to the baby with soft sounds. The baby looked up at her with fear in her eyes, and she started crying. The baby did not want to leave the wolf. Michael grabbed Alysse again and pushed her to the side.

"I will go get the baby," Michael said. He started walking up the wooded incline toward the wolf and the baby. The wolf jumped in front of the baby and started growling. Alysse quickly grabbed Michael and pushed him back. She just knew that the wolf wanted her to approach, not Michael. Her eyes drifted toward Michael, and she gave him that stubborn look, but he would not let go of her.

"Please, Michael, let me go toward the baby, the wolf does not trust you." Alysse laid her hand on Michael's shirt and pleaded with her eyes. He took a step back, as she took a step forward. Alysse knew this was absolutely crazy. *Was this just a dream? Did I want a baby so badly that I am dreaming about this little blond-haired girl?* Alysse walked slowly toward the child. The wolf did not move, and the little girl grabbed harder onto the fur of the gray wolf. Alysse didn't know how, but she absolutely felt that the wolf wanted her to take this baby, to rescue this little girl from this forest and bring her home and love her. Alysse's eyes never left the eyes of the wolf. She seemed to be testing me, to see if I was the right person to relinquish the little girl to.

As Alysse approached the little girl and the wolf, she reached out her hand. The wolf moved forward and put her nose up against her hand. Michael screamed, and Alysse looked back to assure him she was fine. She wasn't afraid as she let the wolf smell her scent. The wolf backed up a step, and the little girl went with her. The wolf stopped and nudged the baby forward. Alysse saw panic in the baby's eyes as the wolf backed away. The little girl let out a big yell as Alysse rushed forward and grabbed her. She was fighting Alysse. Her hands and legs were moving all over the place. Alysse held her tight, and Michael ran up to them and pushed them back.

The wolf gave one look over her shoulder and headed into the forest. Alysse saw sadness in that look, and she somehow knew that it was giving up this child to her. It was a gift. The greatest gift Alysse could ever receive, and she felt gratitude toward that big gray wolf. She didn't know the whole story of this baby, but it was a gift. As silly as it sounded in her head, she let the words *thank you* come out of her mouth, directed toward the wolf. Alysse didn't know how or why, but she had her baby, her little girl, and she wasn't going to ever give her up. The little girl was making some sort of sound, a loud howling sound. She had tears coming out of her eyes. And she tried to bite Alysse several times, but she wouldn't let go. Michael grabbed the little girl and held her tightly by the torso. She was kicking and screaming and fighting with all her might. But they would not let go. No, they would never let go. This little girl was living in the woods. She had been living here until they came. She was their baby now. God worked in mysterious ways. Alysse glanced at Michael, and the look in his eyes was unreadable. They ran down the trails and back to their cottage as fast as they could with their little girl fighting them the whole way back.

Chapter 3

Michael turned off the television in the hotel room and let out a big sigh. This past week had been a whirlwind for him and for Alysse. He put his hands on his head. Was he doing the right thing? Was there even a right direction to take? He knew that it was crazy for him to hire a detective and try to find the baby's mother. The "wolf baby," like the media was calling her, was the biggest story coming out of Colorado. Alysse had not left the little girl's side at the hospital. She was calling this baby "her baby." For the first time in a long time, Michael had seen something in Alysse's eyes, something that made him want to forget about anything except bringing that look of hope into their life again. Alysse was happy! She was talking about the future; shit, she was planning the future with this little girl. Michael did not know what to make of it.

They had brought the little girl to the hospital right away. Michael had called the police on the way. He had known that this was going to be a huge story, and he wanted to try to keep it under wraps. He did not want to drag Alysse into the spotlight. She was still fragile. Just recovering for the first time in months and now this. But she had jumped into the role of mother right away. Ordering little girl clothes online while she waited in the hospital. Talking about what to name her and even planning a birthday party for her! Michael grimaced when he thought about how he had to grab Alysse and pull her close and tell her that this little baby girl came from someone. It may have been raised by wolves, but it was born to a human being. For God's sake! He was a lawyer. He owned his own law firm. He knew the law. They couldn't just take this baby from the hospital and bring it home like it was a toy doll.

Alysse had looked at him with her big beautiful eyes that were quickly filling with tears. Michael saw the look of anguish that had replaced that long lost look of hope that was starting to slowly come back into their life. He felt like the enemy, but he knew that the baby may have family out there, and he had to do everything possible to try and find out where this baby came from. He was very familiar with the legal rights that they had. He had hired the best private detective that he could. He even flew him to Colorado from Washington, DC. He had been recommended as one of the best years ago when Michael had needed one for a case he was working on. His name was Anthony Paulo. He was a former FBI agent and had served in the military as a green beret. A former Division One college football player. He had graduated at the top of his class, and he had come to Michael as a favor. Anthony was the brother of one of his best clients. And this being such a huge media circus, Michael wanted—no, needed someone he could trust. Anthony was more than an employee; he had become a good friend to both him and Alysse.

Within forty-eight hours of finding the baby, Michael had Anthony sitting in a chair across from him at the hotel bar. He still remembered the surprise he felt when Anthony walked through the door the first time he had met him. The guy was over six feet, four inches and at least 240 pounds of pure muscle! How could this guy go anywhere secretly and not be noticed? But from the moment Anthony, who told him that all his friends called him Tony, sat down and started talking, Michael knew this was the right guy. He had a heart of gold, and he was very professional but also understood the complexity of this case and how the outcome could affect Michael and Alysse.

Michael had relayed every last detail of that day up in the forest. He had tried to remember little details, anything that might help find the family or even a clue of how and when this baby girl came to live in the forest. It still seemed like a dream to him. What were the chances of something like this happening on a day where he was trying to make his wife forget about losing a baby? They had found a baby! Babies don't just turn up in the middle of the forest. And babies don't just turn up with a wolf as a guardian. He rubbed his head again at the thought. Michael knew he did not have to tell Tony that the media and the public were to not find out about this job. The sooner Tony was done with this investigation, the better it would be for everyone involved. After all, if that little wolf girl had a mother, he was sure she was either dead or she had thought that her baby was dead. Michael wished Tony the best of luck. He knew this was not going to be an easy job, but definitely interesting.

Tony left about six hours later and said he would check in every other day or so. He had four years of digging up records to do, and this job would keep him very busy. The hospital had said the baby was about two to three years old. This was a quick evaluation. Most likely somewhere in between. That meant looking for a missing pregnant girl up to four years ago. Or a dead girl. Or it could be a totally different angle. Michael's head started pounding again. This was not what he wanted to end up with when he took Alysse for the relaxing trip to Colorado. Alysse said this was fate. Was it? Michael had to stop thinking about what had happened and start thinking about how to prepare Alysse for the chance that his baby would not be hers to keep. And even if it turned out that they could adopt this wolf child, should they? What type of learning problems would this little girl have? She was like a wild animal until the doctors gave her a mild sedative to calm her down.

The hospital had confirmed that the baby was about three years old. She was actually healthy! She was a little underweight and had some sores and scratches over her body. The worst was the little girl's feet. They had been bare and bruised and cut up very badly. The doctors were at a loss. They just did not know how this little girl could have survived up in the woods for even two days. She was not starved. She was deficient in some vitamins, but nothing that was life-threatening. The doctor in charge had pulled Michael aside when Alysse was occupied with the little girl. He had told Michael that no matter where this little girl ended up, her biggest hurdle would be adapting to our world. The wolf baby was still restrained ever so gently because she would try to bite or scratch. Her sounds were still more animallike than human. She had been washed and bathed over and over again to remove all the dirt that had seemed to deposit in certain places.

When Alysse had walked in to see the baby after her cleanup, she had pure joy on her face. The little girl was beautiful! She had blond hair that was so thick and curly, and it framed this round little head that had the biggest blue eyes. She looked like an angel! Alysse immediately decided that the baby girl needed a name. She had started calling her Gabriella, Gabbi for short, and the name took, so the nurses would also refer to the little girl as Gabbi. This had worried Michael; he knew that if the baby's family was found, then Alysse would be devastated, maybe never being able to recover from a hit like this. He realized that he was hoping that the baby was an orphan. That he would not have to tell Alysse that the baby belonged to someone else. Michael looked out the window of the hotel; he saw the lines of people, cameras, and television trucks surrounding the entrance of the hospital. This was a nightmare. Alysse did not need this type of public scrutiny. He had wanted to take Alysse back to their home in Ohio. But of course, she would not even hear him out. How could he suggest that? He wanted to leave their baby here alone?

For the first time in his well-organized life, Michael was at a loss. He did not know what to do. He called his partner back at the law office. Eric. Eric was a great lawyer but an even better friend. He was the best man at their wedding and someone that Michael knew he could count on. Eric picked up Michael's call, and the first thing out of his mouth was "Jesus, Michael, you leave for a little four-day trip to help Alysse relax and you end up starring in the biggest story of the decade!"

Michael smiled just a little. Eric was right. This was going to be a huge story, even with him trying to keep the media presence down. Michael explained the story to Eric the best he could. He heard himself saying the words, knowing they were true, but they sounded like a best-selling novel. Eric was amazed by this story but yet he felt sympathy for his best friend. Alysse and Michael had been through a lot. And Michael had wanted to just get away from everything with his wife and try to heal. And this crazy turn of events happened. Eric had promised Michael that he would take on his cases at the office and had told him to take as much time as he needed. He would hire a few local interns to help field the cases and paperwork. Michael hung up the phone feeling a little better. He hated to leave his office and work, but he had to handle this situation first. Alysse needed him, and he wanted to be here for her.

Michael stood up and took a deep breath. He headed toward the door and then stopped in his tracks and decided on taking a shot of the whiskey he had sent up to him. He was not much of a drinker, but a shot of the Bushmills single malt hit the spot. He had it sent to the hotel the day they arrived, and he did not regret that decision at all. Michael walked out of the hotel and over to the hospital. One reporter saw him walking over and started toward him. Michael ran into the closest door to the hospital, and the police guard barred the reporter from following him. The last thing he needed was to have a reporter asking questions. How could he answer questions when he had no idea what the hell was going on.

Jordan, the head doctor assigned to Gabbi, saw Michael and started over to him. Michael could see the sympathy in the doctor's eyes. Jordan knew most of the story, and he was the first one in to examine Gabbi. Jordan had expressed his amazement: This little girl that was supposedly raised by a wolf? Amazing. Jordan had examined her over and over. He had run all the blood work and repeated it three times. But the end result was that she was a healthy little girl. They were waiting for some more extensive tests, but for the most part, she was a healthy girl. It was amazing, he had told Michael.

Michael greeted Jordan with a handshake.

"How are you holding up?" Jordan asked Michael.

Michael exclaimed, "I am doing the best I can. This is so unreal to me, and I am so worried about Alysse." Jordan shook his head, and Michael could see the sympathy pop back up in Jordan's eyes. Jordan went on to tell Michael how almost all the tests they had originally done were coming back fine. Michael saw the excitement in Jordan's face. He couldn't blame him. Jordan had said he had researched past stories about kids being raised in the wild. There were stories here and there, and most historians did not believe the truth in it. Jordan had told Michael that from everything they knew of the genetic makeup of a wolf, this whole situation would be impossible. He had gone on to tell Michael that wolf pups are born blind, but by two weeks old, they have teeth and could start hunting. He told Michael that the eyes of the wolf pups are born bright blue but turn to yellow at around eight weeks.

This had Michael thinking of "Gabbi." Her eyes were the most vivid blue he had ever seen. They bore into you when she looked at you, and you could easily get lost in them. Of course, Michael knew that the baby had received its genetic makeup from her parents, not the wolves. But nonetheless, it had made Michael think of Gabbi and her blue eyes. Michael turned back to Jordan, who was telling him again how he just could not believe how Gabbi could have survived up there in the Colorado mountains. She would have frozen to death unless the wolf had her covered with its body the whole time. Michael had thought of the naked little girl running through the woods. This was definitely a miracle. A once-in-a-lifetime event, and unfortunately every reporter in the world was trying to get this story.

Michael had paid good money to keep his handpicked body-guards on the floor of Gabbi's room. He also paid good money to try and keep their identities safe. He knew the story couldn't be hidden, but he did not want the press following them back to Ohio. He also had one following his wife, which was actually an easy task, because she never left the side of this little girl. Michael let out a big sigh, and Jordan stopped talking and apologized.

"I am so sorry, Michael, I know this is hard for you, and you probably don't need me telling you about the history of wolf pups or how this is a miracle in itself. Let me answer any questions you may have." Jordan led Michael into his office so they could have some privacy. Michael tried to smile. He knew he failed, and it probably came out looking like an evil grin from a sci-fi movie. As Jordan handed Michael a fresh cup of coffee, Michael sat down and started with his questions.

"What I need to know, Jordan, is it going to be safe to bring this baby home with us? Will this little girl adapt to human life, or will she act like a wild animal?"

Jordan looked at Michael and smiled. "Michael, I can assure you that Gabbi is going to adjust to her surroundings with people rather than animals. It is human nature, she has improved a little each day, and it has only been a short time. You both need to be patient, there will be some learning difficulties to overcome, of course, and also her speech will be something you will need to work with a child speech therapist. I have a great one I could recommend to you." Jordan grimaced a little and put his hand up to brush his hair back from his forehead. He then continued talking before Michael could even answer. "Listen, Michael, I know I am Gabbi's doctor, but I really want this whole thing to work out for you and Alysse. When I hear you asking these questions, I feel like you're forgetting something very vital."

"What am I forgetting?" Michael replied.

Jordan took a deep breath and started telling Michael that Gabbi was not legally their baby yet. That the police and Michael's detective were out looking for a past. Any past. Was there a parent? What happened to the mother of this baby that left this little girl to be raised by wolves? And even if there is no one that shows up to claim this little girl, would Michael and Alysse start the adoption proceedings? Would this be a long case in court? There was so much to take in account here before Gabbi would be theirs permanently. Michael sighed a deep sigh.

"I know, Jordan, I am a lawyer, so of course I know the long road ahead for us. I have many misgivings about this, but for the first time in years, Alysse is coming back to life! She is happy and focused, and she is smiling again. I would do anything I need to make her happy again. And she cannot go through another attempted pregnancy, it would kill her."

Jordan stood up and put his hand on Michael's shoulder. "I know you're a lawyer, and I just felt like I needed to bring this up to you, but enough of this talk. Let's go see your wife and Gabbi!"

Michael followed Jordan down the hall to Gabbi's room. The guard Michael had hired gave him a brief head shake and opened the door for them. The second they stepped into the hospital room,

Alysse stood up and came over to Michael and put her arms around his neck and kissed him.

"Michael, I am so happy to see you!" Alysse grabbed his arm and pulled him over to Gabbi's bedside. Gabbi was asleep in this big hospital bed with all these machines monitoring her heartbeat and blood pressure and God knows what else.

Michael looked at this little blond girl laying there, and he felt something stir inside him. He thought about how this little girl had lived in the woods for all or some of her life. He wished he knew the story behind what had happened three years ago. This little girl that should be playing with toys or learning new words or sleeping with a stuffed animal instead of being hooked up to all these machines. Jordan assured Michael and Alysse that Gabbi was doing well, and they would start to take her off these hookups. Alysse smiled at Jordan and thanked him like she always did. She put her hand on Gabbi's hand, and Michael could see that Alysse already considered this little girl theirs. And almost as if Alysse could read his mind, she turned to Jordan and asked him, "Doctor, when can we take our little girl home?"

Jordan told Alysse that it would be at least another week before he would feel comfortable letting her leave the hospital. He also told them that if they were planning on taking her back to Ohio, they would need to set up appointments with a doctor right away. He went on to say that he could give them a few names before they left. The Cleveland Clinic was an excellent hospital, and he knew a few physicians there that they would be able to trust.

Alysse was so happy, but Michael knew he had to have this conversation with her, so he asked Jordan if they could have some privacy. Jordan smiled at them and walked out the door, reminding them to call him with any questions they may have. Michael turned to Alysse and hugged her close. He loved this lady so much, and he did not want to hurt her. God knows she had been dealt a terrible hand in life already and deserves some happiness. But he needed to let Alysse know that there could be problems with taking Gabbi home.

"Alysse, listen, I know you are falling in love with this little girl, but you need to realize that there are so many questions that have to be answered before we would be allowed to take Gabbi home."

Alysse stopped smiling, and Michael could see the worry cross over her face. "Look, Michael, I know that the police have to see if there are any known family members, and I also know that I can't just pick her up and take her home back to Ohio." She put both hands over his and continued. "Michael, this is a miracle, everyone says so. The miscarriages and the struggles we had were all part of this bigger plan by God. We were meant to find this little girl. Gabbi is meant to be ours, and there will be nothing stopping us from being her parents." Michael went to open his mouth to tell Alysse that she needed to keep an open mind, but she planted a kiss on his lips and said, "Now, Michael, I want you to go and check in with the police and your detective and see if you can move this along at a faster pace, please."

Michael kissed her back and told her that he would not do anything else to move this along until she took a break and came out to a restaurant to eat something.

"Michael, please, I can't let Gabbi wake up and not see me here! She will be so scared. She has been through so much already. I want her to know we are here for her."

Michael grabbed Alysse's hand and pulled her out of the room. "You cannot stay strong and healthy for that little girl if you don't take the time to eat and sleep. The last thing you want is to get sick, and Gabbi won't have you there to count on every day." He could see Alysse's mind processing what he said. "Alysse, I will make a deal with you. We go down to the cafeteria and you eat a whole meal with me, and then I will head over to the police station and see if there is any news."

Alysse sighed and smiled and said that he was right. "Michael you are always right."

As they walked down the hall toward the cafeteria, Michael stole a glance back at the room Gabbi was in. He shook his head ever so slightly.

How did this become our life? Was Alysse right, did this all happen for a reason? Is there such a thing as fate? Are we going home to Ohio as a family?

It was just too much to think about right now. He needed to make sure that Alysse was healthy and eating. And that was exactly his plan for the next hour or so. From there, they would have to see.

Chapter 4

As the plane took off from the tarmac, Michael let out a huge sigh of relief. He felt like he was finally able to start breathing again after holding his breath for the last six weeks. Alysse and Gabbi were settled in next to him. He stole a glance at his beautiful wife and Gabbi. Alysse was sound asleep, her eyes closed as soon as they were all buckled in. Of course Alysse had made sure that Gabbi was nestled beside her before she let her eyes close. They had both been through so much and wouldn't be surprised if they slept the whole flight to Ohio. Michael was grateful that he had the means to charter this private plane. He did not want to take a chance and fly on a commercial flight. He had done everything in his power to keep the identity of Alysse and Gabbi quiet. He had some of his law team and his partner, Eric, working night and day to untangle the legal problems and to start the adoption process.

Michael was not sold on this whole wolf girl being the best bet for Alysse, but she was happier than he had seen her in a long time. She loved this little girl like she was her own flesh and blood. Alysse was committed to becoming a mother to Gabbi. Michael had to admit that Gabbi was starting to cast a spell on him too. Those big blue eyes looking up at him with the little blond curls. Such a harsh contrast to the dirty and bruised little girl they had seen in the woods. She was even starting to trust them now.

Gabbi had a connection with Alysse that was undeniable. Alysse did not leave that little girl's side from day one. She was with her every day and almost every minute for the last six weeks. Michael remembered the little girl that they had brought into the hospital that fateful day in Colorado. She was fighting them and trying to bite them and wailing like an animal. Gabbi had slowly started to conform to her surroundings. After all, she was only three years old. He knew she would adjust, and he had enlisted the best child specialists to see Gabbi while in Colorado. They were all sworn to secrecy, and they all had said that this was nothing short of a miracle. This little girl had spent her last three years in the forest with wolves, and she was slowly becoming a normal little toddler.

He had watched in awe as this miracle little girl started to trust Alysse and then to openly adore her. It hadn't been an easy road though. Alysse was so patient and had talked calmly to the little girl every single day and even in her sleep. She would read books or say soothing words. She had told Michael that she wanted Gabbi to hear human words, to hear human voices and get used to them. To associate the sound to something that was soothing and comforting. Alysse really did have the patience of a saint. Michael was surprised to see Gabbi start to slowly trust Alysse. Not just trust her, but to want to be with her and want human contact.

Gabbi had only made grunting noises when she was brought in to the hospital that fateful day. But Michael saw Alysse talking to Gabbi every day and Gabbi start to respond. She of course was not talking like a three-year-old should be, but she was making sounds that were starting to sound like words. The child speech pathologist that Michael had brought on for consulting had warned both Michael and Alysse that speech would come in time, but not to expect Gabbi to be talking in a week or two. And lo and behold, this past week before they left the hospital, Gabbi had said her first word. Michael grinned from ear to ear as he remembered when Alysse called him, and she was so excited that Michael had to tell her to settle down and take a deep breath. She had said that Gabbi woke up in the morning and looked at Alysse with her blue eyes twinkling and had said something. Alysse said it sounded just like the word *food*. Alysse was so emotional when she was telling Michael this that he had thought she was going to cry.

Alysse went on to tell Michael that she picked up Gabbi and said, "What did you say, sweetie? Did you say the word *food*?"

Gabbi had looked at her and said the word *food* as clear as day.

Alysse had told Michael that she called the nurse and asked them to bring in pancakes and fruit and milk for Gabbi. And she had told them to bring some juice and cookies too. Michael laughed out loud at the memory. Alysse never jumped into anything part-way; she always had to go in with guns loaded. Gabbi would be ten pounds heavier by the time she was back home in Ohio, he had warned Alysse with a smile. As Michael put his arm around his wife, he glanced again at Gabbi. They had released Gabbi, and Jordan had given him a list of pediatric specialists in the Ohio area. He had rec-ommended them himself. Jordan had known that keeping this whole process low-key was Michael's first priority.

Michael had contacted every judge and senator he had known. Especially the ones that had owed Michael a debt of gratitude, either because of a case he had won for them or because he had helped them with a discreet legal problem. Michael had spent the last two weeks trying to get Gabbi out of the child services records and into an adoption process. Michael did not mince words, ever. He chuckled to himself as he thought back to the visits he had paid to these judges and senators in the Colorado state. He told them what he needed help with and that he needed discretion and a promise to not talk about this case.

It was nothing short of a miracle that he was able to convince child services to allow him to take Gabbi home with them to Ohio. He had enlisted the help of the doctor and nurse that had looked over Gabbi. They all were on Michael's side. They all agreed that this little girl needed a home. A family. She did not need to be put through the system, not even for one day. They had argued that this little girl needed help to adjust to the human way of life, and she could not do that in child services. She needed something that was going to be permanent. A permanent home with permanent parents.

The biggest concern had been the little girl's biological parents. She had to have a mother and a father. What had happened to them? How could they take this little girl out of the state of Colorado if they were not sure if her parents could be found here? Michael had been in touch with Anthony, his personal detective, every day. Anthony had been looking into every single pregnancy record around this area for the last four years. He was concentrating on any type of unusual notes or circumstances. Anthony had told Michael that he was investigating any missing girls that may have been pregnant around the time that Gabbi was born.

That information was part of the problem. It was difficult because the doctors and specialists had run Gabbi through so many tests and physicals to try to get a pretty good gauge on her age. She was developmentally behind obviously, considering her circumstances, but by her physical features and development, they had told Michael repeatedly that her age had to be around three years of age. This was based on her growth and teeth. But still they couldn't be a hundred percent sure. Her first three years of life were not normal, so they were estimating to the best of their ability that she was around three years old.

So Anthony had worked off that age, of course giving a few months on each end to account for any missing girls. Michael remembered the last meeting with Anthony. Alysse had been with Michael at the time, taking a very rare break from the hospital to buy some clothes for Gabbi, and she had met Michael for a quick lunch. Anthony had met them at the little outside bistro down the street. This place had the best hamburgers in town, and Michael had been craving one. He had actually ordered an extra hamburger because all this working day and night to try and take care of all the details before they flew home had really taken its toll on Michael's otherwise never-ending appetite. So he had decided to take advantage of this number one rated hamburger place, and he was not disappointed. He had made Alysse sit down and eat. She was not worrying about food, and she was already looking too skinny due to all this excitement and stress with Gabbi.

His blood started to boil when he thought back about the meeting with Anthony. Anthony had greeted both him and Alysse with a smile and had sat down with them and gave some very vague information. Michael knew right away by looking at Anthony's gaze that he did not want to disclose what he had to say in front of Alysse. So Michael had told Anthony to order what he wanted and to order two more beers and he would be right back. He had told Alysse that he would walk her to the hospital so she could give Gabbi her new clothes and maybe talk the nurses into letting her change into one of the cute outfits she had bought for her. Alysse had lit up instantly, like Michael knew she would. She had stood up and said her good-byes to Anthony and grabbed Michael's hand and practically pulled him onto the sidewalk. He had dropped Alysse off at the hospital with a promise that he would be back soon, and he went quickly back to the little bistro and sat down with Anthony.

Anthony had ordered two Dale's Pale Ale, a popular beer in this area of Colorado. Michael took a few big sips, practically finishing off half of the beer to calm his nerves. Michael was expecting big news that Anthony had found Gabbi's mom or maybe her dad or both. The whole time walking back to the restaurant, he was going over in his mind how he was ever going to tell Alysse that Gabbi had a mother or a family and they couldn't adopt her. Anthony had brushed back his thick wavy hair with his hand and took a deep breath.

"Michael, I don't think you are going to like what I found out," Anthony went on to say.

Michael had told Anthony to just say the words; he wasn't the type of man that liked to beat around the bush. He would hear what he had to say and then deal with the best way to proceed. If it meant having to give up Gabbi to her real family, then so be it. He would be there for Alysse, like he always was. He would make sure they adopted a baby as soon as possible. The baby would not be Gabbi, but Alysse would grow to love the new baby and slowly forget Gabbi. He knew this would break her heart, and it killed him to have to tell her this news, if this was what Anthony was going to tell him.

Anthony looked up at Michael and said, "Michael, I did lots of research around this area of Colorado. I was looking into missing girls around the year that Gabbi would have been born. I was surprised at the amount of girls that were missing, so I extended the search for previous years and also including the last few years. I even did some research in other states. Something did not seem right, and I thought it may lend some insight into what had possibly happened to Gabbi. Why she was alone and left in the woods."

Michael stopped eating and looked at Anthony with confusion. So Anthony continued, "Michael, in 2015 alone, there were 10,398 kids that went missing in Colorado alone—10,398! And 84 percent were between fourteen and sixteen. Most of these missing children were girls. As I started looking into this more, I started talking to a few of my buddies in the FBI. I knew that there was around one hundred thousand to three hundred thousand of human trafficking cases in the US. These poor kids were kidnapped or runways that are forced into prostitution." Anthony saw the look in Michael's eyes turn from confusion to understanding, and his eyes grew dark. Anthony took a long sip of his beer before continuing his conversation with Michael.

"Even with those unbelievable statistics, I knew there was a larger than normal missing kids number here in this area. So I had my buddies pull the files. It seems that this area of Colorado has a human trafficking problem that seems to be getting worse. The FBI has been trying to find in particular a certain group that is behind many disappearances. They had a few girls that were rescued and had said they were taken and held in a place that they couldn't identify. They had said they were held there for no more than two weeks. And in those two weeks, they were cleaned up and had pictures taken of them and then shipped off to 'their new owner.'

"These kids are being grabbed off the street and then auctioned off to the highest bidder. They are being sold through a network that the FBI can't seem to break open. Now, the FBI was lucky enough to recover a few of these kids, and some say that they thought there were anywhere between five and fifteen men. And this is probably one or two operations. This is a growing concern. We were lucky enough to identify one of them. From the evidence that some of these girls presented, a few of them had heard the name Niko, and they were able to identify his picture. He is bad news, assault and drugs in the past, and it looks like over the past few or more years he found a more lucrative business in the sale of young girls." Anthony swore under his breath and went on to call Niko a lowlife son of a bitch.

Michael looked up at Anthony and just shook his head. "So what you are telling me is you think that Gabbi's mother was kidnapped? Sold into human trafficking?"

Anthony finished off his beer and ordered two more. Michael did not stop him. He needed another one after this conversation. "Listen, Michael, I don't know for sure, but what we do know is there is some sort of well-guarded stronghold operating out of Colorado. And they are pretty elusive. I am sure they are in the mountains somewhere, but Jesus, 40 percent of Colorado is mountains! That is like searching for a needle in a haystack. If I had to make an educated guess, my thought is that Gabbi's mother either was pregnant when they grabbed her off the street, and for some reason decided to hold on to her instead of killing her, or she became pregnant during the captivity. But I think I would go with the first scenario.

"These human traffickers are scumbags, but they are not stupid. They are not going to let a girl get pregnant while they are holding onto her. Can you imagine all these babies showing up dead? My guess is that she was pregnant and kidnapped." Anthony went on to say that he was still looking into missing girls that could have been pregnant around the time frame of Gabbi's age. If they had a really good lead, then they could always do a DNA test and see if Gabbi was a match. Michael remembered how angry he was hearing these statistics. Of course, he knew there were human trafficking cases, but he did not realize the scope of this problem. *Those poor kids,* he thought to himself and then felt his blood get cold.

If Gabbi was a discarded baby from one of these poor girls, then chances are they would never find out the truth. Which probably meant they would never find any living relatives. Anthony had said that there were no cases of a missing pregnant girl that would match Gabbi's timeline. Michael thought of this poor little girl's mother. Did she know that they put her baby in the woods? Was that baby left there to die? If that was the case, then she probably thought the baby was dead. *This world is messed up,* Michael thought to himself. And looked over again at the little blond girl that had turned their lives upside down. Hopefully for the good though. Would he ever think of this little girl as his daughter? He couldn't even think along

41

those lines yet. He was so busy trying to do all the legwork for getting her home to Ohio and taking care of the legal work. But as his gaze lingered on his beautiful wife and her arms wrapped around Gabbi, he promised himself he would do whatever it took to make this little family of his work. It wouldn't be hard to spoil this little girl. She had endured so much already.

As his thoughts lingered on his newfound little girl, the sound of the pilot interrupted his thoughts. They were getting ready to land into Cleveland. He barely heard the pilot say that the weather was sunny and about sixty-five degrees. Alysse opened her eyes and looked at Michael.

"Are we almost back home, Michael?" she asked. Michael told her that they were getting ready to land so make sure Gabbi and her were secure. The excitement in Alysse's eyes was visible. "Michael," she said, placing her hand in his, "we are going home with our little girl!"

As the plane came to a stop on the runway, Michael wasn't a hundred percent sure what to expect. He had told Eric that they were flying home and to have a car ready to pick them up. And of course, Eric wanted to make sure that they had groceries and some necessities for Gabbi. He and his wife, Nikki, had purchased a little toddler bed and dresser in white with little pink flowers painted on the border. They wanted to surprise Alysse but wanted to get Michael's approval. Of course, Michael was grateful. He didn't even think about what they would need now bringing Gabbi home. Of course they had the extra bedroom, and it was partially decorated from when she was pregnant, and Eric had said he would set up the furniture before they got home. Eric was a great friend, not just his partner, and he owed him so much for taking the time to help him with this twist of fate. And he knew that Alysse would not want to leave Gabbi to go shopping. Hell, he didn't even know if she would ever leave the house without Gabbi. Would they ever have a date night again at a nice restaurant? Would she ever trust a babysitter with this little girl? He knew he was thinking way ahead like he always did. They would have to take one day at a time. Maybe they would even be able to bring back the sex life they had before Alysse had her miscarriages.

Well, thought Michael, *this is something to look forward to!*

Michael, Alysse, and Gabbi grabbed their luggage, and their car pulled up. It even had a car seat in it! Eric was the best! Well, he thought it was probably Nikki that had thought of the car seat, because Lord knows that Michael didn't even think ahead on that one. And by the look of surprise in Alysse's eyes, Michael realized she didn't even think about getting a car seat for Gabbi.

Alysse looked up at Michael and said, "Michael, you are the best! I can't believe I didn't even think of getting a car seat for Gabbi!"

Michael smiled and as much as he wanted to take credit for this, he gave the credit where it was due. Gabbi was still half asleep, and she seemed a little nervous about getting into the car seat. Alysse strapped her in and sat right next to her, talking comforting words until Gabbi relaxed. Gabbi started smiling and grabbed Alysse's hand. The ride to their house was about twenty minutes. When they got there, they saw Eric and Nikki and their little boy, Leo. Leo was turning four this year, and he was a mini Eric. He looked just like him. Eric was a big guy, about six foot two and two hundred pounds. Leo, of course, wasn't that big yet, but he had the same chiseled chin and bright blue eyes. Michael always teased Eric that Leo was the better looking of the two.

Michael checked out the area for any type of news cameras or press. Eric and himself had made sure that their names were not leaked to the press. But you never know what could happen, or who you could trust. Michael seemed confident that they were in the clear and opened the door for Alysse and Gabbi. Eric and Nikki came forward with a big welcome home sign and balloons. Alysse was all smiles as she introduced Gabbi to Eric, Nikki, and Leo. Gabbi reached out and tried to touch Leo's head, and Leo pulled away quickly with little interest. They all laughed at that. Alysse set Gabbi on the ground because she was squirming to get down.

"Welcome to your new home, Gabbi!" Alysse spoke to Gabbi as she was putting her feet on the ground. The neighbors were outside with their two dogs. As Gabbi hit the ground, she saw the dogs and started running toward them. Alysse was caught off guard by how quickly Gabbi had run, and she was halfway across the drive before she was scooped up. As Gabbi had approached the neighbors' dogs, they had started yelping and moving away from Gabbi. They were in their kennel, but the dogs ran to the far end. They were afraid of Gabbi! Even the neighbor wasn't sure what was going on. The dogs cowered in the far corner, as Alysse picked up Gabbi, unaware of the reaction the dogs had to her.

Michael looked at Eric, and he knew that he had seen what had happened There was worry in his eyes. These two big German shepherds were scared to death of Gabbi. Why? Gabbi wasn't afraid of them at all, and if Alysse had not grabbed her, she would have gone right up to the dogs and probably given them a heart attack. Michael nodded at Eric to go inside. This was something that Michael needed to call Jordan about right away.

Did Gabbi have a scent of the wolves on her? Was this in her system? It was a little disturbing, to say the least, but he was not going to let it ruin their welcome home. After all, maybe this was not what it looked like. Maybe the neighbors' dogs did not like kids. He needed to quit letting these little things worry him. He glanced back at the car pulling away and wondered what this new life would bring for them. He looked up at the sky, not really being a religious man, but prayed to God that this was the right decision for Alysse and Gabbi.

As Michael walked into their house with Alysse and Gabbi in her little pink dress and matching hair bow, and Eric and Nikki leading the way, it was hard to believe that less than two months had passed since he made Alysse walk out that door and head to Colorado. What an adventure it had been! He had left their house in Ohio with a heartbroken wife who had been barely living. Now they were walking through that door with a little girl that may be calling him Daddy very soon and a wife that had never been happier. He had a feeling that the future was going to be very, very interesting, to say the least.

Chapter 5

Alysse was up early. She still loved her mornings, her time to reflect and just think about everything or, lately, nothing. She took a sip of her coffee and looked out at the woods in the back of their yard. They had bought a new house with a little more room, and the best part was it had two acres of woods behind their house. They were living in a suburb of Cleveland. She loved it here! It was so serene and quiet, and the animals that passed through every day were abundant.

She broke off a piece of her croissant and threw it out for the birds and squirrels that were busy gathering up food. She saw a deer in the far end of the yard, and it made her think of a day a few summers ago. Gabbi had been walking with her, holding her hand and enjoying the woods like she always did. That little girl had no fear of any living thing. When she saw a squirrel or a bird or any kind of animal, she was drawn to them. Alysse remembered that day like it was yesterday. Gabbi's little hand in hers, and they were just walking through the woods, and all of a sudden Gabbi stopped in her tracks. Alysse had looked in the direction that Gabbi was staring, and she had seen the family of deer standing there like statues. At first, Alysse had thought that Gabbi was afraid, so she had started to explain to her that they were deer, and they wouldn't hurt her. That they were gentle animals. But Gabbi had pulled her hand out from her grasp so fast and started to walk slowly toward the deer. Alysse had glanced at the deer, and they were frozen—they couldn't move!

She remembered thinking that they were frozen in fear. She had felt the goose bumps pop up on her skin as she tried to grab hold of Gabbi. But Gabbi had been crouching low and slowly walking toward the deer. It had looked like she was stalking them! Alysse knew how silly that was, but the deer had not run. They couldn't run. The look that had been in their eyes was a look of fear. And Alysse thought that was ridiculous! Gabbi was a little girl, Why would they be afraid of her? And just as she had finally grabbed Gabbi's hand, she had pulled it out of her grasp and ran straight toward the deer. The deer had made a sound and had jerked their heads up and ran for their lives. Alysse recalled how she had stood there in surprise. She could not be witnessing this. It did not make sense. She had caught up to Gabbi and grabbed her hand. Gabbi had looked at her with wild eyes. Eyes that had haunted Alysse for weeks after. It was like Gabbi had become a different being. She had no longer been her sweet daughter.

When Michael had come home that night and she recounted the story, Michael seemed unfazed by it. He told her that Gabbi loved animals and was probably just curious about the deer. Michael had assured her that she was imagining things and that it wasn't what she had thought, and she had slowly started to relax. Deep down inside, Alysse knew what she saw, and she started to worry that Gabbi was still part wild…or animal? Would she ever be human completely?

Alysse took another sip of her coffee and felt the pang of guilt for even thinking that back then. Gabbi was her miracle baby, sent by God. Gabbi had done everything that any normal child would do. She had gone to school and played sports. Well, actually, she had run track. She was fast! So fast that the other coaches had likened her to a gazelle. She could outrun any girl and half the boys. Alysse remembered how she had been so proud of her daughter. Gabbi had not wanted to join any team sports, but Alysse and Michael had suggested that maybe it would be good for her. Give her an outlet. Gabbi had tried out in high school, and the coach was blown away. Gabbi had gone on to win regional races and state races all through high school. Michael and herself had looked forward to the track meets every weekend. They were more excited than Gabbi had been for them. Alysse had the feeling Gabbi did not love being a participant in a team sport, but she did it to make them happy. Remembering how Gabbi had adjusted well to her new life, and they had been a happy family all together. And in a blink of an eye, her little girl was turning nineteen today! The last sixteen years had been the happiest years of her life. How could time go by so fast?

This day had to be perfect. Alysse had a cake already hidden away for Gabbi, and they were going to grill out steaks in the backyard later that evening. Gabbi's favorite meal was steak. Alysse had been upset that Gabbi did not want a party, but Gabbi had never had that many friends. She was sort of a loner. She had one friend that had been over their house since high school had begun, a cute little red-haired girl named Marissa. She was a nice girl, quiet like Gabbi, and they seemed to enjoy hiking in the woods and eating out on the deck. Neither of them had any interest in going out with other girls or parties or even dances. As they started getting older, neither of them had any interest in boys either.

Alysse remembered her conversation with Michael one night when Gabbi started high school. She was so worried because Gabbi did not want to go to any dances or have sleepovers, and she never seemed to want to date. Michael reminded Alysse about Gabbi and her rough start to life. Maybe, he had said, that whatever had happened to Gabbi those first three years of her life had some lasting effect on Gabbi's ability to trust humans or want social contact with them. He had brought up the fact that Gabbi did not use drugs or stay out late drinking. She had always enjoyed spending time with Michael and Alysse, and she called them Mom and Dad. They had never had any trouble at all with her. She was a good girl. All the teachers had only nice things to say about her. Yes, they had said, she was a little quiet, but some kids were quiet and some were loud. Gabbi had straight As in high school. Her elementary years were a little harder for her because of the transition and her late start at speech. Alysse had felt guilty again. She had a perfect daughter.

They were close, her and Gabbi. They would just sit and talk and sometimes go for long walks together. Alysse had loved taking her shopping to buy new clothes for each season. And Gabbi would pick out some basic jeans and shirts, but nothing too fancy or expensive. She laughed out loud at her thoughts. She should be grateful that Gabbi was not into expensive designer clothes or handbags like some of the other high school girls. Alysse had become friends with some of the moms when she volunteered at school. Alysse had always been the mom to say yes when the school had asked for volunteers. She never wanted to be away from Gabbi. She worried about her all the time. She was her baby, and she loved her more than she ever loved anything or anyone, except for Michael, of course. And just like on cue, Michael walked into the room and came up behind Alysse and gave her a big hug and good morning kiss.

"Good morning, beautiful," he said as he started rubbing her neck.

Alysse moaned as his large hands rubbed her aching shoulders. She smiled up at Michael and said, "Do you believe our little girl is nineteen today?"

Michael shook his head and thought, *Where did sixteen years go?* He grabbed a croissant and a cup of coffee and sat down next to Alysse. "Where is our birthday girl?" he asked.

Alysse laughed at him and reminded him that Gabbi was nineteen, and there was no way she would be up so early in the morning. Alysse knew that they had no way of knowing when Gabbi's real birthday was. They had been told by the doctor and medical staff that her age was close to three when they found her. So they decided to use that fateful date they had found her in the forest of Colorado as her birthday. Alysse sighed and remembered about her and Michael's decision about what to tell Gabbi. When Gabbi was about six years old, they had sat her down and told her she was adopted. She remembered Gabbi looking up at both of them with those big beautiful eyes and just staring. No crying or asking questions, just staring. Alysse had grabbed Gabbi and put her on her lap and asked her if she understood what the word *adopted* meant. Gabbi had said she did and that was that. Both her and Michael had tried to open up conversations with Gabbi about being adopted, but Gabbi had no interest. She never asked questions about it, and it never seemed to bother her, so Michael and Alysse had let it be.

The worry of Gabbi's reaction to being adopted, or lack of reaction, was always in the back of Alysse's mind. Michael had told her time and time again that she worried way too much, to just take one day at a time, and when Gabbi was ready to ask questions, she would.

So Alysse had put it to rest. And then one spring when Gabbi was nine years old, Alysse had volunteered to help the teacher with some classroom activities. She thought back and remembered every little detail like it had just happened. She thought to herself, *Isn't it funny how you forget certain events in life, but some days are ingrained in your mind forever.* And this was one of those moments.

Mrs. Miller, Gabbi's teacher at the time, had a big smile on her face when Alysse had walked into the classroom to volunteer for the day. The children were at recess, so the room was quiet. Mrs. Miller had pulled Alysse over to her desk and handed her a report that Gabbi had turned in the other day. Mrs. Miller had gone on to explain that the report was supposed to be about one of the most important days of your life. Alysse had remembered how her hand had trembled when she reached for the report. She had no idea what she was going to read. She had sat down in the nearest chair and read Gabbi's report. When she was done, she had tears streaming down her face. She couldn't believe it. The report was about Gabbi's most important day, the day her parents told her she was adopted. Gabbi had gone on to say that it had made her feel so happy to know that her parents had picked her to be their child. She went on about how much she loved her parents, and she was so happy that they had picked her to join their family. Alysse had been overjoyed to read this report and finally felt that Gabbi was fine with being adopted.

Mrs. Miller had told Alysse that one of the girls in class had raised her hand and asked Gabbi if she wanted to find her real mommy. According to Mrs. Miller, Gabbi had put her paper down on her desk and looked the other little girl right in the eyes. She then proceeded to tell the other girl that, no, she wasn't going to look for her real mommy because her real mommy was the mommy who adopted her and loves her now. Mrs. Miller had said that the whole class was silent as Gabbi sat down and folded her hands on her desk. Alysse had made a copy of that paper because she wasn't sure if Gabbi would show her, and she had stopped at Michael's office to have him read it. She had been crying the whole time, and Michael had thought that something terrible had happened. When he read the paper, he had hugged Alysse and told her that he had been right; she worried about everything! Alysse had sworn that she saw a little tear in Michael's right eye, but of course, he denied it.

Alysse felt a squeeze on her hand and realized she had drifted off in thought while Michael was trying to have a conversation with her. "Earth to Alysse." He was laughing as he started to get up to grab some bacon that he had made earlier this morning. As he stood up, he looked over at Alysse and said, "Honey, you know that this is the day I have to have the conversation with Gabbi about her mother?" Alysse looked confused for a second, and then Michael saw the minute that Alysse realized what he was saying.

"Michael, please, do we have to tell her about Jesse?"

Michael walked over to her and put his arm around her.

"Why do we have to bring this up to her after all these years?"

Michael shook his head and told Alysse that she knew why, because he had made a promise. That was as far as the conversation got before Gabbi walked outside on the patio. Michael walked over to Gabbi and gave her a big hug.

"Good morning, sweetheart, happy birthday!" he said to her as he pulled her close. It was hard to believe that the little girl they had found in the woods sixteen years ago was the same young woman before him. "How does it feel to be an old woman of nineteen?" he teased.

Gabbi hugged her father and giggled. "Thank you, Dad," she said. "I really don't feel any different than I did yesterday at the young age of eighteen," she replied with a big smile.

Alysse watched this interaction with tears in her eyes. She loved this girl so much. This gift from God that was sent to her. She was chosen out of everyone to be this beautiful girl's mother. She stood up and walked over to Gabbi. "Happy birthday, beautiful!" Alysse said in a tearful voice as she grabbed Gabbi and held her tight. Gabbi rolled her eyes and laughed at her mother.

"Really, Mom! Are you still crying on my birthday? You have done that as long as I remember!" She hugged her mother for a long time before they let go of each other. Gabbi sat down and poured herself some coffee and added a touch of milk. She loved coffee in the morning, and she loved coming out on the deck and watching all the wildlife in the backyard while she finished drinking it. Alysse walked out of the house with a plate full of pancakes and another big bowl of strawberries and blueberries.

"Chocolate chip pancakes for the birthday girl!" Alysse sang as she set them down in front of Gabbi.

"Mom, there are like twenty pancakes on this plate! Are you trying to make me big and fat?" Gabbi said. Michael sat down by Gabbi and helped himself to a few of them off her plate as he winked at her.

"I will help you out with these, it's a tough job, but I will do it for your birthday."

Gabbi giggled again and thanked her mom for the wonderful birthday breakfast. Alysse sat down across from her daughter and watched her eat her pancakes. Alysse knew that every parent thought their child was the most beautiful or the most handsome of all children, but Gabbi was gorgeous. Gabbi was about five foot, eight inches tall, which was quite tall for a girl. She had long blond hair that glistened in the sunlight, making it look more like the color silver. She was thin, but she had a thin athletic body. She loved to keep active, just walk in the woods or hike as long as she was outside.

Alysse recalled how she had walked in the house one day about three years ago, and Gabbi was just pacing and pacing. Alysse had asked her what was wrong. Gabbi had gone on to tell her that she hated being in the house when the weather was bad. There had been a terrible lightning storm, and thunder could be heard every fifteen minutes. Alysse had suggested that Gabbi watch a movie, and Gabbi had looked at her with wild eyes. She had said to her in a strained voice that she felt trapped when she could not go outside on days like today. Gabbi was definitely happiest when she was outside. Alysse looked at her daughter eating up those pancakes and smiled. She really was a beauty. Perfect skin and those big bluish-green eyes. Those eyes were something else! Everyone they met commented on Gabbi's eyes and her overall good looks. But the funny thing was, Gabbi didn't seem to know or care about her looks. Yes, Alysse had shown her how to use makeup and would make appointments for her at the beauty salon, but Alysse always felt that Gabbi was doing it more for her than for herself.

Gabbi didn't take selfies of herself or post on social media. She definitely was not like a normal teenage girl. By the time Gabbi started high school, everyone could tell that she was going to be a beauty. Of course, some of the girls would say mean things to her. Alysse had assumed it was jealousy when Gabbi told her about it. She had gorgeous looks, but her personality was even better. Gabbi was a sweet girl who really did not interact with too many of the other students. She was a little different, sort of a loner. And different always brought out meanness in people. Not that the male population of their high school had not tried to get Gabbi's attention. Alysse had noticed the same few cars going slowly past their house over and over again. The one car she recognized as the neighbor boy's car, Jacob. He had tried to come over a few times to talk to Gabbi, but Gabbi was not really receptive. She was never rude, but eventually the boys got the hint.

Gabbi had never dated or had gone to a school dance. Except one. The last dance of her senior year. It was her senior prom. Alysse had told Gabbi that she couldn't miss her last dance, that the senior prom was special. A celebration of the ending of high school. She had even talked to Gabbi's only real friend, Marissa. She had taken her aside and asked her to please talk Gabbi into going to her prom. Alysse had known she was being selfish. She wanted Gabbi to look for a dress and get her hair done and do her make up and take pictures like all the other parents do and post them on Facebook. Alysse wanted to be part of Gabbi's senior prom.

Michael had told Alysse that she shouldn't push her. He had told her all girls are different, and Gabbi may just be a late bloomer when it came to boys and dating. Alysse had known Michael was right, like usual, but she wanted Gabbi to experience this once-in-a-lifetime event. Between Marissa and herself talking to Gabbi, she had finally agreed. Alysse remembered the day Gabbi had come home from school and informed her that she was going to prom. Alysse had hugged Gabbi and started to cry. Gabbi had rolled her eyes and had told her straight out that she really wasn't looking forward to it, but she would go because Marissa had been asked by a boy she had liked, Devin. Devin was a cross-country runner, and Marissa had always had a crush on him way back from the first day of high school. When Devin had asked Marissa and Marissa had said yes, she had told Devin that Gabbi needed a date too. Marissa had told Gabbi that Devin had said that any guy would go with Gabbi. She was gorgeous, but she had never dated and had turned down every single guy that was brave enough to ask her out. No one had asked Gabbi, mostly because they all had given up on her, thinking they had no chance. They didn't want to be turned down again. Marissa had made Gabbi promise her that if she got asked that she would say yes. Gabbi reluctantly promised her friend Marissa. And Jacob had asked Gabbi the next day, and Gabbi had said yes.

Alysse had wanted to take Gabbi shopping that evening for her dress and shoes and make a hair appointment, but she saw that Gabbi started to pull back, so she had taken a big breath and had hugged her daughter again and told her that she was so happy she had decided to go to prom. She had told Gabbi that she would be happy to take both Gabbi and Marissa shopping for dresses the next day. She also told her they could make a whole day out of it and get manicures and pedicures, and she would pay for all of it for the two girls. She said it would be her treat! She also would throw in lunch at whatever place the girls wanted. Gabbi had smiled, and Alysse saw that Gabbi had even looked a little excited about their adventure the next day. Alysse sighed as she remembered that day. It was one of the best days of her life with her daughter.

They had all had an amazing day, picking out dresses and shoes and jewelry. Gabbi had picked a blue-and-silver long dress with a small slit up the side. She was breathtaking in it. The colors of the dress with her light skin and hair made her look like an angel. And Marissa had picked out a dark-green dress with diamonds around the top of the bodice. She had looked beautiful in that color. Her red hair was a perfect match for the green dress. Alysse had talked Gabbi into high heels. They were sparkling silver with little diamonds along the front. The heels were very small though, and Gabbi had laughed and said she would have to practice walking in them every day until prom. She was used to running shoes or loafers. She had never worn high heels before.

After the girls had picked out matching jewelry, they had all gone to the steak house situated on the river. Alysse smiled to herself as she remembered the food the girls ordered. While most girls would order salads or wraps, these two ordered steak and lobster with sides of french fries. And they had eaten every single bite with room for some brownies with ice cream on top for dessert! Even the waitress was amazed that these two slim girls could eat all that food. After dinner, they had gone to get their nails done, and by the time they dropped off Marissa and walked in the door, they were both exhausted. Alysse would never forget that day or later that evening when Gabbi had come into her room and lay in bed with her and hugged her and thanked her for such a fun day. She was so happy that day, and she would never forget it.

"Mom!" Gabbi was talking loudly to her now. Interrupting her thoughts. "Are you listening to me or daydreaming?" Alysse came back to the present and smiled at her daughter and Michael.

"I was reminiscing about the day we spent looking for your prom dress," she told her. "I am sorry, honey, what were you saying?"

"I was just telling you and Dad to please don't make any big plans for my birthday tonight, I honestly just want a cookout here on the deck with some big, juicy steaks."

Alysse looked startled for a minute. "Gabbi, your father and I wanted to take you out to dinner tonight for your birthday, anywhere you would like."

Gabbi told them that she would really rather just spend it at home with the two of them. She didn't even want to invite Marissa over, which had made Alysse sad. But she had brightened up a little when Gabbi looked over with a big smile and mentioned how she hoped that there would be a birthday cake! And then Gabbi had said she was going to go for a hike in the woods. Michael had given Alysse that look out of the corner of his eye. And she knew what that meant. He did not want her to start on Gabbi like she always did about spending so much time alone. Gabbi loved to spend hours in the woods just walking or running. She had told them that she felt at peace there, and she wasn't sure why. Gabbi had never mentioned anything about the wolves from her early years. And Jordan had told them that she probably had forgotten entirely about it.

Watching Gabbi tie up her running shoes, Michael stood up then and told Gabbi she could do whatever she wanted today on her special day. "But first," he had started to say as he grabbed her hand, "your mother and I have a birthday gift for you!" Gabbi looked surprised. She never asked for anything. She honestly did not care about clothes or material items. She didn't want her parents to spend their money on gifts for her. But Michael took her hand, and Alysse grabbed her other hand as she told Gabbi to shut her eyes. Gabbi smiled and closed her eyes as they guided her to the front of the house. Michael told her to open her eyes, and as she did, Gabbi screamed!

There was a red jeep with the top off sitting in their driveway with a big ribbon on it. Gabbi looked at her parents and screamed, "This is for me? This is too much. I love the jeep, you know I do, but this is way too expensive."

Michael and Alysse both started talking at once, telling her that she had never asked them for anything ever. So they were giving her this jeep as a graduation present and a birthday present, but she had to promise to drive slowly and be careful driving it. Gabbi jumped up and down and kissed her parents and hugged them. She ran to the jeep and jumped in. The keys were in the ignition, and she started it up. She told them to come for a ride with her, and they both smiled, and Michael took the front seat by Gabbi, while Alysse jumped in the back seat. Michael had taught Gabbi how to drive both stick shift and automatic. She was a natural. She picked up on driving both right away.

She beeped the horn and backed out of the driveway and took her parents around the block with her new birthday jeep. Michael glanced back at Alysse, and she was smiling from ear to ear. Michael smiled back at her. She was so happy that Gabbi had loved her present. They had talked about it and wanted to give her something that she could use. She had not decided on a college yet. She was taking her time and said she may just think through the next year until she was sure about what she wanted to do for the rest of her life. Alysse and Michael were fine with that. Gabbi wasn't the type of girl that would put off college to party or have fun. She was not like most other girls and boys. She took life seriously and was always thinking things through. They did not want to push her to make a decision that she may not be ready to make. So they had decided to get her the jeep. She had always borrowed one of their cars when she needed it, which was not very often. Gabbi liked to stay home and, of course, once in a while hang out with Marissa.

Gabbi loved the outside and nature and knew she would love driving the jeep especially with the top off in the warm months. And Michael felt so happy looking at Alysse and knowing that she was thrilled with Gabbi's reaction to her gift. Michael glanced over at Gabbi. Her blond hair flying in the wind and the smile on her face melted his heart. He had grown to love this girl, and he couldn't help but worry about the conversation he needed to have with her tonight. He knew she deserved the truth; after all, it was her life, but he was worried about the effect it would have on her. He was going to tell her everything, and it was not going to be an easy story to tell, but Gabbi deserved to know, and he had promised Jesse that he would tell her everything at her nineteenth birthday. Gabbi pulled into the driveway and jumped out and stared at her beautiful red jeep. She hugged her parents again as they walked into the house.

"Gabbi, sweetie, what are your plans for the day?"

Gabbi went on to tell her mom that she was going to go for a run along the trail in the woods and then come home and shower and spend her birthday having a cookout with her favorite family.

"Are you sure you don't want to invite Marissa over for some cake and ice cream? You can pick her up in your new jeep."

Gabbi smiled at her mom. She was always trying to get her to have a social life, and Gabbi honestly preferred being alone. She looked forward to her walks in the woods and being in nature. That was what truly made her happy, but she knew it would make her mom happy if she at least asked Marissa to come over for cake later.

"Okay, Mom, I will text Marissa now and see if she wants me to pick her up and have some cake to celebrate my birthday."

Alysse smiled and told Gabbi to enjoy her run. As Gabbi was stretching out for her run, Michael stopped and put a hand on her shoulder.

"Hey, Gabbi, do you think you can spare some time after cake and ice cream tonight? There is something I need to talk to you about later."

Gabbi looked up at her father with some concern in her eyes. "Is everything okay, Dad?" she asked him.

"Everything is just perfect," Michael assured her. "I just need some of your time later to discuss some things."

Gabbi smiled up at him and agreed and put her long blond hair up in a ponytail and took off running through the trail in their backyard.

Later that afternoon, Michael started the grill as Alysse brought out the steaks. Michael pulled her close and kissed the back of her neck. "I love you, baby, I just want you to know how happy I am with our life here."

Alysse smiled and turned around and kissed him. "Everything is so perfect, Michael, I wish you did not have to tell Gabbi about her past or her mom. I know you promised Jesse, but she is gone now, and what is there to be gained by letting Gabbi know about her past?" Alysse closed her eyes and tried to imagine the way Gabbi was going to take this news.

Of course, Gabbi knew she was adopted, but she never found out about being raised by wolves or any information about her mom. Of course she had asked, but at that time, Michael did not have the information he had received from Anthony, the private detective that he had hired. And after asking a few times early on, Gabbi never brought it up again. Alysse smiled to herself. Gabbi was mature beyond her years. She may be turning only nineteen, but she had the mental attitude of a thirty-year-old. She was so proud of her daughter, and she meant the world to her. She did not want to see her sad on her birthday when Michael told her what he had to tell her. Michael hugged Alysse tighter.

"You know I would do anything to protect our daughter, but I promised Jesse, and she was her mother. Jesse had her whole life ripped out from under her because of the abduction, otherwise she would be raising Gabbi now. I feel the least we can do for having the honor of raising her child and calling Gabbi our own is to let Gabbi know about her mother and what happened to her. Jesse had her reasons for wanting Gabbi to know everything about her past. She wanted her daughter to know that she gave her up to protect her, not because she didn't want her."

Alysse felt a tear running down her eye as Michael said those words. She knew he was right. Gabbi had every right to know that she had a mother who loved her and by no fault of her own had lost her little baby girl. Alysse remembered the agony that almost destroyed her when she had the miscarriages. That fateful day in Colorado had saved Alysse and her marriage to Michael. That dirt-filled little girl that came to her in the woods that day was a gift from God, and she truly believed that there was a reason they found Gabbi that day. And maybe telling Gabbi the whole background of her life was part of God's plan. Either way she knew that Michael was right, like always! Gabbi deserved the truth even if it would hurt her temporarily. She was a strong girl, and Alysse knew she would deal with the news on her own terms.

"I don't even have to say it, Michael, you are right, like always." Alysse smiled up at him and hugged him closer as she pulled his mouth down to kiss him again. "And you can wipe that smug look off your face, buddy," she said to him before she kissed him. After all these years, they still loved each other even more every year.

At that exact moment, Gabbi walked out, and they could hear her clear her throat and say, "Honestly, I think I have the only parents in the world that still make out like teenagers!"

Michael and Alysse smiled at their daughter. Alysse could not help but feel so proud when she saw her daughter walk out. Not only was she smart and considerate and mature, but she was gorgeous. She walked up the deck in a cute baby-blue sundress and a pair of white sandals. Her blonde hair was almost silver in the sunlight. It almost sparkled as she walked. It was so long, almost down to her hip bones. She had a smile on her face, and her eyes sparkled. Oh, she was so beautiful, and it made her sad to think she had never even been on a date yet! She knew Gabbi was not interested in socializing with boys, or even most people on that account, so she pushed that thought aside. She knew that Gabbi would find her soul mate one day, just like she had found Michael.

"Gabbi, my birthday girl, you are breathtaking!"

Gabbi smiled at her mother and came to stand by her parents. "I know you probably want to check to see who this girl is that looks like your daughter but can't possibly be her wearing a sundress!"

Both Alysse and Michael nodded in agreement and laughed. Michael said, "I did do a double take, you look wonderful, sweetie."

Gabbi kissed her father on the cheek and hugged her mom. "I know I usually don't dress up, Mom, but I figured it would be a good time to wear this beautiful dress you bought me for my birthday last year." Alysse kissed her daughter and agreed with her. Gabbi informed them both that she was so hungry she could eat a whole cow. Michael took the foil off the pan holding the steaks that were being marinated, and Gabbi's eyes lit up. "Those are the biggest steaks I have ever seen!" Alysse also pulled out a big green salad and a watermelon and put them on the table.

"Is Marissa coming for dinner?" she asked Gabbi. Gabbi told her that she was going to pick up Marissa after dinner because she really wanted to spend it with her two favorite people. She told them that Marissa would join them for cake and ice cream.

A half an hour later, they all sat down to dinner on the patio. It was a beautiful day. Not too hot, but the sun was shining still, and there was a nice breeze making it a picture-perfect day. They ate almost all the salad, and both Michael and Gabbi had finished a whole steak, while Alysse had only been able to eat half. Michael put his hand on his belly and looked at his beautiful daughter.

"I honestly don't know where you put all that food. You have a great appetite, but you never put on a single pound!"

Gabbi giggled and informed them in her exaggerated voice that she was a growing girl. She also added that she loved to run daily, when she could. Alysse gave both Michael and Gabbi a dirty look and told them they both better have some room left for cake and ice cream. She told Gabbi that she had made the cake herself. Carrot cake, Gabbi's favorite. Gabbi rolled her eyes and told her mother that of course she would have room. She always had room for carrot cake and ice cream. Gabbi left a few minutes later to go pick up Marissa, and Michael helped Alysse clean up the table. Alysse came out with nineteen balloons all done in gold and silver. Michael laughed at his crazy wife.

"Of course, it doesn't surprise me that you would get balloons for our family party."

Alysse also pulled out a small wrapped box and told Michael that even though they had spoiled their daughter rotten with the red jeep, she wanted to get her these earrings when she had seen them in the store. They were diamond stud earrings, but next to the diamond was a blue sapphire that sparkled just like Gabbi's eyes did. Michael told her they were the perfect gift and that Gabbi would love them. Alysse set the box down on the table just as Marissa and Gabbi walked out on the patio.

Gabbi looked at the balloons and said, "Mom, it really doesn't surprise me that you have nineteen balloons sitting out here." She laughed as she kissed her mom again. Marissa walked over and hugged Michael and Alysse. Marissa was still gushing over Gabbi's jeep. She was smiling from ear to ear and telling them about the ride over with the top off. Alysse couldn't help but smile too. Marissa's thick red hair was flying back and forth as she was very animated in this conversation. Alysse told Marissa and Gabbi to sit down and brought out a huge carrot cake that was decorated with a forest and a deer and a few squirrels on it and a couple of wolves at the base of the mountain on the one end of the cake.

Gabbi was smiling ear to ear and exclaimed that this cake was absolutely perfect. She took out her phone and took a few pictures and said, "I may even have to start a Facebook account just so I could post my cake on it."

Marissa stared at her friend with this news and said, "Gabbi, I can help you, and I could be your first friend on Facebook!"

Gabbi agreed to let Marissa help her with her first social media post, and Marissa seemed thrilled at the thought. They all ate a huge slice of cake along with some butter pecan ice cream after they sang

"Happy Birthday" to Gabbi. And of course Gabbi made a wish. When they were done, Marissa pulled a wrapped present out of her purse and handed it to Gabbi. Gabbi was surprised and told Marissa she did not have to get her anything, but Marissa just waved her hand and told her to open it. Gabbi smiled and opened the present and pulled out a light-blue journal with Gabbi's name on the front in silver letters.

"Oh, Marissa, this is perfect, I love it. I wanted to start a journal because now that I am done with school, I have a feeling my life is going to get very exciting!"

At those words out of Gabbi's mouth, Alysse felt herself shiver. Why all of a sudden did she feel that something bad was going to happen? She looked at Michael, and Michael was smiling at his daughter and telling Marissa that it was such a thoughtful gift. Alysse stopped herself. She was not going to let that sudden feeling ruin her daughter's birthday. Alysse tried to put away that feeling that something bad was going to happen, but Michael saw something in her eyes. When Gabbi and Marissa went to take a walk out back in the woods before the sunset, he asked her about it. Alysse had told him it was nothing, just a feeling she had. A premonition of something bad. She had told him maybe it was just because their daughter was turning nineteen and would eventually leave. If not this year, then next year when she decided where she wanted to go to college.

Michael hugged Alysse and said, "Would it be so bad to just have the house to ourselves again?" He wiggled his eyebrows, and Alysse couldn't help but laugh at him.

"You are right again, this will be a new chapter in our lives. Our daughter will still be a part of our life, but she has to spread her wings and find herself," she said to Michael in a voice that sounded a little sad still. When Gabbi and Marissa came back, they all sat around and talked for a few hours, and then Gabbi took Marissa home.

When she walked back into the house, she thanked her mom and dad again for a wonderful birthday. Alysse pulled out the earrings and gave them to Gabbi. Gabbi took the box and opened them while she simultaneously told her mom she shouldn't have. The jeep was enough of a present to last a lifetime. But when Gabbi saw the earrings, she looked like she would cry.

"Mom, I love them, and I will never take them off, ever!" She put them in her ears and showed both parents how they looked. Michael told her that any earrings would look good on his beautiful daughter, and Alysse hugged her daughter for the millionth time that day. Gabbi yawned and then turned to her father and said, "Dad, I didn't forget about our talk you mentioned, are you ready?"

Michael looked at Alysse and nodded at his daughter. "Sure, sweetie, let's go sit outside." Alysse told the two of them that she was going to clean up and then take a bath to relax.

Gabbi sat down on the patio chair across from her dad. Michael could see the worry in her eyes and took her hand that was sitting on the table and put his hand over it. "Gabbi," he started and then took a deep breath. "I have something I need to tell you, and I need you to listen to the whole story first, and then I promise you that I will honestly answer any question you may have, even if we are out here until morning."

Gabbi looked at her dad and squeezed his hand. "Is everything okay with you and mom? You are not sick, are you?"

Michael sighed and felt guilty that his daughter had thought this was going to be some bad news about himself or Alysse. "No, sweetie, nothing like that. I need to tell you the story of you, and the story of your mother."

Gabbi looked up at him with shock in her eyes. "I thought you did not know anything about my mom, you told me you didn't."

Michael squeezed her hand and assured her that when she had asked him early on that he did not know anything. He then looked at his daughter and said, "Gabbi, this is not going to be easy, but it is important that you let me tell the whole story before you make any kind of judgement about anything. The one thing I want you to know is that your mother and I love you more than anything in this world, and it is hard for us to tell you this story. I would much rather keep you from the sad news you will hear today, but this is your life, Gabbi, and it is only fair that you know everything about it, or at least as much as I found out.

"We owe you the truth, and if you hear this story and you want to bury it forever and never bring it up again, then we will support you. If you want to try to find out more about your mom and family, then I will help. If you need to talk to a counselor, then we will support you. We only want you to be happy, Gabbi, but we also want you to know the truth."

Gabbi smiled a weak smile at her father but assured him she would listen to the whole story before she asked any questions. She also told him she appreciated the truth but asked him why now, why on her nineteenth birthday? Michael sat back in his chair and pushed his hand through his hair before he started to talk.

"Gabbi, that is what I promised your mother, that I would tell you this story when you turned nineteen. She did not want you to know before this day because she wanted you to be old enough to process the details."

Gabbi nodded, and Michael took that as a sign to begin. He started with the miscarriages and telling Gabbi how they had wanted a child more than anything, but with each miscarriage that happened, Alysse had become more and more depressed. Michael went on to tell Gabbi about how he had forced Alysse to go on the trip to Colorado. He told her about the city of Loveland, Colorado, and how the cabin in the woods was overlooking the mountains and forest. It was secluded, and how on the first day, her mother had started to show some signs of life again.

Michael told Gabbi that he had thought he was going to lose the love of his life, and he had to try and help her, so this trip was his last hope. Gabbi looked sad and only shook her head, but she moved up closer to the table. Michael told her about the day they walked in the woods and how it felt like the weight of all the miscarriages were lifted off Alysse. He told her with a smile how they went off trail and had a little picnic lunch and how Alysse had laughed for the first time in months.

This part of the story made Gabbi smile. She wanted her mother to be happy, not sad, even in the years she wasn't part of their life. Gabbi couldn't wait to hear more of the story now, and as that thought raced across her mind, she saw the change in Michael's eyes.

Michael squeezed Gabbi's hand again and started to tell the story of how as they were ready to continue on their hike, Alysse had seen something run past. She said it was a little girl. Michael told Gabbi how he didn't believe her at first. But as they started in the direction that Alysse saw the creature run, Michael was blown away when he saw a little dirt-filled toddler. This naked little toddler with a tuft of blond hair.

Gabbi looked confused and started to speak, but then remembered her promise. So she did not say anything. Michael went on to tell the story of how they saw the gray wolves that were watching over this baby. He told her that no matter how crazy it sounded, Alysse and the one wolf had a connection. It was like the wolf had raised this human but knew she did not belong with the wolf pack. Michael told her how he witnessed the wolf nudge the baby toward Alysse, and Alysse, without hesitation, grabbed that screaming, crying little girl and held onto her with everything she had. He continued on about bringing the child to the hospital and the news media frenzy about this baby that was raised by wolves.

He stopped a minute to catch his breath and try to see how Gabbi was taking all this. He couldn't tell. She was just sort of staring at him with confusion. He wanted to answer her questions so badly, but he knew he had to tell the whole story first. He had to get everything out tonight, and he was afraid if they started with questions, the story would not be told. A promise was a promise, but he realized he was feeling a little better himself finally telling Gabbi about all this. It was always his fear that she would find out from some source and accuse Alysse and himself from keeping the truth from her.

He went on about how Alysse never left the little girl's side in the hospital and how he had posted a guard to keep out curious onlookers and the media. He also told her about Anthony, whom he had hired to try and find the little girl's real mom, or the story behind this toddler living in the Colorado forest. He told her about the transformation from a wild little toddler to a beautiful little girl that Alysse worked with daily to try and teach the girl English words and gain her trust. Michael smiled and told Gabbi that he knew from day one in the hospital that Alysse would never let this little girl go.

How she said it was God's plan that Alysse and Michael were in those exact forests at exactly the same time that the little girl ran by.

Michael saw that Gabbi had tears running down her eyes, and she was trying to wipe them away. Michael admired her. She was such a strong girl, keeping her word to not ask any questions even though she must be going crazy trying to figure out what had happened. This story he was telling her sounded more like a cross between a sci-fi movie and an action movie. More like the *Jungle Book* than real life. He went on to tell Gabbi that Anthony could not really find out much information about any missing babies that matched the age and description, but he said he wouldn't stop until he found some type of story about this particular missing baby. He told her how weeks had passed, and they stayed in Colorado working with child specialists to determine the health and any other information they could on this child. This child was a miracle and nothing short of that. Michael pulled out the magazine from sixteen years ago that he had saved and had protected with a plastic cover. There on the front was a picture of a gray wolf pack and a baby with the headlines "WOLF BABY FOUND IN COLORADO FOREST STILL REMAINS A MYSTERY."

Gabbi looked through the magazine briefly. She wanted to hear the whole story and then take the time to research later. Michael added that he paid good money for security to keep his family out of the media. He said this baby was not her. The media was just desperate for any kind of pictures. He had his security guys arrest many people for trying to get into that hospital room.

He laughed then and told Gabbi, "If one or two made it past the guards, absolutely zero made it past your mother."

Gabbi tried to smile at that, but she just didn't even understand all this. She was raised by wolves? What had happened? Gabbi took a deep breath and put her attention back on her father. She knew that there was a lot more to this story, and she needed to know the whole story. She needed to know who she was. Michael had given her a few minutes to process this. Jesus, how do you process this kind of information? He wished he knew what Gabbi was thinking. She was mature for her age, but how could anyone swallow this type of infor-

TJ RITOSSA

mation? But he knew he had to go on. She was waiting now, anxious for the rest and to see what follows. Michael went on to tell her that because they could not find any information pertaining to a missing child, child services wanted to take the case and put her in a foster home. Michael told her how he pulled out all his favors that he could from judges and anyone in authority on this matter.

After a small fight, he and her mother were allowed to take her home. And Michael told her how Alysse was a changed person. She had a daughter that she loved even more than if she had borne her herself. The adoption was finally granted because no real mother could be found. Also, Anthony had tested DNA on many girls claiming the baby was theirs, but none came out a match. Everyone wanted a part of this million-dollar story. Michael went on to say how the years passed by, and they had loved her more than any parent had ever loved a child. Alysse had believed that they were chosen by God to raise this special child. Gabbi was crying boatloads of tears by this point in the story, and Michael got up to get a box of Kleenex he had inside the kitchen. Gabbi started to wipe her tears but told her father to please continue. So that was what Michael did. He told some funny stories throughout to make Gabbi laugh, like how Alysse had bought probably about ten thousand dollars' worth of frilly, girly clothes, but even at a young age, Gabbi had been more of a tomboy, preferring simple shorts or sweatpants. Much to Alysse's dismay. And Gabbi had even rolled her eyes at that, because Alysse had always tried getting Gabbi to wear dresses and high heels, while she preferred shorts and T-shirts and tennis shoes.

Michael explained to Gabbi that he had Anthony on retainer even years after they had brought her home. He said he needed to know why a little toddler girl was left in the Colorado forest and how she survive. He said that years had passed with very little information, and he had started to lose hope that they would ever find out anything about her. And then about ten years later, he told Gabbi that she was about fourteen years old, Anthony had called him and told him he wanted to bring a girl by the office. He said this girl, Jesse, was insisting that she was the mother of the wolf child. Anthony had told Michael that of course he was skeptical, until he picked this girl up from a storefront that she had asked him to come to. He said this girl was different. She was scared to death, scared for her life. So Anthony went with his gut feeling and picked her up and told her he was going to need to test her DNA. She had agreed with a sigh of relief.

Anthony had told Michael over the phone that the minute he picked this girl up and brought her to the clinic, he knew she was the one. He said that Gabbi was a spitting image of the girl. But the girl was older of course and had a worn look to her. But he remembered Anthony's words to this day.

"Michael, this girl is a gorgeous girl that definitely has a story to tell."

Michael had been excited and wanted to meet her right away. But he told Anthony to let him know how the DNA test came out first. He did not want to see another pretty blonde that *may* be related to his daughter. He wanted a hundred percent certain DNA match before he would speak with her. He had told Anthony to rush the tests and to put the girl in a hotel with a guard. Anthony said he would stand guard. He had said this girl was scared of something, and he would make sure she stayed safe.

The next day, Anthony had called Michael, and the excitement in his voice could not be contained. He had told Michael that it was a match. That this girl's DNA matched Gabbi's DNA. He had even talked to the doctor himself that ran the test. He wanted to make sure there were no mistakes on this, and he wanted to make sure the doctor he used could keep this confidential. Michael did not need the media hype starting up again for Alysse and Gabbi. Anthony had said he was on his way over to a discreet building where they decided to meet. It would be too risky to bring her to the house or to his office. After all these years, this story was still being pursued by the media. Michael looked at Gabbi and took both her hands.

"Honey, the minute that Anthony brought Jesse into the building, I knew without a doubt that she was your mother. She was not as tall as you, but she had the same silver-blond hair down her back and the sparkling blue eyes. She was beautiful by all means, but you could tell that she had been through a lot."

Michael pulled out a picture at this time and gave it to Gabbi. Gabbi took one look and knew it was her birth mother. She started to cry. She was a beautiful girl, but she had sad eyes. Michael came over and hugged Gabbi for a few minutes, and then Gabbi stopped crying and ordered Michael to please tell the rest of the story. Michael nodded his head in agreement. He went on to tell how he sat with Jesse for hours with Anthony there also.

She had told him the story from what she knew was the beginning. She told him how she was pulled off the street and forced into sex trafficking. But that was after she had told them that she was pregnant. She had just found out she was pregnant, and she wasn't sure how she was going to tell her boyfriend or her mom. No one had known about her pregnancy when she went missing. Her dad was not in the picture, and she had lived with her mom. She told Michael how she had fought to convince her captors to let her keep her baby, and she believed they were going to let her until she went into labor and delivered the baby.

Jesse had cried as she told Michael that she fell in love with her baby the minute it was born. She also said they wouldn't let her hold the baby for more than a few seconds, and then they grabbed her and wrapped her in the blanket and took her away. She said they never told her what happened but had said they had given the baby to a good home, like they promised they would if she cooperated. She said she had believed them, and it made her want to live so she could escape and find her baby. She said she never really knew where they were. She knew it was a cabin in the forest and could see mountains. She was sold into slavery to a very rich man. He had kept her locked in his house with guards for years, and it was horrible. She had told them about Niko and some of the other names she had heard during the time she was held captive and how she had heard girls crying and screaming while she was at the cabin before she was sold.

She also told them that the man she was sold to was always nice to her, treating her well but never letting her out of the locked house. She was his slave, and he did whatever he wanted whenever he wanted. Michael had debated telling Gabbi this part, but Jesse had been insistent. She wanted her little girl to know what type of people were out there and to not trust anyone. Gabbi had a look of anger, and Michael was worried that this could be too much.

He stopped the story and asked Gabbi, "Are you okay, honey?"

She nodded her head and said she was fine, so Michael continued. Jesse said the man that bought her was starting to lose interest and had other girls he bought at the house. So he wasn't watching her as much. So one night she heard Niko's voice, she would never forget that voice, ever. She tried to listen to the conversation and had heard them talking about her. How finally the media hype about the baby found in the woods was diminishing.

Niko still sounded angry that this so-called wolf baby was bringing reporters into the surrounding forests and mountain areas. And this was a risk to his operation being found out. "Being raised by wolves, how does that happen?" He was drinking and loudly said the little girl was adopted by a couple in Ohio and that was all he knew. He also said he didn't even believe in all this hype. That was a risk their operations did not need.

Jesse had told Michael and Anthony that she had felt like her life had meaning now. She just knew that this baby was hers. It had to be. It was a little girl and about the same time her baby was taken. Her baby was alive and adopted by good parents! She had told them that she knew she had to get out of that house and escape. So she devised a plan. She had maids in the house, so one night she knocked one unconscious with a vase when she came in to draw her bath. It was late at night, and most of the guards were asleep with only one or two she would have to get by. She took the maid's clothing and put her hair in a bun. She grabbed the tray of food and headed out. She had snuck out the back and into the woods with hardly any problems. She was surprised that she had actually escaped her captor.

She was running for her life for months while trying to stay alive. She had found out her mom had passed away a few years after she went missing, and she had really no other family. Jesse told how she spent her days in the library of all places. She knew she was safe there, and she didn't stay in any city for too long. She knew that Niko would be looking for her, and they would kill her. She was a threat to their business. She knew too much, and she was getting older now, so they wouldn't think twice about killing her. Her age made her worthless.

Michael went on to tell Gabbi that Jesse was a smart girl. She had said that she had gone to the library, where she had researched all the information she could get her hands on about the wolf baby and the family that adopted her. She said it wasn't easy, and Michael had remembered how proud he was of her spirit and determination. Jesse told him how she stole food and tried to sleep wherever she felt it was safe. She said one day she got lucky and found an old flyer hanging on a telephone pole. It was an article looking for anyone that might have information regarding a missing three-year-old baby. The flyer was torn up, and she could barely read it. This had been in the state of Texas.

Slowly Jesse had been trying to make her way to Ohio. The flyer had Anthony's number on it and had been handed out years ago when they were trying to find the baby's mother. Anthony had a special phone set up just for this type of call. Michael remembered how Jesse had smiled and said that the flyer had been a sign for her. She just knew that she had to call the number listed and find out about this baby. Her baby. But soon after she found the flyer, she had seen Niko's men in Texas, and she knew they were tracking her. She knew she had to work fast. So Jesse had found a safe place to make a phone call, and she called Anthony, and the rest was history. Michael had asked Jesse to let them involve the police so they could try and stop this sex trafficking ring. She had agreed, but she was scared. Michael and Anthony had assured her that they would protect her.

Michael told Gabbi how he was scared to ask her mother, Jesse, what her intentions were about her daughter. Michael had seemed sad when he told her, "I was afraid we were going to lose you, Gabbi, if your mother wanted you back."

Jesse had known that Michael was worried about losing his adopted baby. She could tell that he loved her baby, and she knew she did not really have a choice. There had been only one right choice to do what was right for her little girl. Michael told Gabbi he would never forget that conversation with Jesse. She had softly told him that she loved her daughter too much to ever try and raise her. She told

70

them that she knew her life was in danger if Niko's men found her. She asked Michael for just three favors in exchange for her giving up her baby to them, and Michael agreed to all three of them. Gabbi looked at her father, and he knew she wanted to know what the three favors were. He smiled at his daughter as he told her what the three favors were.

"She first wanted to see you, and that was the toughest one because I knew your mother would freak out about this. But I explained to your mom that she needed closure, she needed to see her baby girl and know she was safe and in a loving home so she could move on. You see, it was her wish to help fight this human trafficking business and put Niko in jail for life. She knew she couldn't have you in her life, it wouldn't be fair to risk your life like that. She told me she just wanted to see and hug you just one time. So we did that, Gabbi. Remember when we told you that your mom's cousin was stopping by for a brief visit?"

Gabbi nodded her head and asked, "You mean the cousin from California?"

Michael nodded his head yes. "Well, that was your birth mother."

Gabbi nodded her head that she did remember, and she looked so sad again. She had actually been in contact with her real mother and didn't realize it. For some reason, Gabbi felt better that at least her mother had been able to meet her. Michael looked at his daughter and felt her pain. He remembered that night they brought Gabbi to an apartment that they had rented for Jesse. Jesse had looked at Gabbi and hugged her tightly and handed her a little bracelet with a charm, and on that charm was a compass. She told her that she hoped her life would lead her to wonderful things and to always think of her when she looked at the compass. Of course, Gabbi was about fourteen, and she was polite about the meeting, while Alysse was a nervous wreck. Michael was afraid that Gabbi would realize that this cousin looked so much like herself. But Gabbi really didn't say anything, and they went their separate ways. But that was a changing point for Jesse. Jesse was determined now to stay alive and be a witness to the sex trafficking charges that she hoped would put

Niko and his operation in prison for a long time. They just had to find them first.

Jesse had also asked Michael and Alysse for two more favors. She made them promise that they would make sure Gabbi took self-defense classes. She made them swear that they would make sure she knew karate and self-defense and could take care of herself. Jesse had wanted her daughter to be able to fight against anyone that may try to harm her. Alysse was all for this, but Michael was a little leery of it until he saw how Gabbi had loved it. And at the mention of this, Gabbi smiled. She had loved learning how to take care of herself. She especially loved the karate classes. She had moved up to black belt before any other students in her class. And the self-defense classes helped her build self-confidence too. Gabbi was a tall girl, but she was a skinny girl. Neither Michael nor Alysse had any doubt that she could take care of herself if she had to. The thing was they both prayed every night that she would never have to use any of it.

Michael stopped his conversation for a minute and took a deep breath. He wanted to make sure all this information wouldn't overwhelm Gabbi. Michael got up from the table and went into the kitchen and came out in a matter of a minute. He had grabbed a bottle of water and offered one to Gabbi too. She opened it and started sipping while waiting for Michael to finish.

He told her, "The last favor of the three was that when you turned nineteen years old, I would tell you about your past. All of it. That I would tell you about your mom and how much she loved you and wanted only the best for you."

Gabbi started crying again and Michael knew that she must have had a million questions building up. Gabbi tried processing all this information. It sounded like a movie, a dramatic, make-believe movie. And she was the star of this movie. She knew all this information was hard to process, but she also knew her father would never lie to her. He loved her, and she knew this conversation was one that he had been dreading for years. She wiped her tears, and Michael handed her a tissue. She waited because she knew Michael had more to the story. Michael hesitated just a second too long, and Gabbi

72

knew the story was going to end badly before the words even came out of Michael's mouth.

"Gabbi, I just want you to know I tried to help your mom. Anthony and I both did. The police had her under surveillance because they knew she would be a potential witness when they were able to find Niko and his men. Jesse was a wonderful person. She had a good heart, and she was strong, even after all she went through. I paid for her medical bills and a complete checkup. I made sure she had clothes and food and a place to live. Anthony and I helped her get with the police and give accounts of everything she knew so they could put a stop to this terrible business of ruining these kids' lives.

"I had a guard on your mom for the first year, but then she did not want it anymore. She had told me that Niko would have given up or thought she was dead. She wanted to try and live a normal life and get back into a job and career. She wanted to live in California, so we helped her buy a little condo in a small city, right by the ocean. But Niko and his gang found her. I don't know how they did, but they did. Her body turned up in the water at the beach in San Clemente. Some fishermen found her. She had been shot and dumped in the water.

"I am so sorry, Gabbi. I should have insisted she stay here, but she knew the danger and did not want you anywhere near it. We made sure she had a Christian burial, and your mother and I put flowers on her grave every few months. I tried to find any distant family, but I couldn't. And Jesse never talked about your father, she did not want him in your life." Michael stood up and hugged Gabbi because she was crying uncontrollably at this point.

"I will never get to see my real mom," she cried. Michael just hugged her and held her close. That was all he could do for her. He knew she needed time to process this all, and then they could talk about it when she was ready. Gabbi was a strong girl, and he knew that she would need all the strength she had to get through the next year.

Chapter 6

Gabbi opened her eyes slowly. She sat up and saw that she was still wearing her blue birthday dress. She had slept in her clothes. She had never slept in her clothes before. Her mind was foggy as she tried to put the pieces together. She saw the faded picture of her mother on the floor. It all came flooding back to her. She reached down and picked up the picture of the beautiful blond girl. The girl who had lost the best years of her life. The girl that was forced into sex with who knows how many men. It wasn't fair! Life isn't fair! She held the picture close to her as the tears started forming again. She remembered the whole conversation with her dad. Every last word was engraved in her mind and her heart. She remembered the look in his eyes, the worry for her. She closed her eyes again. Maybe if she closed them again and went back to sleep, this would all go away. It could just be a bad nightmare. She opened her eyes and wiped the tears away. She felt like she had no energy.

It was late when she had made her way to bed. Her father had held her for a long time, and then she had wanted to ask him questions about her mother. He had agreed even though it was late. He told her everything he could about her, and Gabbi put every detail into her mind. She wanted to remember everything about the mother that was lost to her. Gabbi lay in bed until her mom poked her head in the door and saw her lying in bed with her dress still on and her hair a mess. Gabbi saw the worry on her mom's face. She had always been close to her, and now that she had learned how she had fought for Gabbi, she loved her even more. The last thing Gabbi wanted was to make her mom worry. Alysse came over and hugged her daughter.

"Sweetie, I know this is hard for you, but I also know you are a strong girl, and in time you will be able to come to peace with all of this." Gabbi just smiled up at her and hugged her harder. "I met your mother twice, she was so beautiful, just like you. She was a tiny little thing, but she was as tough as nails, and she knew from the beginning that the best thing for you was to stay with us. And for that I will always be grateful. Gabbi, you are the best thing that ever happened to us, and all I want is for you to be happy."

Gabbi nodded her head. She just needed time to think things out. She felt like all this had happened for a reason. And she had this overwhelming feeling that there was a plan for her. There had to be a plan for her. Something this bad does not happen for no reason. She jumped out of bed and smiled at her mom.

"Mom, if you don't mind, I am going to jump in the shower, and then I will be down for breakfast."

The worry vanished from Alysse's eyes instantly. Maybe Gabbi would be all right. She was a girl that had been through so much in her young life, so maybe she would just bury it and move on.

"That is fine, honey, I am going to make you some pancakes and sausage, how does that sound?"

Gabbi rubbed her stomach in approval. She actually was not that hungry. She needed to shower and then talk with her parents and then spend the day in the woods. That was the one place where she could think and feel at ease. She was feeling very anxious. She knew she had to think things through, but she also knew that she needed a plan. A plan had just popped into her head, and she knew it was what she was going to do. Gabbi felt like she had a purpose now. She had always felt a little different than other people. She loved being alone and in the woods. And now it was all coming together. She was raised by wolves! It made sense now that she felt safe in the woods, and she felt out of place in public. As silly as that sounded, it had happened, and Gabbi believed there was a reason for it. She was going to turn her misfortune with her early life into something good. Gabbi rushed into the shower. After all, she had a million things to do today.

Gabbi came down the stairs and walked into the kitchen. She could feel her parents' eyes on her, trying to gauge her mood. She smiled at both of them and poured herself a cup of coffee. She saw her mom get up, and Gabbi raised her hand.

"Don't worry, Mom, I am not really that hungry. I will grab some toast and a banana."

Alysse sat back down and asked Gabbi how she was feeling. Gabbi pulled out the chair across from her parents and smiled.

"I am doing well, please don't worry about me. You know I am a fighter. But I do have a few more questions if you don't mind."

Michael patted her hand and said, "Of course not, sweetie, ask away." Michael was surprised at the direction of the conversation. He had thought Gabbi would ask all these questions about her living in the woods and how she survived, but her focus was on the sex trafficking and her mom being kidnapped. Michael did not like talking about this subject with his daughter, especially because of her mom being involved, but Gabbi was insistent. She spent the next few hours wanting to know everything about the guys that kidnapped her mom and the area where she was found. She wanted to know how these guys can get away with kidnapping girls and boys right off the street. Gabbi had sadness in her eyes as she asked her father how thousands of kids disappeared off the street every year, and most of them were assumed to be sold in human trafficking rings?

Alysse had looked at Michael with concern in her eyes, but Michael just gave her a nod. If this was what Gabbi needed to know to move past this, then he would try his hardest to give her the answers that she needed. At least the answers he knew. He only knew about Niko's group that worked up in Colorado. They seemed to get lucky with never getting caught. He knew Niko was a heartless son of a bitch that only cared about money. But when talking to Jesse, he had picked up on some of the information that she gave to him.

According to Jesse, in the beginning when they had picked her up, Niko seemed to have a soft spot for her. He let her stay pregnant when most others would have killed her. For a minute, Michael's mind went to his daughter. Gabbi was a spitting image of Jesse. Michael was glad that they were in Ohio and far away from Niko and his gang. The thought of Gabbi being kidnapped and held by those guys for who knows what purpose made Michael's blood boil. He was determined to try and get Anthony out that way again and help track these lowlifes down and put them away for good. He looked at his daughter and remembered that now he had to make sure she was okay. His focus had to be on her.

This information she had received about her mom and her life was traumatic. Even for an adult, it was a lot of bad news to process at once. He had to make sure she was handling this okay. He reached out and grabbed Gabbi's hand and said, "Sweetie, I was thinking, if you would like to take a drive with me, we could visit your mother's grave. I had her buried here, and it may bring some closure for you."

Gabbi smiled at her dad and got up. "I would love to, Dad, I am going for a run in the woods first, I just need some time to think. But when I get back in a few hours, I would love to be able to say goodbye to the mother I never knew."

Alysse felt her eyes watering and got up to avoid Gabbi seeing. It would do no one any good if they all started crying again. Gabbi came over and hugged both her parents and said, "I love both of you so much. And thank you for fighting for me to give me this life." She then ran out of the door and into the woods. A few hours later, Gabbi came back, and she seemed refreshed, almost better. Michael and Alysse looked at each other and smiled. Their little girl truly was a fighter. She may have had a rough start to life, but it made her stronger than most people.

When Gabbi came back from her run, she changed her clothes and grabbed a sandwich. Michael drove to the cemetery that Jesse was buried at, which was in Columbus. It was a few hours away, and they mostly sat in silence. Alysse had decided to stay back. Michael knew Gabbi was thinking of seeing her mom's final resting place, so he didn't try and make conversation. When they finally got there, Gabbi sat in the car, not moving to get out. Michael came around and opened her door and offered her his hand. She looked at him with gratitude and grabbed it like she was grabbing on for her life. She did not realize how this trip to the cemetery was going to affect her this much. She couldn't help it; she started crying.

Michael pulled her close and just hugged her tightly, not saying a word. What could he say? This beautiful, sweet girl lost her mother, the mother she never even got to meet. And she lost her to a crime that was so terrible and cruel. He felt a tear drop from his eye. He never cried. Well, hardly ever. His heart bled for his little girl and all the suffering she had to endure the past few days. This was more than anyone could endure. But he knew that seeing the grave and just being here would bring some kind of closure. He took Gabbi by the hand, and he walked over to Jesse's grave site. He had picked up some flowers on the way so Gabbi could lay them on her grave. Michael stopped at the end of the grave site. The stone just simply said Jesse Conner on it, with the words "A beautiful soul that was taken way too early."

Gabbi put the flowers on her mother's grave site and then put her hand there. She felt the cold stone beneath her hands, and the tears just started pouring down her cheek. She looked at her mother's name and vowed right there that she would avenge her mother's death. Somehow, someway, she would make Niko pay. She would spend her life fighting against human trafficking so no other family would be torn apart like Jesse's family. Like the family she could have had. She was more determined now than ever. She sat there for about half an hour. And during that time, she talked to her mother in barely a whisper. She did not want her father hearing her. She told her mom that she loved her and wished that she could have spent time with her. She wished she could have hugged her and had conversations with her.

Would her life have been much different? She knew that she was fortunate that she was found by Michael and Alysse and saved from the forest. She probably wouldn't have survived for many years out there. It was a miracle she had survived three years. Nursed by wolves? She had looked up the articles about the wolf girl found in Colorado and how it was a huge media story for a few years. But then it had disappeared over time, just like many other stories. The forgotten wolf girl. Something new to talk about took preference. Some other big story. Her parents had done an amazing job of keeping her hidden, and she knew that could not have been easy. There was even a little plaque in the Loveland, Colorado, forest trails leading to the mountains, where they named it Wolf Girl Path. She personally thought that was a bit much. Gabbi stood up with that thought and smiled at her dad.

"Thank you for taking me here to see my mom, I feel like it will bring some closure."

Michael hugged Gabbi again and took her hand and told her anytime she wanted to come out this way and see her mom, he would take her. They walked to the car, Michael's hand holding Gabbi's hand. Gabbi glanced back one last time when they reached the car. They drove back home with no words being spoken. Michael wanted to give Gabbi time to think, and Gabbi had appreciated the silence. She needed to think. Gabbi was silently devising her plan. She knew where she was going and what she was going to do. What she had to do.

By the time they got home from Columbus, it was late. Alysse was waiting for them with some homemade chicken soup. One of Gabbi's favorite dishes. She had eaten two bowls with about a whole loaf of bread. Alysse honestly did not know how her daughter stayed so skinny, but she was happy she had eaten. That meant she was feeling better. After dinner, Gabbi had told her parents that she was going to bed. She was exhausted. Alysse and Michael had understood and did not blame her one bit. She had been through so much, and they just wanted to help her get over all this so she could continue on with her life. Alysse was so deep in thought that she didn't realize Michael had come up behind her and put his arms around her.

"I think our little girl is going to be fine, she is a fighter like her mom, and I mean her adoptive mom."

Alysse smiled and turned around and said, "I think we should both turn in a little early tonight, we all had a rough day." She gave Michael an overexaggerated wink and kissed him on the lips. The kind of kiss that promised so much more. Michael picked Alysse up in his arms like he used to do when they were first married and carried her up to the bedroom. Even with all the emotional moments today, he couldn't keep that big grin off his face as he gently threw Alysse on the bed.

Gabbi woke up early the next day, eager to start her day. Today was Sunday. She had already planned out her trip. She was going to Loveland, Colorado. She wanted to see the place she was born and where her mother's life was turned upside down. The place where her own life had started. She wanted to see what was going on up there with the human trafficking and find Niko and put a stop to this now and forever. She knew she would need a more solid plan; after all, she was smart enough to know she was going up against a solid group of criminals. Men that though it was okay to steal little girls and boys and sell them for sex or slavery. But she would think about how she would try to find information about Niko and his men when she got there. It was going to be a long drive, and she had plenty of time to think things through while she was driving.

She knew she had to go to Colorado. She felt the draw within her. It was a force pulling her there. She would do this for her mother and for herself. She knew it would devastate Alysse and Michael when she left, and the last thing she wanted to do was hurt them. But this was something she must do. This would be her closure. And hopefully her revenge. She would spend the week looking at maps and the best way to drive there without being detected. She knew her dad had access to the best detectives, so she had to be careful. She would write them a note and have Marissa give it to them.

She needed a few days head start, so she had a plan for that. She had worked off and on for years at the zoo, helping care for the animals, so she had money saved. She never spent money on any-thing and never really went out, so she had a few thousand dollars in the bank, and she would take that out. She spent the week as usual, mostly walking in the forest and hanging out at home. She could tell her parents were still worried about her emotional state, so she tried to show them that she was fine. She even asked her mom if she would like to go shopping with her. Alysse was thrilled! Gabbi never cared about shopping, but she knew it would make her mother happy. So on Thursday night they both went to the mall, and Alysse had insisted on buying Gabbi whatever she picked out. Gabbi was feeling guilty about her plan, and it made her feel a little better knowing that this was making her mom happy.

Even though it was the middle of summer, Gabbi opted for a few sweatshirts and a pair of hiking boots. Alysse had looked at Gabbi with questioning eyes, and Gabbi had told her that these were the new style for the fall and Gabbi had loved them. That seemed to work. Alysse had bought her two pairs in her size and a few shirts and sweatshirts along with a pair of jeans. Alysse insisted on a pretty summer dress, and Gabbi agreed. Mostly because it seemed to make her mom happy. Like numerous other times, Gabbi wished she could have been a girly girl that loved makeup and dresses and going out. This was what her mom had hoped for in a daughter, but instead she got a tomboy.

On the way home, Gabbi informed her mother that Marissa was having a sleepover on Friday night, and then on Saturday, her and a few girls from class were going to a music festival. Gabbi told her it was going to be a weekend event. Alysse had been shocked. She had turned and stared at her daughter. Her daughter going out with a group of girls? She was delighted about this happening all weekend that she did not even question Gabbi about too many of the details. Gabbi was thankful for that. She hated that she had to lie to her parents, she had never lied before, but she did not have a choice. She had to use the weekend to get out of Ohio and into Colorado. She would explain everything to them in a note and would have Marissa give it to them when they got suspicious. That night she spent the night watching a movie with her parents, and then before she went to sleep, she wrote the note she would give them.

When she felt like the note would explain enough but not too much, she called Marissa. She asked Marissa to please give her parents the note when they came looking for her. She didn't give Marissa any other information, and Marissa had finally agreed with worry in her voice. She had told Marissa she would put the letter in her mailbox on her way the next day. Her best friend told her that whatever adventure she was going on to please be careful. Gabbi had assured Marissa that she would. Gabbi had hung up the phone. She was feeling terrible for having to go behind her parents' back, but she also felt excitement and purpose. She felt a purpose in her life, a goal, a direction, and she couldn't stop herself now even if she tried. She would make this up to her parents, but she was nineteen years old and legally allowed to travel by herself. But deep down she knew this was going to cause her parents to worry, and that made her so sad to leave.

Chapter 7

Friday morning came, and Gabbi had already packed a bigger suitcase and put it in the jeep. She had her money and she had gotten a GPS for the jeep so she didn't have to use her phone for directions. She did not want her dad tracing her and planned to leave it off and use it only for an emergency. She walked downstairs, and her mom was drinking her coffee, and she was all smiles. Gabbi knew something was up.

Alysse had jumped up when she saw her daughter come down stairs and said with excitement in her voice, "I thought since this is an exciting weekend for you that we could go get your hair done and maybe a manicure and a pedicure?"

Gabbi tried to force a smile. That was the last thing she wanted to do today, but she knew her mom had probably planned this since last night and had already made the appointments. So Gabbi told her mom that, okay, she would go. She tried very hard to smile at her mother. Gabbi had made it clear to her mom that she wanted to be over Marissa's before dinnertime. The sparkle in her mom's eyes was too much. Gabbi couldn't help but get excited too, so she said, "Maybe we can stop for lunch too?" Alysse was ecstatic!

Gabbi actually had a wonderful day with her mom and came home feeling happy. She had light-pink toenails that never looked better and matching fingernails too. She did not want a haircut or color, so the stylist just trimmed a few inches, which you could not even tell when you looked at Gabbi's beautiful long hair in the back. It came almost to her waist. Gabbi had actually liked the little tapering of the sides of her hair, it had added some body, and she was feeling very pretty, which was something she never really thought about.

She laughed to herself. So the wolf girl grows up into a princess. She thought about what a news story that would make.

They had finished up the afternoon at Alysse's favorite restaurant, which was a little Italian place that had the best salad and breadsticks, and they had both ordered the veal parmigiana too. Gabbi had thought this meal may have to last her for a while. But it was a good one to end the day with. She couldn't eat another bite. When they got home, Gabbi went upstairs and grabbed her backpack and keys and told her mom she was going to go. She told her mom not to worry about her, and she would text her maybe Saturday night to just let her know how things were going. She then grabbed a jean jacket and hugged her mom. Gabbi couldn't help herself as she walked out the door.

She turned around and said, "Mom, you know I think you're the best, and I love you so much! And tell Dad I said goodbye!"

Alysse had smiled and told Gabbi she loved her too. She watched as her daughter walked out the door, and Alysse had felt hope for the first time in a long time. Maybe Gabbi was finally going to start acting like a normal girl her age and start dating and going out. She had never been happier.

Gabbi brushed her back with her hand as she drove past the "Welcome to Indiana" sign. *One state down,* she thought in her head. This was a twenty-hour drive, and she was determined to make it as quickly as possible. Her thoughts were all over the place. She felt free! She knew this was something she had to do for herself and for her mother. She needed to see the place where she spent the first three years of her life. She wanted to see how she would feel there in the Colorado forest. Would she remember anything? She was only three when she left, but the human mind was an amazing thing. She just needed to "feel" the place where her old life had been left and her new one had begun. She was excited, and it amazed her that she did not feel the least bit scared or worried about driving to Colorado by herself.

Her dad would have a panic attack when he found out where she went. Gabbi knew it was inevitable. Her father had resources everywhere, and even though she begged him to not come after her in the note she wrote her parents, she knew he would access all the detectives he could and come find her. That was why she needed to be careful. She had already put her phone away in her purse. She would not turn it back on at all unless she needed it for an emergency. She knew that would be the first thing that her father would do, track her phone. She would have to keep a low profile when she got there. She even thought about camping in the woods. She was not afraid to be by herself. She felt at home in the woods, and now she knew why. But she also needed to research the sex trafficking cell up there. She needed to find out as much as she could. She really didn't have a plan. She knew she could not march in there and start letting the girls go or killing Niko. Her thoughts went black for a minute. Could she really kill a human being? Even one that was pure evil and had ruined her life and was responsible for her mother's death? Honestly, she felt she could. She had to do something to help bring down this group of kidnappers that only cared about money.

Even though Gabbi could care less about her own looks, she knew she was attractive. She knew it from school when the boys would smile at her and later try and ask her out. She knew it from the other girls in school who would give her that look of hate, of jealousy. She never understood and really never cared if other girls hated her because of her looks. She couldn't control what she looked like. She never worked on her looks or even put makeup on. She remembered her mom trying to have a talk with her when she turned fifteen. She giggled to herself at the memory. It was awkward. Her mom had told her that she was a beautiful girl and that boys would try and take advantage of her. Gabbi had looked at her mom with confusion in her eyes.

"Mom," Gabbi had said to her mom with sincere confusion. "You know that I can take down any boy around here, or any girl."

Gabbi had misunderstood her mother because she had never had any interest in boys at all. Her mom had smiled at her and had started to tell her that she could not fight anyone for any reason. She went on to tell her that she was talking about boys trying to kiss Gabbi or even more. Gabbi had shut her mother right down.

"Mom, you don't have to worry about any boys kissing me. I do not like boys, I never want to date a boy, and I am never going to get married."

Her mom had been a little upset, but she smiled at her and had told Gabbi that she would change her mind, and she would date and she would fall in love. She had also gone on to say that she would not want to throw a boy to the ground just for showing interest in her. That had ended the conversation. She had said good night but then overheard her parents talking that night. Her mom was expressing concern about Gabbi's self-defense classes and her black belt classes. Gabbi had not wanted to take them at first, but of course Michael had insisted. He had promised Jesse that Gabbi would be able to take care of herself, and Michael had told Alysse that he had agreed with Jesse's wishes. He wanted his little girl to protect herself.

She thought back on the day she had won her first black belt championship. She had beat out five boys and two girls. Her father was so proud of her, and she was so happy to hold that trophy up high and stand on the first place podium. Looking back now, Gabbi understood her mother's wishes for her. Jesse's wishes for her. This world was a crazy place where little girls and boys could be snatched off the street in a second and sold for sex. Gabbi was not afraid to run into anyone. She could take care of herself, and now she was thankful for the first time that she was attractive. She was going to use her good looks to attract the attention of Niko and his gang. She would research everything first and try to find out what she could from the local police station. She had thought up a story to use. She would say she was doing a project for her college course on sex trafficking in Colorado and what we could do to end this craziness. They would love to help her and give her some facts. She also had great instincts, and she would use them to help her get the information she needed to make sure she found Niko and destroyed him.

She felt her hands squeeze the steering wheel. She was angry now even thinking about it. But she was not going to rush into anything. She first wanted to get to know the area in Loveland, Colorado. From the pictures she had looked up on her computer, Colorado was a beautiful state. Gabbi looked at the sunset and realized she should stop to get gas and maybe some coffee. Her goal was to get to Colorado as quickly as possible even if she had to drive all night to do it. She wouldn't waste her time with any stops other than one last fill up at the gas station. She wasn't even hungry, but she knew she had to keep up her strength, so she grabbed a coffee and a few granola bars. She was back on the road in less than twenty minutes and crossing into the great state of Missouri within the next half an hour. Gabbi felt her pulse race. She was so excited to be going "home."

Gabbi drove through Missouri and then Kansas, and almost nineteen hours after she had left her home in Ohio, she drove into the state of Colorado. She was so, so excited that she was finally here! She stopped to eat some breakfast and stretched her legs. Her next stop would be Loveland. She could see the mountains in the distance, and the whole state seemed amazingly beautiful. She pushed the gas pedal down a little further, trying to get there as soon as possible. She didn't even know where she was going to stay, but she would go into town later. Right now she knew she was headed to the forest on the outskirts of town. She looked at her GPS and started the few hours' drive north past Denver. She could not contain the excitement she was feeling. It was more of a pull, some force pulling her closer to her destiny.

Gabbi had always felt a little different, a little lost with her life. She had felt like something was missing. Something important. She, of course, loved her parents, Michael and Alysse. She again put her thoughts on her adoptive parents. Michael had told her there was really no information on her real father. Jesse had not wanted him in the picture obviously if she hadn't told him about the baby. But there was her mom. Her beautiful, selfless mother who fought to keep the daughter she had never even held safe from any harm, even when she knew she couldn't be a part of her daughter's life. She would take revenge on her mom. She would help fight human trafficking the rest of her life. She would make her own life mean something more than just living. She would do all this in her mother's honor. This last thought fueled her motivation even more.

As Gabbi drove, she looked up at the horizon and saw the mountains and the forest. She had asked her dad details about the area where they had found her with the wolves. She knew she was close; she just felt it. A few miles down the road, she saw an overlook at the entrance to the forest and she pulled her jeep in and grabbed her backpack with a bottle of water in it and a sweater. She took her phone out of the glove department and threw that in too. She would only use it for an emergency purpose. She did not want to put out any signals that her father would trace. She was going to call her mom later in the evening to just check in and buy herself some time. She felt a tinge of guilt as she got out of the jeep. She had washed up at the last gas station she had pulled into.

She put on a clean T-shirt, one of her favorites, a light-blue shirt that had the words "Save the Animals" on it. She put a sweatshirt around her waist and had thrown on some deodorant and white shorts. Her hair she had put up in a ponytail that went all the way to her waist. She had brushed her teeth in the gas station bathroom and glanced in the mirror. She had never been the type of girl to stress about her looks. She knew she was considered pretty because of being told that often. She would just smile and say thank you. She honestly really didn't think about her looks too much. Of course, she cared about personal hygiene, but that was about it. She giggled to herself. She just did not really care too much if she had makeup on or not. Or if the boys thought she was pretty. That seemed frivolous to her, and she had more important things on her mind. She had never found a boy that she was interested in. She didn't know if one actually existed.

With that thought, she took a deep breath and thought to herself, *Here I go!* She glanced back at her jeep and headed into the forest. She had researched and drawn out on the maps the location of where she was found by her parents. She had been careful to get as much information from her father, and she did lots of research on her own. She knew the forest was vast, and she had even researched the dangers to be found there. She wasn't the least bit worried about danger. She could take care of herself. She took a deep breath of the mountain air and knew she had made a good decision about stopping here. She had just felt that this was the place to stop. She knew it was the same forest her parents had found her sixteen years ago.

But the forest was huge, and according to her father, it had been deep into the woods. Their cabin had been higher up in elevation. Gabbi pulled out her map. She would need to hike for a few hours to get to the spot that she had pinpointed on the map. The place where she was found. Or close to the area. She was looking forward to the hike almost as much as the destination. She loved the forest and the fresh air up here in Colorado. It was nothing like the air in Ohio. She felt exhilarated!

Ever since her father told her about her past and her years in the forest with the wolves, she had wondered if this had made her the type of girl she was now. More of a loner and loving the outside but always feeling a little like she did not fit in. This was where she belonged. She felt free and happy. The view was amazing. She started to hike on the trail, taking in the forest and sensing the presence of animals. Her senses had always been good. She now believed it was because of her first three years living with her wolf family. Her wolf family? She let her thoughts stay on that for a minute. She had a connection with some animals, and others were nervous around her. Alysse had worried about that from the beginning. It was never a big deal to Gabbi though. Was it from a scent? From her being nursed by her wolf mother? Sometimes she would let herself be engulfed in these thoughts, and it would drive her crazy! But she came back to the future like she always did.

Gabbi knew she was a down-to-earth girl. She remembered her first teacher conference and her parents coming home telling her that her teacher had said that she was a down-to-earth girl. Gabbi wasn't sure if that was a good thing or a bad thing. Gabbi heard a faint noise, and it brought her back to the present. The trail she was walking on was narrowing as it inclined. She stopped and looked around. She was heading up on a trail leading farther up the forest, closer to the mountains and at a much higher elevation. She did not see anyone on the trail at all. She looked up at the trees. These trees were so big, and they seemed to go on forever. She took another big breath and started walking again. She saw a few squirrels playing up in a tree that was to the left of her. That could have been the sound she had heard. She started to pick up her pace a little. She had a good five hours before the sun set, and she really wanted to take her first trip to the forest today instead of waiting until tomorrow.

After sitting in the car for almost twenty hours, she needed this exercise. She hiked briskly for another hour or so and then realized the trail sort of stopped and turned back toward the way she came. Gabbi stopped and looked around and felt a sense of peace. She really did love it here. She looked to the right and noticed an overgrown trail. It didn't look like it was used much, and it was definitely off the beaten path, but it was the direction she wanted to go. She tied a piece of string to a tree before she walked forward onto the so-called trail. She was great at direction, but she did not want to take any chances of getting lost. Not that she would mind spending more time up here in the forest, but she really needed to find a place to stay tonight and for the next few days. Plus, a shower sounded like heaven to her.

Gabbi trekked up the trail, and the farther she went, it seemed to get a little steeper. She walked about a half hour more before she decided to stop and take a break. She looked around at the area, and she felt something stir inside her. There was a sense of familiarity. She was remembering some small flashbacks of running through a forest. Was it this forest? Until now, her first three years of life had been all but erased from her mind. Maybe coming back here, to Colorado, will bring back some early memories. Gabbi saw a cave up ahead with a cluster of rocks around it. And there was a big flat rock that would be perfect for her to rest on. She walked over to the cave and sat down and glanced around. Her eyes were drawn to the cave opening. There was an energy here.

Her heart started pounding faster, and she jumped up to look inside. She felt something here, some kind of presence. Was this the area she had spent her early years? Gabbi closed her eyes, hoping that some memory would come back to her. Anything! She needed a sign. She was desperate for a sign. Could this be a cave where the wolves stayed in the winter months? Gabbi knew she would never get a real answer to her questions, but without a doubt she knew she felt some kind of belonging here. She smiled to herself and sat back down on the flat rock.

Her thoughts went to her mother. She couldn't even imagine what her mother went through. Gabbi didn't want to dwell on the sadness. She wanted to think of her birth mother as being happy. But the thoughts of her being kidnapped and killed wouldn't leave her head. She wanted to do something for her mother. She wanted to avenge her and every other child that was ripped from their parents. Their lives changed forever because of greed and evil men. She started to feel her anger build up, and Gabbi knew she needed a clear head if she was going to make her plan work. She had to be smart and alert. She knew her father would probably come look for her, so she had to be careful. Gabbi froze for a second. Without a doubt she knew she wasn't alone anymore. She saw something pass through the edge of the forest to her left. Something bigger than a squirrel. She didn't move. She did not feel any fear, but it was her instinct to stand still. She wasn't sure what it was. Could it have been a wolf? She knew there were many wolves up here in the forest, and she was sure there were even more up here toward the mountains.

When she was researching the area, she also learned that there were many animals that she could come across up here. There were coyotes, bobcats, and bears. And of course, the gray wolf. She sensed she was being watched, but oddly, she didn't feel like she needed to be afraid. Gabbi relaxed and took out her water and an apple she had brought with her. She really wasn't even that hungry, but she knew she had to keep up her strength. It would not help her at all if she became dehydrated. So she took a few sips from her water bottle and realized she was so tired. She had driven almost all night to get here and had only slept for a few hours. Gabbi took a glance around again and realized she was so far off the regular path that there was probably not another human being within at least a few miles. Whatever animal that had come upon her earlier must have left. Probably lost interest. So she decided she would just rest for a few minutes and then head back to town. She would be back out here again tomorrow anyways. She leaned up against a tree and shut her eyes. She felt the mountain breeze softly blow over her body, and she felt so happy. She was at peace here.

Gabbi awoke suddenly feeling startled. She felt out of sorts. Glancing around, she realized she must have dozed off. She instantly felt that she wasn't alone. She slowly glanced around and saw a gray wolf sitting on the rock maybe twenty feet from here. Her heart skipped a beat. Oddly enough, she wasn't afraid at all, only curious. The creature was beautiful! It had fluffy fur and pale-yellow eyes. It was bigger than a dog and had a majestic stance to it. Gabbi stared at it with no fear. She saw a movement to her left and realized there were more. She could see three or four, but the rest stayed back farther. They were probably just as curious as she was. She just sat there very still, and to her amazement, the bigger wolf slowly came closer to her.

Gabbi put out her hand, and for a minute she thought that the wolf was going to make contact. But at the last minute, the wolf took off running toward the trees, and the others followed. Gabbi watched them until they were out of her sight completely. She somehow felt honored. Most wolves would try to avoid human contact instead of trying to be seen. She knew they were endangered, and most people would go their whole life without seeing a wolf. They did not seem hostile toward her, and she found herself wishing that they would have stayed longer.

This would be a day she would never forget. This forest and this cave area was where she felt a connection. She did not want to leave, but she knew she would be back tomorrow, so she got up and glanced at her watch. She realized that she had only been sleeping for about fifteen minutes. The wolves had woken her, or she had subconsciously awoken because she felt their presence. Gabbi started to head down the trail as her thoughts kept going back to the wolves. Was she dreaming? Why would they have just sit there staring at her? She couldn't wait to get back and do some more research. She picked up her pace to the point where she was almost running. She stopped dead in her tracks halfway down the overgrown trail. This time she was a little frightened.

There standing in front of her was a man. She could tell from his expression that he was even more surprised to see her than she was to see him. The man pulled himself together and smiled at her. He walked up to her and at the same time she walked backward a few steps. He spoke first.

"Hello, you scared me half to death. What are you doing out here all by yourself?"

Gabbi stopped and did not say anything.

The man walked a little closer and held out his hand. "My name is Phil, my friends call me PJ."

Gabbi managed to mumble the word hi but did not shake his hand, but she did tell him her name was Gabbi. PJ looked at Gabbi. Boy! She was a beautiful girl, and she was out here by herself? All of a sudden he got a little angry and said to her for the second time, "What are you doing out here by yourself, especially off the trail? Don't you know how dangerous it is for you to be hiking alone. Especially a girl that looks like you."

For some reason, that last sentence brought Gabbi back to life and made her angry. Another typical man that thinks women cannot protect themselves.

"What do my looks have to do with anything? Do you think I can't take care of myself because I am a pretty girl out here hiking by herself?"

PJ could not help himself and started laughing. Here in the middle of nowhere was this absolutely gorgeous girl standing in front of him with her hands on her hips and her baby blue eyes flashing with fire. She looked like she wanted to punch him in the face. He started laughing even harder. He realized that this was not helping the situation. Boy, did he have a way of making bad first impressions. PJ stopped laughing, but he couldn't wipe the smile off his face.

He stepped closer to her and said, "Listen, Gabbi, I apologize. I meant nothing bad at all when I said that. I just am surprised to see anyone on this trail, especially a young girl by herself. And I have no doubt you can take care of yourself, but these woods could be dangerous if you're not familiar with them."

Gabbi was still angry at this guy and she wasn't even sure why. Obviously the guys in Colorado were the same jerks like in Ohio. She was usually polite to everyone even if she didn't talk that much. She decided she did not have time for this, so she just walked right past PJ without saying another word and headed down the trail. PJ caught up with her and grabbed her hand to stop her. That was a mistake. Gabbi turned around toward PJ and gave him a look that wiped his smile right off his face.

"Do not touch me," Gabbi said slowly.

PJ dropped his grip on Gabbi and came up beside her. "Can you please just listen to me for a minute? I work here in the park system, I am a park ranger part-time, and I also work for the police department, so I will not hurt you."

Gabbi seemed to relax a little, but she still turned away from PJ and started down the path. PJ followed her for a few minutes until she turned around and looked at him.

"Are you going to follow me for the rest of my hike?" Gabbi asked him.

PJ put his hands on his hips and sternly said, "Yes, I am. It is my job to make sure any person in the park is safe, and it is getting close to sunset, so I would feel better if you would let me walk you back to your car. Is your car parked close?"

Gabbi was getting very aggravated with this guy. She had so many things to do and so little time. She did not need a protective park ranger following her around. She turned and said to PJ, "I am sorry if I came off angry, I just came into town, and I don't have time to waste. Like I told you before, I know about the animals here, and I will be very careful. I honestly can take care of myself." She turned and started down the path at an even quicker pace. PJ was not going to be turned away that easy, especially by this girl. She was the most interesting thing that has happened to him in a while.

He came up beside Gabbi and said, "It is not just the animals that you have to worry about up here. There is a big human trafficking threat up here around the area of Loveland and the other towns adjacent to Denver. If you're not familiar with human trafficking, then let me tell you that in a matter of minutes, you could be kidnapped and have the rest of your life ruined."

Gabbi stopped in her tracks so fast that PJ ran into her and almost knocked her down. His arm reached out around her waist and pulled her toward him to stop her from hitting the ground. Gabbi caught her balance and looked up into a pair of mesmerizing green eyes that seemed to twinkle with laughter. She pushed herself out of PJ's arm and felt herself blushing. What the hell was wrong with her? She didn't get this way around guys. She never even had any type of reaction to any of the many guys that had tried to flirt with her. She took a deep breath and remembered why she stopped so abruptly. PJ had mentioned the human trafficking ring. He might be able to help her get the information she needed. He may even be able to save her many hours of research in the Loveland library. She decided to do something she had never done before—flirt! She smiled at PJ and put her hand on his arm.

"Thank you so much for catching me, PJ, I apologize for stopping so fast."

PJ felt his heart beat a little faster when she flashed that smile at him. "No problem at all. I am glad to see you don't hate me anymore," PJ said with a returning smile. Gabbi brushed her hair back that had escaped from the ponytail. She started asking PJ what he knew about the human trafficking here in Loveland. PJ went on to tell Gabbi that he was helping the FBI try and track down a few missing girls from this area. He told her that there was a big problem in this area with missing girls, and they were almost positive that they were all being kidnapped by a group that had been working in this area for close to twenty years. Gabbi was excited about this news coming from PJ. She turned to him as they were heading back down the path and told him that she was from out of state and she had always felt a connection with Colorado. It was a state she had always wanted to visit. She told him that she also was doing a project on human trafficking for a summer college class she was taking.

"So you came to Colorado just to find out about human trafficking? Specifically here in Loveland?" PJ asked with a little bit of surprise.

Gabbi replied, "No, I love the outdoors and the big forests, and I have a slight family connection to Loveland, so I decided to do a road trip and come out and research a little."

PJ was happy that Gabbi had changed her opinion of him. He looked at her again. She really was a beautiful girl, but there was more to it than that. He saw something wild in her baby blue eyes. He was definitely attracted to her, but he did not want to let on and scare her off. He was hoping for a second meeting. PJ saw the parking lot up ahead and glanced at the sun that was almost ready to set. The only car in the lot beside his ranger car was a red jeep. He pointed to the jeep and said, "I am assuming that the jeep is your ride?"

Gabbi nodded in agreement, as they both walked over to the car.

PJ did not want this to be the last time he saw Gabbi, so he said, "So where are you staying in town?"

Gabbi hesitated for a minute. She really did not trust him, but she really needed PJ to help her with her goal, so she told him she had just driven into town a couple hours ago and hadn't even looked for a place to stay. She asked PJ if he could recommend a hotel. "I can do better than a hotel," he said with a huge smile. "My brother rents out a little cottage in the back of his yard. He has a few acres, and the suite has a bathroom and small kitchen along with a bedroom." He went on to tell Gabbi that it was a small cottage, but the view from the large window in back faced the forest and the mountain, and best of all, it was on the outskirts of town, so about fifteen minutes from this parking lot.

Gabbi wasn't sure about this. On one hand, the location was perfect for her, and if her father, or she should say *when* her father came looking for her, it would be harder for him to track her down. She realized whether she liked it or not, she needed PJ and his connections to the police. Gabbi looked again at PJ. She couldn't really tell his age. He could be anywhere from twenty-five to thirty. He was tall, probably about six foot, four inches, but he had more of a thin athletic body. He did have a very contagious smile, and she realized for the first time that she thought he was very handsome in a rugged sort of way. He had thick blondish brown hair and beard stubble. Gabbi stopped her thoughts right there. She had never been interested in any guy before and this was not a good time to start. Her reason for this trip had to take top priority. She wasn't sure what she should do. This was all so unusual for her. She remembered how she saw him on the trail that was overgrown and wondered why he was up there off the beaten path. She decided to ask him.

"PJ, why were you on the trail that was overgrown, you said yourself no one ever goes up that way, so why would you?" For a second she wondered if she should trust him at all. She didn't know anything about him. What if he worked for the traffickers? She was starting to take her keys out and slam the door on PJ. PJ smiled at her and told her that it was his job as a ranger to keep all the forest safe, so he knew all the trails whether they were used or not. He went on to say how he loved the outside and especially felt at peace when he climbed up the trails that were usually deserted. He went on to tell her how he felt a connection with the animals that lived in the forest, and many days he would go up the trail as far as he could go and just lay there and think.

PJ told her that he felt the forest was the one place on earth where he felt free and happy, where he could get away from the city life. Gabbi felt something stir inside her. PJ and her were alike in this way. She decided to make a decision and told PJ that she would like to take the cottage that his brother had if it wasn't too expensive. PJ was ecstatic about this, but he tried not to show it. This would give him a reason to see her while she was in town.

"Let me call my brother real quick and see if it is available, how many nights are you looking to stay?"

Gabbi said, "I'm not sure yet, but if I could rent it for a week, that would be good." PJ walked off a little while he was talking on the phone. Gabbi thought that was a little suspicious. Did he not want her to hear him? *There I go again.* She smiled to herself. She was always suspicious, but she felt she had a fairly good reason. After all, look what happened to her mother Jesse. Maybe if she had been a little more suspicious, then she would be alive today. This world was a crazy place, and she needed to be alert and cautious so she could do what she had set her mind to. She glanced at PJ as he walked back over to her. He told her that it was all set. His brother had said the room was available for the next week, and he would save it for her. He told her it would be $500 for the week, and Gabbi agreed that was a fair price. She actually felt that the price was cheap for a place so close to the mountains and forest here in Colorado, but she wouldn't argue the point.

PJ told Gabbi where the cottage was at, but he told her to follow him back into town. His shift was over anyway, and he could introduce her to his brother and get her settled. Gabbi couldn't help herself; she smiled at PJ. Not a fake smile because she needed him, but a genuine smile because she realized she liked him. So she thanked him for all his help and jumped in her jeep and started to follow him out of the parking lot. She glanced back at the forest. She felt a sudden feeling of sadness at leaving. But she had plans to come back first thing tomorrow and visit the area again. It just felt like she needed to be in this place where she had spent her beginning years. Where her mother had once been. She yawned and realized that she was very tired and couldn't wait to sleep in a real bed for tonight.

Gabbi followed PJ to a street about fifteen minutes away. The houses were few and spaced far apart. It was a beautiful street, and she looked up to see the sun starting to set against the outline of the mountains. She pulled into the driveway that PJ pulled into, and he motioned for her to go in front of him and pull the car around back. There was a driveway going to the back, and there was the cabin all the way in the back. Again, Gabbi stopped and wondered if she should trust him. This could be some kind of setup to kidnap her. But as she sat there not moving, she saw another man come out of the house. He had a big smile on his face and a boy about two years old in his arms. He let the boy down and he started running toward PJ.

"Uncle Phil! Uncle Phil!" He was so excited and flung his little body right into PJ. PJ picked him up and swung him around a few times, much to the little boy's delight. Gabbi decided that no kidnappers would have a cute little boy around, and she realized she was being crazy. Gabbi parked the jeep and jumped out, grabbing her backpack. She headed toward PJ and the other man. PJ introduced Gabbi to his brother, John.

Gabbi held out her hand to shake hands with John and said, "Thank you so much for allowing me to rent your room on such short notice, I really appreciate it."

John smiled a huge smile. She could see how both men were related. They both had these infectious smiles!

"It's a pleasure to meet you, Gabbi, and of course, anything for my brother."

Gabbi didn't miss the wink that John gave PJ. She even noticed that PJ was blushing a little. What did that mean? PJ walked over to Gabbi and introduced his nephew, Jax. Jax smiled at Gabbi and shyly said hello. Gabbi took the little boy's hand and shook it just like she did with his father.

"Why, Jax, hello!"

Jax seemed to love that she shook his hand and looked at his dad with a very proud smile on his face. John gave Gabbi the keys and told her to follow him, and he would give her a quick tour. Gabbi, John, and Jax went into the house. PJ came up beside her and grabbed her backpack from her. Gabbi normally would argue that she was quite capable of carrying it herself, but honestly she was exhausted, so she let it go. They walked up to a cute little cottage. When they walked in, Gabbi let out a big "wow" and walked right up to the big picture window in the living room. PJ was right.

The window overlooked the forest and the mountains in the distance. The sight before her was breathtaking. John and PJ both smiled. John asked Gabbi where she was from and picked up the slight hesitation before she answered Ohio. He wondered why this beautiful young girl drove from Ohio to Colorado by herself. He was hoping that she was not in any kind of trouble. He looked at PJ. His brother was definitely taken with this girl, and he was in law enforcement, so John decided not to worry about it. He showed Gabbi the small kitchen and the bedroom and bathroom upstairs. The rooms were on the smaller side, but the house was impeccably clean and decorated in a modern type of western decor. Gabbi absolutely loved the place! The view from the living room and her bedroom were amazing, and when John opened up the door off her bedroom to a little deck outside, she was all smiles.

Gabbi said sincerely, "This is absolutely amazing! I love it." She reached into her purse and pulled out $500 cash.

Both men were surprised by the amount of cash this girl was carrying around, and PJ had to stop himself from lecturing her about safety. He really needed to get to know this mystery girl that showed up in Colorado. But he would wait until tomorrow. He did not want Gabbi to get spooked by him. Well, not spooked, but more like aggravated. John took Jax by the hand and jotted down his phone number on a pad on the table. As he walked out the door, he said, "If you need anything, Gabbi, you call me, I am just right up the driveway. My wife, Megan, should be home any minute from the store, but it is getting late, and I will introduce you tomorrow to her."

Gabbi thanked John and said good night to Jax. As they walked out the door, Gabbi turned to PJ and said, "Thank you again, PJ, this is perfect for me."

PJ smiled and said he was glad he could help. He looked at Gabbi and then went to the refrigerator and saw it was bare. "Do you want to go grab something to eat? I don't think there is any food here if you get hungry."

Gabbi looked at PJ and realized she was half tempted to go with him. Would it be a date? she wondered. She stopped herself again. What the hell was wrong with her. She had a mission to accomplish and could really use PJ's help, but that was it. She was not looking to find a boyfriend. She thanked PJ but told him she was exhausted and needed to call her parents to let them know she arrived safely. She smiled and asked him, if he had time tomorrow, if he would be able to help her with her project.

PJ looked a little uncomfortable. He didn't like the subject of human trafficking but then smiled and said he would be happy to. He asked Gabbi what her plans were for tomorrow, what time she would be free. Gabbi told PJ that she planned on doing some hiking and exploring the town a little tomorrow, but anytime in the late afternoon she would be free. PJ turned to face Gabbi and said, "How about if I take you out to dinner tomorrow, and then afterward we could come back here, and I will bring my laptop. I have some of my research about the sex trafficking ring stored on it."

Gabbi felt her heart beat a little faster. So she would be going on a date. Her first real date! She told PJ that it sounded like a good plan, and he wrote his phone number down next to his brothers on the piece of paper.

"I want you to put this number in your phone tonight, you promise me?"

Gabbi rolled her eyes but took out her phone and copied his number in her contacts. She turned to him and said, "Are you happy?"

PJ nodded his head yes and headed for the door. He turned around before he walked out and told her that if she took a right out of the street and went up about four miles, there was a coffee shop on the left that had great muffins and breakfast sandwiches and, of course, the best local coffee. Gabbi thanked him for the information and said good night to him. She watched PJ walk out to his car and pull away. She locked the door and texted her mom that she was having so much fun and that they were all planning on hanging out at the pool tomorrow after breakfast. She asked if that was okay.

Her mom seemed so happy for her and said of course it was. She texted Gabbi that she was so happy she was having a fun weekend with the girls. She asked her what time she would be home tomorrow because she couldn't wait to hear all about the weekend. Gabbi felt instantly guilty. She did not want to hurt her mom or her dad. And she absolutely hated lying to them. But this was something she had to do. She texted her mom that it might be late tomorrow evening, but she would text if that changed. She told her mom she loved her and told her to tell Dad that she loved him too, and then she took a quick shower.

Gabbi realized she was hungry, so she pulled out a power bar and some nuts she had left over from her drive up. She walked upstairs and fell into the soft bed. She was so excited about tomorrow and the hike back into the forest, but she also had to admit to herself that she was excited about meeting up with PJ and finding out what he knew. Everything was coming together. The last thought before she fell into a deep sleep was what she should wear tomorrow night when she went out to dinner.

Chapter 8

Gabbi woke up startled. She felt confused. The way you feel when you're not sure what is going on. She glanced around the room, and then it all came flooding back to her. She relaxed and smiled and saw the sun streaming in through the big window. She jumped out of bed and went out on the patio. Oh, this view was gorgeous! She inhaled the fresh mountain air and felt charged. She was so excited about today, and she wanted to get it started as soon as possible.

The excitement of exploring the forests here! There was nothing Gabbi liked more than hiking or running through the forests. It always made her feel happy. It made her feel free. Her mom always referred to her as a free spirit. If she was having a bad day, she would lace up her running shoes and head out into the forest. And she was even more excited about being in a whole new state with a big, beautiful landscape to explore! She spent about fifteen minutes pulling on a pair of shorts and a T-shirt that had the word *wanderer* written across the chest. She washed up and pulled her long hair into another ponytail. She never really wore makeup, and she found herself wishing she had some she could use for tonight. Maybe she would stop and buy some. That thought made her giggle. Even if she was to stop at a store that sold makeup, she would have no idea as to what kind she should buy. She put on her running shoes and headed for the door.

The coffee shop that PJ told her about sounded so good right now. She was going to stop and grab some coffee and see if there was a little store close-by where she could buy some essentials for the week. Gabbi glanced at her phone and saw that it was about 9:00 a.m. This was good. It was early enough still. It would give her lots of time to explore the forest and maybe even the town. She shut the door behind her and jumped in her jeep. There was no movement outside at the main house, so she drove out the driveway and followed the directions that PJ gave her. Dark Heart Coffee Shop was the name on the sign, when she pulled in and got out of her jeep. The smell of the bakery was tempting even from outside the door. Gabbi ordered a large coffee and an egg and cheese biscuit. She was so hungry, and she knew she would be burning quite a bit of calories, so she decided to buy a muffin and save it for later. A chocolate chip muffin that was almost too big to fit in her hand. Oh, did it look good though! They smelled so good she couldn't pass it up.

She ate her breakfast in the jeep and then headed toward the forest where she had parked yesterday. When she was about five minutes away, she passed a sign for a roadside market off to the left. The sign looked like it had seen better days, but she decided to stop. She wasn't sure why, but she felt like she needed to check out this little market off to the side of the road. As she drove down the dirt road that led to the open air market, she smiled. Such a cute little place greeted her when she walked into the open air market. There were fruits and all types of vegetables. She saw some Native American blankets and was drawn to the dream catchers that were handcrafted and hanging from the ceiling throughout a building she went into. Gabbi saw one that was blue and gray, and it had pink and white feathers. It was beautiful! She had to have it, and she grabbed one for her mom too. The one for her mom had a green and yellow color scheme. Gabbi grabbed a few pieces of fruit and some water bottles and went to pay.

The lady at the cash register was of American Indian descent. It was hard to tell her age, but she was a very old lady, and she had eyes that seemed to change from green to gray. The lady started ringing Gabbi up, and all of a sudden, she stopped. She stared at Gabbi and grabbed her hand. Gabbi was taken back and shocked at this sudden move. Her instincts were to pull her hand away. But before Gabbi could do that, the old lady put both of her hands around Gabbi's hand and held tight. The lady stared into Gabbi's blue eyes and smiled.

"I am from the Ute tribe, we have long lived here in Colorado."

Gabbi didn't know what to say, so she told her that her name was Gabbi. The old lady let go of Gabbi's hand and finished ringing her up. After Gabbi paid, the old Indian lady grabbed Gabbi's hand again and put a bracelet around her wrist. Gabbi was surprised and looked at the bracelet. Gabbi felt some kind of emotion when she looked at the bracelet. The bracelet was handmade from a thick string wound together in different colors, and at the center was a charm. The charm was of a wolf head, and it had a single stone that was supposed to be a blue eye. The bracelet was beautiful, and she looked at the old lady. Gabbi asked her how much the bracelet was, and the old lady shook her head no.

"This is for you and you only. You have the spirit of the wolf inside you, I sense it."

Gabbi was shocked again. How did this lady know about her past? Did she know her mom? Gabbi was going to ask her, but the old lady stopped her.

"Gabbi, I feel it in you, and you must protect the wolves always and follow your path with this wolf blood that runs through you. This is a gift."

With that, the old lady handed Gabbi her bag of items she purchased and walked in the back room. Gabbi touched the bracelet again and felt something. She wasn't sure what but definitely some kind of power, or so she thought to herself. It was just an Indian bracelet given to her by a superstitious old lady. She glanced again at the bracelet and smiled. It was definitely a gift fit for her. It was also really cute. Gabbi brushed it off and headed back outside. She put the fruit under the seat except for a peach that she stuffed in her backpack with two bottles of the water.

She finished sipping her coffee just as she pulled into the parking lot of the park she went to the day before. Gabbi noticed that there was another car in the parking lot. It was a beat-up pickup truck with a cover over the back. As she got out of the jeep, she thought to herself that she hoped she could get to the secret trail without running into anyone. She really needed to explore on her own. After she locked the jeep, Gabbi made her way to the edge of the forest and started up the trail. She felt alive when she stepped into the forest. Her body was feeling energetic, and the morning sun was not that strong yet.

It was a perfect day for hiking, and she planned to take full advantage of this beautiful day. She headed into the forest and found herself almost jogging up the path. She needed to be up at the top and just think about how she was going to get revenge for her mother's death. She found the unused trail and headed up to the top. When she got to the same cave she was at yesterday, she sat down on the big flat rock. Looking around, she thought that this place up here in the forest was one of the most beautiful places she had ever seen. The tall trees reached the heavens, and the sun coming in through the tops of the trees made everything glisten and sparkle. It was magical, and she breathed in the fresh air and took out the sweatshirt she had brought and laid it under her head. She closed her eyes and thought about her mom. She felt closer to her mom up here in Colorado. Up here on her mountain trail. Her eyes started to tear as she thought about never being able to see her mother or spend time with her. Jesse would never be able to see herself get married or be a grandmother to her kids. That is, Gabbi thought, if she would ever have children or even get married.

Her thoughts moved to her date tonight with PJ. Was it a date? She giggled to herself. No, it was just a dinner to try to get PJ to open up about what he knew regarding Niko and the human trafficking crime up here. Her eyes started getting heavy, and she didn't fight the feeling to fall asleep. After all, she had all day long to explore, and a little nap wouldn't matter that much.

Gabbi opened her eyes and was not sure where she was, until she saw that she was back in the forest. She must have dozed off. All of a sudden, she sensed that she was not alone. She slowly sat up and looked around. And behind her on the same slab of rock was the wolf pack she had seen the other day. They were just looking at her. There were five adults, and two were just lying not more than four feet from her. They were just lying there looking at her! She felt excitement, not fear. She saw the other three back at the edge of the forest, and there were two baby pups frolicking in the brush, and one of them had a stick in his mouth. The mother kept a close eye on the pups and on me. I knew right away they were just curious.

I slowly started talking to them. Just soothing words so they could get used to my voice. They weren't afraid, more curious than anything. The biggest wolf slowly inched closer to me, his big gray eyes looking right at me. I held out my hand. The wolf came and sniffed my hand for a few minutes. I took my hand and put it on his head and started stroking him. He didn't move at all. The old Indian woman was right. There was some kind of connection with these wolves. The male was so close to me that I could see his big teeth perfectly aligned in his mouth as he was breathing. Even that didn't scare me. My God, this creature was gorgeous! So strong but graceful. Almost looking like a scruffy dog but so much bigger and stronger. He let me pet him for a few minutes, and then all of a sudden, they all froze. The male wolf stood, and I could see his muscles tense as he took one look around and started to run. They all ran into the forest.

Gabbi tensed up. Did they sense something? Maybe a bear or a mountain lion? Gabbi stood up and walked around. She didn't see anything, so she sat back down. She started to relax again. She could almost picture herself as a baby running through this area. Playing with the wolves. That thought was crazy! How did she ever survive one day out here with no food or water or warm clothes? She laughed at that. She had no clothes at all. Her parents told her that she had been as naked as could be, with mud covering most of her little body. Gabbi drank some of her water and looked around, hoping the wolves had come back, but they were nowhere in sight. She sighed and started to walk in the direction that they had run. There was really no path but enough space to walk through the trees. She noticed a little stream up ahead to the left and stopped to wash her hands in the cold clear water.

All of a sudden, she heard a noise that made her duck down. Was it a gunshot? It couldn't have been. Hunting was illegal in the park. She ran toward the direction of the noise and stopped dead in her tracks. There was a man holding a shotgun and aiming at something in the forest with one hand and with the other he had one of the baby wolves that he was putting in a cage. She couldn't tell if the baby wolf was hurt, but he was making a loud whimpering noise. Then she noticed that he was lifting his paw up. His paw was hurt. Gabbi saw the metal trap on the ground by the wolf. That son of a bitch set a trap up here for the animals? For her wolves. Gabbi was so angry at this sight that she didn't even think twice about walking into the clearing and screaming at the man.

"How dare you set traps up here and hurt these wolves? You let that baby go now!"

The man had just finished locking the baby wolf in a cage he had brought with him. He turned toward Gabbi with surprise in his eyes and the gun raised at her.

"Who the hell are you?" he asked Gabbi. And then all of a sudden, he took a step back and realized that this girl that was screaming at him was beautiful. More than beautiful with her long silver-blond hair and tall lean body. She didn't stop walking towards him, so he cocked the shotgun and she stopped. "Well, what do we have here? What is your name?"

Gabbi stared at him and started barking orders at him again to let the baby wolf go. She had never been so angry in her life. She headed right toward the cage, and as she bent down to unlock the door, the man pushed the gun up against her head. Gabbi froze. She was angry, but she wasn't stupid. She didn't know this man at all, so she decided to change her tactic. She slowly got up and turned toward the man.

"My name is Gabbi, what is your name?"

The big man seemed to smile a crooked smile as he told her his name was Jeff. Gabbi looked over at Jeff and sized him up quickly. That was what they had learned to do first in her self-defense class. Jeff was about midthirties with reddish-blond-colored hair. He was starting to show a receding hairline, and the very top of his head was balding. He also had a thick beard. But what Gabbi noticed most of all was that Jeff weighed about 240 pounds, she would guess, and that put her at about half of his body weight. Plus he was about six foot one.

Gabbi thought to herself that she would have to be smart when she made her move; otherwise he could overpower her. She looked to see if there was anything on the ground that she could grab as a weapon and realized there was nothing but sticks. Jeff reached out his hand to touch her cheek, and Gabbi shuddered as she backed up.

"Well, this is my lucky day," Jeff said. "Not only did I find myself a baby wolf that will make me a couple hundred at least when I sell him, but I found myself a beauty that will be spending the night with me." He took another step toward her, and before he could reach her, he saw out of the corner of his eye, the wolves sneaking up and coming closer. He grabbed his shotgun and took aim at the closest wolf.

Gabbi saw this all take place and knew she had to act fast. She charged at Jeff and pushed the shotgun out of his hands while she used her foot to make him fall. The gun went off but did not hit anything. He stumbled for a moment as Gabbi ran toward the cage to let the wolf out. Just as she had her hand on the door, she felt her body being lifted up from behind. She went into fighting mode and tried to flip Jeff over, but he was just too big. He grabbed the gun and aimed it at the baby wolf. Gabbi stopped fighting and froze.

"Please don't shoot that baby wolf!" Gabbi begged.

Jeff stopped and put the muzzle of the gun right into the pup's mouth. Jeff told Gabbi to sit down or he would kill the wolf and just end up with her as the prize. He told her that he may not even waste his time with the wolf. He had a better prize in her.

"Ha, I bet I could get some good money for you in the trafficking market. Of course, after we have had our little fun for a while."

Gabbi stood up, and Jeff cocked the shotgun so she sat back down. He shut the cage and walked toward her. The look in his eyes was unmistakable. Gabbi knew she had to figure out a way to save the pup and free herself. He grabbed her by the shirt and pulled her up against him. Gabbi felt his big body against hers, and she felt disgust. The smell of sweat and alcohol overwhelmed her. She could see the sweat beading on his face. The only choice she had was to fight and fight fast! She ducked down and used her feet to push against him and was able to knock him to the ground as she went for the gun. She had it in her grasp, but Jeff used his full body weight and slammed into her, knocking the breath out of her. Gabbi lay there stunned. She told herself to breathe.

Jeff stood up and lifted Gabbi up like she weighed no more than air. He grabbed her arms and held them back as he looked for some rope. He fired one more shot into the forest to keep the wolves at bay. Gabbi had seen them watching, and she was hoping they would stay hidden. She did not want any of them to get killed. He was holding Gabbi's arms so tight behind her back that she was wincing in pain. She tried to get free but could not release herself from his grip. The next thing she knew, Jeff had released her. The surprise of being free put her into quick motion. and she took advantage of that and turned around to fight. That was when she saw PJ standing behind Jeff with a gun pointed at his head. PJ did not look happy at all as he took out his handcuffs and radioed in for backup.

Gabbi smiled at PJ and said, "Boy, am I happy to see you." PJ asked her if she was hurt and she replied, "No." She ran over to the cage and unlocked it, and the baby wolf stepped out. He was shaking, and you could see the fear in his eyes. Gabbi stroked him and tried to soothe him with words as she looked at his paw. It was bloody but did not seem to be broken at all. Gabbi noticed the wolves coming over by her. PJ screamed at Gabbi to watch out and slowly move back. Gabbi looked over at PJ and told him she was fine. She took her first aid kit and tried to clean up the paw as the mother walked over and started licking the baby. Gabbi looked over at PJ and Jeff, and they were both staring at her and the wolves. Gabbi ignored them for now. She knew she would have to explain to PJ later.

As she was talking to the mother wolf like she understood her, she cleaned up the paw of the pup and wrapped it up in a thick bandage tape she had in her kit. After hugging the pup, Gabbi laid him down by his mom. The mother wolf was clearly relieved, and she came right up to Gabbi and rubbed against her. Gabbi hugged the mother wolf and the pup before they ran into the woods. She got up and walked over to PJ and Jeff. Jeff turned around and tried to walk toward Gabbi.

"I will find you again, my beauty, and when I do, we will finish what we started." He winked at her just as PJ pulled Jeff away from Gabbi. PJ looked like he was going to punch him.

Gabbi walked right up to Jeff and said, "We will never finish anything. People like you that prey on poor, defenseless animals deserve to be sent to prison for life." And with those words, Gabbi kneed him right where it counts, as Jeff yelled out with pain and dropped to the ground. Gabbi walked away just as the area was filled with four other policemen and rangers. PJ handed Jeff over to the police and told them what had happened from the point he entered the scene. The police and rangers called Gabbi over and wanted her to be checked over. She refused, saying she was perfectly fine. They asked her if she would come into the Loveland police station to make a statement. Gabbi did not want to spend her time doing that, but PJ said he would bring her in since she was new in town. They all headed out, and Gabbi could tell that PJ was not at all happy with her.

They started down the trail in silence. Gabbi looked over at PJ and said, "Listen, I know you're mad for whatever reason, but I am fine. And more importantly, the wolf pup is fine, and you got yourself an illegal poacher on top of it." PJ did not seem amused with her words at all. He walked Gabbi to his ranger car and opened the door on the passenger side.

"Just drive in with me and we could get your jeep later."

Gabbi agreed, mostly because she did not want to argue with him, and they drove to the station in silence. As they pulled into the station and the car stopped, PJ came around and opened the door for her. She gave him a little smile and followed him into the station. After about two hours of Gabbi telling the sheriff exactly what had happened, they were ready to go. PJ had sat in on the interrogation but did not say anything. The police had looked at her in amazement when she told how she walked into the clearing yelling at Jeff. This made her laugh at herself. Alysse had always told her that she was so much like her dad, Michael. She never thought things out before she reacted. Gabbi had to agree with this. She was very passionate about animals and would not stand by and see one get hurt. They asked her if she would testify in court, and she agreed to do that. Whatever she had to do to keep this man from being out on the street again. He would not be hurting any helpless baby animals for a long time. She would do anything to put him in jail for a long time, and she knew the attempted kidnapping charge on top of the poaching would give him many years to think about his mistakes.

When they were done, PJ drove her back to her jeep, and again they sat in silence. Gabbi got out, and PJ walked her over to her jeep. She was going to get in when all of a sudden, PJ put his arm in front of the door and grabbed her shoulder.

"Do you not understand that there are people out here that could get you killed? Or even worse, kidnap you? You can't keep putting yourself in danger like that, what if I hadn't heard the gunshot and ran up to investigate? That guy was going to rape you and maybe even worse than that."

Gabbi saw fear in PJ's eyes, and she softened a little. He was right; she had to be more careful from now on. She turned toward PJ and said softly, "I know you are right, PJ, and I am sorry. That poor little wolf pup was being taken, and I couldn't allow it, I reacted without thinking. And I could take care of myself, but that man knew I would listen to him if he threatened to kill that pup, and that put me at a disadvantage."

PJ relaxed a little and put his hand on her other shoulder so she was facing him directly. "Please, Gabbi, promise me next time that you will call for help before you take on the bad guys." Gabbi could see he started to smile as he said those words, and she smiled too. PJ removed his hand and said, "It's about 4:00 p.m. right now, we are still on for dinner tonight, right?"

Gabbi nodded her head yes. PJ told her that he would pick her up around 6:00 p.m. She shut the door of the jeep and drove back to the cabin. PJ was following her all the way to the street that led to his brother's place. For some reason, that made Gabbi really happy.

Gabbi took a shower and was ready to throw on some shorts and a top but stopped. What was she doing? She had never really dated, and she knew this was just a dinner, but for some reason, she wanted to make an impression. A good impression. Was she falling for PJ? Or did she just need to get on his good side to help with her plan? Gabbi stepped over to the mirror. She looked at the person looking back at her. She never really cared about her looks, but she decided she wanted to look pretty for once. Remembering that she had no makeup because she forgot all about stopping to try and look for some made her stop to think. She looked at the clock and saw that it was nearly 5:00 p.m. What could she do with only an hour to work with? She decided to call PJ's brother and ask where a drugstore was. He answered right away and asked her what she needed. She was a little embarrassed but told him what she needed to buy. He told her to hold on for a minute and he would send help.

Within a few minutes there was a knock on the door, and there was a girl not much older than her. She smiled and said she was John's wife, Megan. Gabbi introduced herself and smiled back. Megan was a few inches shorter than Gabbi and had midlength dark hair, but she had a welcoming smile, and that put Gabbi at ease. Megan told Gabbi she was here to help her and pulled out her makeup kit. Gabbi was a little uncomfortable, but Megan said she loved to do makeup and wanted to see if Gabbi would want a quick makeover. Gabbi told Megan that she and PJ were going out to dinner to talk about her research project for college.

Megan smiled and said, "So you and PJ are going on a date?"

Gabbi was quick to inform Megan that it wasn't a date, just a dinner meeting, and she just hadn't really brought anything from home. She knew Megan was probably thinking, what kind of girl does not bring any makeup with her? So she told Megan the truth.

"Honestly, Megan, I never really wore makeup before or took time to curl or straighten my hair. I am actually sort of a tomboy."

Megan looked at Gabbi and smiled. "Come on, Gabbi, this will be fun!" She took Gabbi's hand and went upstairs.

"You are a beautiful girl, and once in a while it is fun to dress to kill and do your makeup to match."

Gabbi couldn't help but smile. Megan may be petite, but she was definitely a girl you did not say no to. As Megan had Gabbi sit in the chair by the mirror, she thought, *Why not?* It would be fun to look more like a girly girl for one day. Megan proceeded to work on her makeup and then brought out her curling iron and put some curls in Gabbi's hair. Megan had positioned herself in front of Gabbi, and after about a half an hour, she looked at Gabbi with pride in her eyes.

"Gabbi, you are beautiful! Breathtaking! Let's take a look and let me know what you think."

Gabbi got up and went to the mirror, and she gasped. She had never put this much effort into her looks, and the girl looking back at her was a stunning resemblance of herself. Her eyelashes were so long and her eyes looked beautiful. Megan had put some brown and gold eyeshadow on, and it brought out her greenish-blue eyes. Her cheeks now had a touch of color, and her lips were a medium shade of pink. She looked at Megan and thanked her.

"Oh, Megan, thank you so much. I just never worried about makeup or doing my hair before, but this was so much fun!"

Megan asked Gabbi what she was going to wear, and Gabbi showed her the shorts and shirt. One look at that outfit and Megan walked right over to Gabbi's closet. Shaking her head dramatically, Megan giggled and said, "You really did not pack to go out," as she glanced through Gabbi's closet. All of a sudden she smiled and pulled out Gabbi's blue dress, the one that she had thrown in at the last minute. Megan gave it to Gabbi, who protested for less than a minute, to try on. Gabbi came out, and Megan smiled and said, "My job is done here."

Gabbi looked in the mirror and honestly was surprised at how pretty she felt. She thanked Megan, and Megan gave her a hug.

"I am leaving you the makeup I put on you today for you to keep. A little gift from me to you."

Gabbi hugged her again. She slipped on her shoes just as the doorbell rang. Megan opened the door and could tell that PJ was surprised to see her with Gabbi. PJ started to say something to Megan but stopped midsentence with his mouth hanging open. Gabbi had come down the stairs and was walking toward PJ, grabbing her purse on the way. PJ forgot all about Megan and smiled at Gabbi.

"Wow! Gabbi, you look beautiful!"

Gabbi smiled back and thanked him and asked if he was ready to go because she was hungry. PJ opened the door and followed her outside. He thought she was gorgeous before, but looking at her now with her hair in waves and a little makeup on and that dress. Yes, he thought to himself, that dress was something on her. Wow, she was perfect, and he tried to pull himself together. He opened the door of the car for Gabbi, and as she sat down in the passenger seat, she stole a glance at him. PJ had on a button-down white-and-gray striped shirt with a pair of dark khakis, and Gabbi thought he looked very handsome. He joked with her and said, "So you go from fighting men that are double your size to a supermodel all in one day."

Gabbi blushed a little at this. She was not used to flirting with guys, but she managed to come back with "I may have cleaned up a little, but do not be mistaken, I can still fight." PJ smiled and drove to the restaurant.

When they pulled into the parking lot, Gabbi was surprised at his choice. This was a cute little restaurant that had the most unique little courtyard in the back. They walked into the restaurant, and PJ gave his name to the waitress who took them to their table. Gabbi looked at the menu and decided on some shrimp and salad. PJ ordered the steak with potatoes, and they made small talk until the dinner came. Gabbi started asking him questions about the trafficking ring here in Colorado, and PJ seemed uneasy talking to her about it. But she persisted and reminded him it was for a project.

He went on to tell her that for the last twenty years, sex trafficking had been huge in the state. Shaking his head, PJ told her that just last year alone there were over 130 cases. About 80 percent were girls, he told her, but there were boys that were also being taken and used and sold. He said they were able to track down a holding house with about five girls in it only once in the past five years. The men had been able to escape before the police broke into the house. He went on to say that with the help of the FBI and local police, they knew that a guy named Niko was running the whole thing. PJ stopped and looked over at Gabbi.

"You are way too young and beautiful to be doing a project on this horrible topic, why did you pick this?"

Gabbi wasn't sure how much to tell PJ. So she decided to tell him that she was hearing in the news how all these kids were being taken right off the street and their lives were being destroyed. She told him how it sickened her that there was a market for this type of slavery in this day and age. Gabbi went on to tell PJ that she wanted to call awareness to human trafficking and one day find a way to put a stop to it.

PJ was impressed, thinking to himself that this mystery girl that unexpectedly came into his life was not only beautiful but she also had compassion for animals as well as people. He had dated a few girls here and there through college, but no one ever really made that much of an impact on him. Not enough to make him take that dating to the next level. At least not enough to change his status from being single to married. His brother kept teasing him that he was going to be thirty in a few years and wasn't it about time he started settling down. But that was just it, he thought, he did not want to settle. He knew there was a right person for him out there, and he was going to continue to look until he found her. Maybe, just maybe, he had found her. He looked over at Gabbi and asked her how old she was.

"I will be twenty in a few months," she lied. For some reason she didn't want PJ to know she had just turned nineteen. PJ was visibly surprised.

"You are only nineteen?" he asked again. Gabbi smiled at him and asked him how old he was. He clearly didn't want to tell her that he was going to be twenty-seven soon. That made him about seven years her senior. PJ told Gabbi his age and waited for a shocked response, but there was none. She just said that it was exciting he was going to be the big 3-0 in a few years. PJ laughed and assured her it was not exciting. PJ relaxed. It was not like they were even dating, and Gabbi seemed so much more mature than her age. And in reality, if she didn't seem to care about the age difference, why should he?

They finished dinner, and the waitress asked if they wanted dessert. PJ answered for them and thanked her but said he was taking her to another place for dessert. Gabbi was curious, but she also was glad that they had more time together. If this was dating, then she might just have to do it again. Many of her questions were answered, and she wrote a few notes down for future use. Even though she had found out a lot of information, she needed to know if there was a location or at least an area that the FBI was investigating. After all, if she was going to get revenge on Niko and bring down this trafficking ring, then she needed to find out where they could possibly be located. Gabbi thanked PJ for the dinner and walked with him toward the car, but he took her hand and kept walking toward town.

"Where are we headed, some secret dessert spot?" she asked with a smile.

He just said "We will see" and kept walking with her. Even though she tried to ask a few more questions, PJ was done with the subject for tonight, he told her. She decided not to push it and found herself excited to see where they were headed. They walked into the center of Loveland, which was a cute town, with so much character and charm. There were many little shops and coffee shops lined up on the street. Some had outside patios stringed with lights. And with the moonlight glow, she could see the mountains in the distance. The air was crisp, but she loved it.

She heard some music and realized they were walking into a street festival of some kind. PJ told her that this was Colorado's bluegrass festival, and every year at this time, the whole town celebrated country music and good food. Gabbi was excited, she had never been to a festival like this. Actually, she had never been to a festival at all. The country music was blaring, and people were dancing. The smell of food coming from the food stands was amazing. Gabbi had always had a big appetite, and she loved food!

PJ looked at Gabbi and saw her big smile and was glad he decided to take her here. He pulled her over to a food stand where they were selling homemade brownies topped with your choice of ice cream, and on top was nuts and whipped cream. Gabbi gladly accepted the yummy creation that PJ handed her. He asked her if she would like to split one or have a whole one to herself. She gave him a big smile and said, "I would definitely want one to myself," and she offered to pay, but PJ wouldn't hear of it. They sat down on a bench off to the side, and a few of PJ's friends came by to say hello.

PJ introduced Gabbi to a few of his college friends, and they talked a few minutes before they went off to sample more food. PJ and Gabbi finished their ice cream brownie treat and went up and started walking down the street.

The band playing started a country slow song, and PJ grabbed Gabbi's hand and asked her to dance. Gabbi said she wasn't a good dancer, and PJ ignored that answer and pulled her out to the middle of the dance floor anyways. His hand circled around her waist. Gabbi tensed up for a second and then decided to let go and have some fun. Besides, she liked the feel of PJ's hands on her waist. She put her hands on PJ's shoulder, and they swayed to the country music. Gabbi looked up at PJ and realized she was having so much fun with him. He was so easy to talk to, and he was such a gentleman. Gabbi realized she did not want this night to end. After the dance, PJ glanced at his watch and told Gabbi that they should head back. She was sad that their night was ending.

They drove back to the cabin Gabbi was renting, and PJ walked her up the stairs to her front door. Gabbi really wanted to talk more with PJ, so she invited him in to sit out on the deck with her since it was such a nice night. PJ agreed with a smile. He settled on a lounge chair that was out back, and she sat next to him in another chair.

"Hey, Gabbi, I wanted to ask you about what happened today with the wolves. I know enough about wildlife to know that these animals just don't come up to people and show affection, especially not wolves."

Gabbi again wasn't sure how much she should tell PJ. She found herself wishing she could tell him everything right from the very beginning. But she knew that it would be too much information, and she still had her plan to put into motion. PJ was an unexpected advantage to this trip, but her main focus was her revenge for her mother. Nothing could get in the way of this. Gabbi was silent a moment, and then she started telling PJ about growing up with animals and how they reacted to her. She told him that ever since she was little, she had a unique connection with animals.

One story she told him was about the dogs that were scared of her sometimes when she passed them on the street, even when she was just a little kid. They would whine and run away like they were terrified of her. She also told him about the time she went horseback riding with her parents one year, but they had to leave early because the horses were skittish and scared around her. The owners of the horse ranch did not understand the horses' reaction and apologized and refunded their money. Remembering that day and how Alysse had been very upset and looking at Gabbi like she was different. It had made her sad. She loved animals and did not like that some were afraid of her. Alysse had assured her that it was probably something that Gabbi wouldn't encounter too many times. But she was wrong. It still happened to this day. Gabbi also told PJ about the wolves she encountered earlier in the forest and how she felt a connection with them. Not wanting to tell him too much about herself, she decided to tell him about the old Indian lady and the bracelet. He took her hand and looked at it and was shaking his head in amazement.

"So you don't know why the animals are attracted to you or scared of you?" PJ asked. Gabbi just shook her head no. PJ looked at Gabbi and said, "This reminds me of a story that is told in this part of Colorado quite a bit. Some people think the story is a made-up story, but there are many who believe it happened, and it was a big media story too. About seventeen years ago, there was a little girl that was found in the forest living with wolves. The little girl was about three years old.

"When she was found, she was naked and running with a family of wolves. She was found by a couple that were up here on vacation. They tried to keep it out of the media, but a story like that doesn't happen very often. If I remember correctly, the couple ended up adopting the little girl. I remember even though I was only ten at the time. The story was huge! It was all over the paper and television. Many people did not believe the story that a little girl could be alive after living with wolves, but many did, especially the Indian community."

PJ looked at Gabbi, and a huge smile broke out as he said, "I wonder, could you be that wolf child? You're about the right age."

Gabbi froze, but then she realized that PJ was joking with her. She laughed at the story and told him she found it fascinating. PJ got up and walked to the deck edge and looked up at the stars. He turned around and said to Gabbi, "I find you fascinating."

Gabbi was glad it was dark so he couldn't see her blush. She wasn't sure why, but she got up and walked over to PJ. PJ put his arm around her and he slowly kissed her. Gabbi pulled back for a moment, but after seeing the hurt in PJ's eyes, she leaned back in for the kiss. Gabbi had only kissed one other guy before. And it wasn't even a guy she had wanted to kiss. It was her prom date, and she only allowed one kiss. Thinking back, she remembered that she had no desire to kiss him at all the night of prom, but Marissa had talked her into it. Giggling, she had told her that she needed to practice kissing before she met someone she really liked. So Gabbi had agreed, and the guy was very eager.

She did not feel anything that night of prom when she had her first kiss, no feelings at all, but something was turning her legs to Jell-O when she kissed PJ. She put her arms around his neck, and PJ took that as a sign to continue and started kissing Gabbi even more. He pulled her close, and the kisses became more intense. Gabbi had never felt like this. She never imagined that this feeling could exist when you kiss someone. She didn't want him to stop. She pushed her body closer to PJ's body, and PJ let out a sound that sounded more like a growl than a sigh. PJ started to pull her into the bedroom off the deck but then stopped. What was he doing? This was some young girl he just met. He had to move slowly and not scare her away. He pulled himself away and stroked Gabbi's cheek.

"I think we both should get some sleep. Today was a very eventful day."

Gabbi did not want to get some sleep. She wanted to stay here and kiss PJ. She wanted more. PJ pulled her into the house and started walking toward the door. He gave her one last kiss and held her tight for a moment. Gabbi thanked him for the fun evening and asked him if she could meet with him tomorrow sometime to go over some additional questions so she could finish her project. PJ looked at Gabbi and said he had a few meetings tomorrow and had to finish the paperwork on the arrest of Jeff.

"How about if we meet for breakfast? Morning is going to be the best time for me tomorrow." Gabbi agreed, so he told her where and what time they could meet and left out the door. He stopped for a second and turned back to her and said, "Please promise me you will lock your door tonight, and don't do anything to put yourself in danger for the next week or so."

Gabbi smiled and said she couldn't make any promises, but as she closed the door, PJ heard her lock it. He walked back slowly to his car and sat inside for a minute just thinking. His hands were on the steering wheel, and he put his head down in between them. There was nothing he wanted more right now than to go back into that house and make love to Gabbi. What was he thinking? This was a young girl who was smart, exciting, and beautiful. She was a college kid working on a project. This may be the last week with her. He may never even see her again. He couldn't just have a weeklong fling with her. It was tempting, very, very tempting, but that wasn't what he wanted with Gabbi. He realized he wanted something more with her. He was falling for her and falling fast. This thought made him laugh at himself. He was going to be three years shy of thirty years old, and he finally found a girl he wanted to get to know better. The problem was, ironically, that she had to be from halfway across the United States. She may have well been from outer space. He would see how the rest of the week played out and see what Gabbi was planning to do. Ohio was a long way from Colorado, and she was way too young to be in a long-distance relationship. That last thought put him in a lousy mood. Reliving that last kiss with her, he realized that he did not want her to go. He wanted her to stay here with him. It wasn't going to do him any good worrying about it. If it was meant to be, then it will be. Fate was something he did believe in.

Gabbi walked upstairs after she locked the door and sat on her bed. She couldn't help herself from smiling. Touching her lips with her fingers, she remembered the feeling of PJ's body close to hers and the taste of his lips. She was definitely falling for him, but she didn't want to think about what that meant right now. And to prove her point, she heard her phone ring. She glanced at it and saw that it was her mom. Oh no! Gabbi had forgotten completely about what day it was. Her parents must be worried sick. They had to have already visited Marissa and read her letter. The guilt consumed her, and she forgot about PJ and the kiss.

She saw that there were twenty-five missed calls. Lying on the bed with her phone in her hand, she had realized that she had run out of time. Without a doubt, she knew that her father would use his resources and find her. Everything had to happen tomorrow. She had to make her move tomorrow. She put PJ out of her mind. He was something she could afford to think about after her plan was put in motion but not before. Her life was put on hold so she could come out here and stop the sex trafficking group that had killed her mother. The mother that she never got to even know. She had to narrow down the location and see if she could find something about Niko. Or maybe Niko could find her.

Pulling up her laptop, Gabbi started researching the human trafficking stories that were coming up and all the information she could find. She concentrated on the ones that were within this area. And there seemed to be quite a few. Some were speculation, and some were proven. How could Niko and this group avoid arrest and never get caught? They had to be smart. She could not afford to underestimate them and let her feelings get in the way. Her need for revenge. As tired as she was, she spent the next three hours looking for any information she could. She devised a plan and realized all along that she knew what she would have to do. One last glance at her phone again showed the missed calls and the messages. She ignored them and plugged it in to charge. The phone may be needed tomorrow. Because tomorrow was the day she was going to find Niko. It just had to be the day. Gabbi thought that she would just have to make sure she was seen all over the area. Make her presence known. Her day would consist of visits to every sleazy gas station or little store. She would ask around and mention Niko's name. If she couldn't find Niko and his gang, then he would find her.

Sleep would not come easy tonight. There was too much on her mind. Between the guilt she felt for hurting her parents and thinking about how fate was so cruel. Finally after all these years she had found a guy that she wanted to be with, or at least get to know better. It took nineteen years, but it had happened, and it couldn't have happened at a worst time.

Gabbi got ready for bed and packed what she would need tomorrow and set her alarm for early. She needed time to go over everything before she met with PJ. Realizing that if everything went her way tomorrow, she would be back here in the evening, and Niko and the rest would be in jail. Her mission would be complete. She realized she was eager to get this plan in motion. Her last thought before she finally fell asleep was of PJ.

Chapter 9

Back in Ohio, Alysse was pacing up and down the kitchen. She was an emotional wreck. She just did not understand what had happened. Yesterday, she was so happy! Her daughter, whom she loved so much, was finally going out and having fun. She had spent all weekend with Marissa and a group of others, and Alysse had been thrilled. She couldn't wait for Gabbi to come back home and tell her all about it. She had planned for the two of them to go out and grab some late dinner or appetizers. It was supposed to be an epic mother-and-daughter moment, and Alysse was going to get every last detail out of Gabbi.

This was the first time that Gabbi had spent the weekend away, and Michael had been slightly worried about her being gone all weekend with barely any contact, but Alysse had assured him that Gabbi was nineteen now, hardly a child. Plus she was responsible. They had never had any trouble at all from her. She was the perfect child. Alysse had often thought too perfect. She sometimes secretly wished that Gabbi would stay out past curfew or even just do something to get a detention in school. Anything so she wasn't so perfect. Perfect was boring, and Alysse wanted her daughter to have events she could talk about for years. Michael had thought she was crazy! Honestly, it wasn't the first time that he had thought she was crazy, she thought to herself with a smile on her face.

So this weekend Alysse didn't want to call or text her every minute. Gabbi had deserved to be treated like the responsible adult that she was. She wanted to show Gabbi they trusted her. And after all, Alysse had heard from Gabbi a couple times when she had texted her. Alysse stopped pacing and looked at her watch. It was already ten in the morning. Where was Michael? She stopped and grabbed a cup from the cupboard. She was going to pour wine in it to relieve her stress but opted for the coffee instead.

This waiting was driving her mad. She needed to keep a straight mind. Again her pacing started as she remembered yesterday evening. The start of this nightmare she was living right now. Gabbi still had not been home by seven, and that was the first time that Alysse had felt the knot in her stomach. She had tried to call Gabbi, and there was no answer. She had texted and no answer. She waited another hour, and Michael started worrying with her. He wanted to go to Marissa's and see what was going on. After all, Gabbi had been gone all weekend. Alysse knew that Michael was thinking about Jesse and what had happened to her.

Finally after ten phone calls and an hour passing, Alysse had called Marissa. Marissa had sounded different, almost scared. Alysse knew right away that something was wrong. She had told Alysse that she would be over in a few minutes, and then Marissa had just hung up. By then, Alysse had been in panic mode. Something wasn't right, what had happened to her daughter? Why did no one call Michael and herself if there was an accident or, worse yet, a kidnapping? Michael had tried to calm her down, but he was worried too. That had been the longest fifteen minutes ever, and she had kept looking out the window.

As the car Marissa was driving pulled into the driveway, Alysse was still expecting to see Gabbi get out of the car with Marissa, but that didn't happen. When she saw Marissa's red hair and that she was by herself, she ran outside, and Michael was right behind her. Marissa had looked like she was ready to cry when she saw Alysse flying out of the house. Alysse had grabbed Marissa by the shoulders and shouted, "What has happened, Marissa? Why is Gabbi not with you?"

Michael had pulled Alysse away from Marissa and told Marissa to follow them in the house. He had felt sorry for her, but he also knew he wasn't going to like what she had to say. Michael was a lawyer, and he had seen so many different cases play out all the time. He tried not to think that this was going to be a missing persons case or even worse than that. Michael and Alysse had sat down across from

Marissa, and Michael had asked her if she would like something to drink. Alysse remembered feeling terrible when he asked Marissa that. This was their daughter's best friend, and she had almost attacked her outside, while Michael was as gracious as ever. Alysse put her hand on Marissa's hand, and that little gesture made Marissa start crying hysterically.

"I am so sorry," she blurted out. "I did not want to be a part of this, but Gabbi made me promise that I would not say anything and that I would give you the letter when you called." She then pulled an envelope out of her purse and handed it to Alysse.

Michael moved in closer so he could read it along with Alysse. Alysse took the letter from Marissa. Her heartbeat quickened, and her hands were shaking as she opened it. Her and Michael read the letter, and Alysse started crying. Michael had gotten up right away and said he was going to make a phone call. The one thing he knew for certain was that he had to act fast. Time was the one luxury you didn't have in a case like this. But he stopped suddenly, and he went over by Marissa and put his hand on her shoulder.

"Marissa, don't cry, we understand that you were just being loyal to Gabbi, you have always been a good friend to her. We are so glad that you and Gabbi are close."

Marissa had stopped crying. Through leftover tears and a voice that was so soft that it was hard to understand, she went on to tell them that when Gabbi told her about this plan, she initially didn't want anything to do with it. Marissa told them that she had even started to call Alysse a few times but always stopped. She had been torn about protecting her best friend's plans and protecting her best friend from harm. Marissa had said for the last two days, she has done nothing but worry about her best friend.

"If something happens to her, I will never forgive myself," she had said as she got up to leave. "I am so sorry I helped with this, but Gabbi had been so sure of what she had to do, she seemed like she had a plan, and I figured, what is the worst thing that could happen to her?"

Alysse smiled at Marissa and told her that they were going to go search for Gabbi and help her get through this. Michael had asked Marissa if there was any other information she could give them before she left, and Marissa had replied that Gabbi had just said that she needed to avenge her mother. That last sentence brought chills to Michael, and Alysse turned pale, and when Alysse looked over at Michael, she knew that he was thinking the same exact thing that she was. Gabbi had gone to Colorado to try and find out about her real mother's kidnapping. Michael and Alysse had thanked Marissa for giving them the letter, and after asking her a few more questions, they walked her out to her car and said goodbye and that they would keep her updated.

Michael picked up his phone, and Alysse had heard him call Eric, his best friend. Right after, he had called Anthony, his own ex-FBI agent that had worked on Jesse's case through the whole ordeal. Anthony had been the one that had found Jesse in the first place. He told them to be at his office at 8:00 a.m. the next morning.

Alysse came running in the kitchen where Michael was and had yelled out to Michael, "No, we need to go now and look for her!" But Michael had come over and put his arm around his wife and told her that it would do no good to go off right now in the dark without making a plan first. He assured her that he was calling in every favor he could to start a search for Gabbi, but they had to do it right. He said he was going to book their flights to Denver for tomorrow. As he walked into the other room, Alysse picked up the letter that Gabbi had written and started to read it again. Her hands were shaking so bad she could barely make out the words.

Dear Mom and Dad,

I want you to know that I love you more than you will ever know. You have done so much for me, and I promise you I will make this decision I made up to you. I will make up for this hurt I know I am putting you through right now. It kills me to do this to you, but I have been thinking long and hard about my past and what had happened to my mother and to me because of her being kidnapped. It makes me so angry that her life was taken so needlessly because of some bad guys that think it's okay to kidnap and sell young girls. This has to stop! I have to put closure to these feelings that I have. I have to go and find out more about my past and visit the place that I was born. My calling is to do something to try and help with the sex trafficking that is going on. Something had to be done, and Niko had to pay for what he did to my mother. I promise you that I will be careful, and you know I can take care of myself, thanks to you! I will be back, and I will go to college and continue my life, but I HAVE to do this. I have to take this road trip and think things out. Please don't be mad at Marissa, I begged her to help me. And please, please do not come after me. I need to do this by myself in order to move on. I will contact you as soon as I can.

Love always,
Gabbi

Alysse stopped pacing when she heard the front door open. She ran toward the living room and stopped when she saw Eric and Anthony. Michael followed behind, but he was on the phone, and he gave her a quick wave. She hugged Eric as soon as she saw him walk in. Anthony gave her a quick hug too. Eric told her that they would get Gabbi back and not to worry. Alysse gave a false smile at that statement. She could do nothing but worry about her daughter. Even just her driving out of state by herself gave her a sick feeling in her stomach. Michael walked up and gave Alysse a quick hug and asked her if she was ready to go. Her nod told him what he needed to know. He picked up her suitcase and made sure the house was locked up as they all four made their way out of the house. Michael told Alysse that he called in a favor from a senator that owed him, and they would be flying a private plane over to Colorado.

Alysse looked up at Michael and said in a voice she didn't even recognize as hers, "Are you sure Gabbi is in Colorado?" Michael opened the car door for her and closed it behind her as she sat down and put on her seat belt. He walked around and threw their bags in the trunk.

"Yes, Gabbi has not been using her phone that much, but the last signal was from Loveland, Colorado."

Alysse paled at those words. That was where they had found Gabbi, or in the forest close to there. Eric jumped in the back with Alysse, as Anthony piled into the passenger side of the car. Anthony was a big guy, and she wanted to give him the leg room that was more plentiful in the front seat.

Eric saw Alysse's face when Michael told her where they were headed. He knew the history, and he also knew that Alysse was imagining the worst possible scenario with Gabbi right now. He hugged Alysse again and told her that Michael had the best possible people on this, and they would find Gabbi and bring her home. Even as Eric's words flowed out of his mouth, his mind was thinking that they needed to hurry before it was too late. Eric, being Michael's partner in the law firm, was very familiar with runaways and kidnappings. Things could go bad fast. They had to get to Gabbi and track her down and bring her home.

As the car pulled out of the driveway and headed toward the airport, Alysse closed her eyes and silently prayed that God would keep her daughter safe until they could get to her and bring her back where she belonged.

Chapter 10

Gabbi woke up early and grabbed her packed backpack and made sure she had her phone charged fully. She also pulled out the old phone that she had lying around at home. It didn't work, but no one would know that, and she may be able to put it to good use today if her plan works out. She threw on a pair of jeans and a bright pink T-shirt. She looked in the mirror. She wanted to make sure that she would stand out today but not look too old or overdressed. She had thought about her plan all night, and she needed to have everything working for her, including the way she looked. The jeans and T-shirt definitely called attention to her lean tall body, and tying the T-shirt at her waist showed a little sliver of her stomach. This would do the trick! She left her long blond hair straight and long. As an after-thought, she put on a small amount of blush and mascara and threw on some light-pink lipstick. She threw on a baseball cap and a sweat-shirt and grabbed a couple bottles of water. There! She was as ready as she would ever be.

She looked around the room and hoped she would be back here tonight. Gabbi grabbed her keys and locked the door as she headed outside in the bright sunshine. It was still early, but she could see that it was going to be a beautiful day today. Her mind was racing with everything she had hoped to accomplish today. The nice weather would help her with her plan. She glanced at her wrist, the one that had the bracelet that the old Indian lady gave her. Her wolf brace-let. Putting her fingers on the bracelet, she unconsciously rubbed it. Somehow knowing the bracelet was on her wrist made her feel safer. As if it was supposed to be there.

She jumped in the jeep and started it up. Glancing at the main house, she was glad that no one was around. It was about a ten-minute drive to the outside café PJ wanted to meet her at. The name of the café was called Taste Local, and he had told her they had the best breakfast in town. She felt the butterflies in her stomach again at the mere thought of PJ. She took a deep breath and pulled into the café. Right away she spotted him, he was standing outside in his rangers uniform. He smiled and started toward her as she parked. Gabbi smiled back and walked right up to him and hugged him. PJ pulled her face to his and kissed her long and hard. Gabbi felt like she was floating on air. Never in her life did she think a man could have this effect on her.

PJ left his arm around her shoulder and asked, "Are you hungry this morning?" He walked over to the table that was closest and empty, and Gabbi sat down in the chair that PJ had pulled out for her.

"I am always hungry," she said to him.

PJ smiled at that comment, thinking that it was true; she had a great appetite for a girl. It was refreshing. They ordered their breakfast. She had the vegetable omelet with wheat toast and coffee, while PJ had the steak and eggs and a side of hash browns with a coffee too. PJ started talking about his busy day today. He seemed to stop talking for a second and looked at Gabbi. It almost seemed to Gabbi that he was trying to decide to tell her about some information he had. PJ grabbed her hand and went on to tell Gabbi that they had found a girl's body up on the park trail late last night. A family from California had stumbled across the body. He told her that it was a girl that had been missing for a few months, from the next town over. She was only sixteen years old. Gabbi gasped at this news, and it seemed to flame the fire of revenge even more for her. The look of anger on his face told the story of what he was feeling.

"Gabbi, this is why you need to be very careful. This girl had her whole life in front of her. Her life was going along fine, and then one day she was gone, kidnapped and pulled off the street in her neighborhood. And then they find her lifeless body. Sixteen years old!" PJ was shaking his head with disgust.

Gabbi asked PJ if it was related to the human trafficking operation around here. He said he wasn't sure, but it certainly was a possibility.

"If a girl tries to escape, she usually ends up dead," he said.

Gabbi asked many questions about the body and where they had found it. PJ just brushed it off as her just trying to get information for her project. Gabbi could tell that PJ did not want to talk about the body. He was disgusted with the kidnappings and the killings. He told her that they needed to stop these men, and they needed to stop them now and put the whole group of them in jail for life since they abolished the death penalty in Colorado. PJ went on to say that in his opinion, they should make exceptions for convicted killers of little girls. Gabbi wanted as much information as she could get, but PJ wanted to change the subject. He looked at Gabbi and gave her a smile that melted her heart. PJ asked Gabbi what her plans were today, and Gabbi said she was going to hike some more and hopefully finish up her project. Which was not a lie. If everything went well today, then her project would be done. Her plan for revenge would be done. Niko and his men would be arrested and locked away for life.

For the first time since she had met him, she felt guilty for lying to PJ about her agenda here in Loveland. He had been nothing but supportive and helpful. He deserved the truth and not these half lies she was telling him. She hoped to have the end result accomplished today. And then she would sit PJ down and tell him the truth about her life and why she came here to Colorado. PJ again told her to please be alert and have her phone handy. Gabbi put her hand on his and smiled.

"I appreciate your concern, but I can protect myself."

PJ laughed and said that he couldn't help but worry about her. He then asked her if she would like to go out to dinner tonight. "Maybe a late dinner?" he asked again. Before Gabbi could answer, he began telling her that he had a full day, and he wanted to walk a couple trails in the park to warn any hikers to keep a lookout for anything suspicious. Gabbi told PJ to stop over later and check with her because she also had a busy day, but maybe they could order in some pizza if it was too late. PJ seemed to like that idea even more than going out to dinner.

"That sounds perfect, Gabbi," he said.

They finished their breakfast, and he walked Gabbi to her jeep. He leaned over and kissed her quickly at first, but then pulled her close and kissed her with intensity. This nagging feeling in his gut had been building all day. He had a bad feeling that something was going to happen. His worry for Gabbi was probably intensified because of the body that had been found. He wanted to warn Gabbi again, but he felt like he was acting too protective. He pushed that feeling to the back of his mind and concentrated on the beautiful girl standing right in front of him. Gabbi smiled and got into her jeep. PJ said goodbye, and for some reason before she could stop herself, Gabbi called PJ back over.

"PJ, I am really glad we met each other, and I can't wait to see you again."

PJ smiled his infectious smile and told her that he was really glad they had met too. He grabbed a strand of her hair and rolled it in his fingers and said, "It was fate, Gabbi. And I am a strong believer in fate." He let her hair drop and walked back to his car. Gabbi stared at him for a while and hoped that it wasn't the last time she would ever see him. She was a smart girl and had somewhat of a plan, but she also knew that she was dealing with some bad guys. And from what she researched, she knew that the amount of money that was made from human trafficking was the kind of money that would make men kill to keep the business going. Money had a way of over-taking all morals, especially with the type of guy Niko was. Gabbi was feeling confident that she could help to get these guys arrested and help avenge her mother's death. She needed a little bit of good luck today. Any type of information to help her would be good, she thought to herself. She looked back one more time in the direction of PJ's car, and she sighed.

Here I go, she thought to herself.

She took off toward the highway. She knew exactly where she was headed. She was going to stop at every park and try to run through the trails and off trails. Her plan included stopping at every truck stop and gas station and any little store along the way. She was also going to drive up to some mountain homes and see if she could find any clue at all. Any hidden driveways or any clues of something that was illegal or that looked unusual. Lastly, she was going to drive up to Boulder, which was about a forty-five-minute drive. There had also been trafficking activity up there and recently some attempted kidnappings near the college town. Gabbi was confident that she would be able to find something that could lead her to Niko. She knew it was a long shot, but she had to end this today.

Without a doubt, she just knew that her parents were probably booking a flight to Colorado as she drove on the highway. It was a risky move, but she was going to ask anyone she saw if they knew a Niko. Dropping his name around town might bring Niko to her. Maybe if she threw his name around a little, she could get some kind of reaction or clue. Gabbi knew that she really didn't have an exact plan in place, if she should find Niko, but she would handle that when she got to that point. After all, she had the element of surprise on her side. Her phone was charged, so she could even call for help if she could find out where their operation was or even if she could find Niko.

Her mind raced back to when PJ had given her some information about human trafficking here in this area of Colorado. PJ had told her that Niko had been either really lucky or really smart since he never got caught over the last twenty years. She remembered PJ saying that they had descriptions of him but no certified actual pictures. So she was at a little disadvantage, but she didn't think Niko was one to show his face too often anyway. She had spent days researching the whole subject of trafficking, and she knew enough to know that as terrible as these men were, they were smart. Because this particular operation had avoided the police and FBI for over twenty years, she knew that it wasn't going to be easy at all, but she had to try and find them or any kind of clue.

Knowing that she could not take down the whole organization by herself, her ideal plan would be to call for help. But if she had to do it alone, then she would. Feeling a little anxious, she took out the old picture of Jesse, her mom, that Michael had given her the day of her birthday.

"Mom, I am doing this for you," she said as she took her finger and ran it down her mom's face in the picture. She felt the tears start to fall, so she put the picture back in her glove compartment. If someone was looking through her backpack and pulled out the picture, it could ruin her whole element of surprise, and she needed all the luck she could get today. Gabbi knew she couldn't afford to make any mistakes today. Absolutely none at all.

Chapter 11

Michael glanced at his watch and frowned. It had been almost an hour since they landed at the Northern Colorado Regional Airport. That had been the closest airport to Loveland, and Anthony had cleared their landing ahead of time, so the process was relatively easy with no major holdups. Alysse had been a nervous wreck the whole flight, and Michael had to make her drink a glass of wine to ease her mind a little. He had told her that they would find Gabbi, and they would bring her home. Michael was not feeling so confident at the moment. Eric and Anthony had worked on the plane ride for most of the trip. They had contacted local authorities in Loveland and gave them a very brief overview of what was happening. Michael and Eric both had many connections in high places from their work at the law firm, and that really helped. Eric had contacted the governor of Colorado, and he had made a few phone calls to clear the way for them when they came into Loveland. Michael knew that sometimes local police or FBI did not want to work with other state authorities, and he didn't want to waste time trying to get information. Anthony was well-known all over the United States, and it had helped that he knew many of the FBI agents that were working on the trafficking investigations in the Colorado area.

But the fact of the matter was that they had no proof anything bad had happened to Gabbi. She was over the age of eighteen and was legally allowed to take a trip to Colorado or any other state she wanted. All three of the men knew that it was better if they didn't have to bring up Gabbi's past as the wolf girl. The media would swarm to Loveland, and that could cause them trouble when trying to find Gabbi. It wasn't that much of a surprise that Gabbi wasn't answering her phone, and Anthony had traced the last few places she had used it. Michael put his hand on his head. He knew he was going to have to let Anthony do most of the legwork because of his background. There were too many unanswered questions, and Michael knew that Gabbi was a smart girl, and she wasn't going to make it easy for herself to be found if she didn't want to be found.

Eric had rented a Jeep Grand Cherokee, which was waiting for them as soon as they got off the airplane. Michael had told Alysse that he would need her to check into the hotel and grab something to eat. She had said she wanted to help, but Michael knew he could not let her sit in on the meetings with the police and FBI. It wasn't going to do her any good to hear the statistics about kidnappings or human trafficking. He had Eric print out flyers of Gabbi on the plane. He had used her birthday picture for the flyer. Looking at the picture had made Alysse break out in tears. He told Alysse that the best way she could help was to walk around and see if she could find any information about Gabbi or anyone that might have seen her. Telling Alysse that Gabbi may even be in town. Alysse had reluctantly agreed to do that part of the search.

They had just dropped Alysse off at the hotel, and after he had taken up her luggage for her, he had pulled her close and told her not to worry. He reminded her that Gabbi was trained in self-defense, and there was not any proof that she was in any kind of danger. Those words coming from his mouth made him want to choke. If Gabbi was looking for revenge, then she was in danger. He had kissed Alysse goodbye and told her that she was probably hiking up in the mountains and would be back later for some rest and dinner. Alysse had even smiled at that comment, knowing how much Gabbi loved to hike or run or just be outdoors. She said she would show Gabbi's picture around and see what she could find out. Michael had told her that he would update her every hour before he left.

Michael got back into the car, and as Eric started driving toward the police station, he looked back at Anthony. Anthony was trying to track down where Gabbi was staying by running her credit card trace. But again, Gabbi was a smart one. She was only using cash for purchases. They had run a trace on her debit and credit card, and nothing showed up. One of the first bits of information they had was that Gabbi had taken out a large amount of money the week of her disappearance, and Michael knew she had planned this out, knowing that he would be able to trace her card information. Part of him had to smile to himself a little. His daughter was a smart one. That girl was going to be a good detective or lawyer one day. He couldn't help but feel proud of his daughter. Even though he was angry at her for putting himself and Alysse through this, and even more for putting herself in danger, but in a way he understood what Gabbi was feeling.

Her early life had been traumatic, and the information about her real mom had hit her hard. He could even understand her wanting to get away and try to make sense of everything, but her coming to the same town that Jesse was being held captive and where Gabbi was born was just too dangerous. Michael knew that they had not been able to catch Niko or shut down this trafficking operation around this area. He was really hoping that Niko had moved out of this area, or if they were really lucky, he had died. Either way, he couldn't take the chance of Gabbi being in this area. She was a spitting image of her mother, and if any of Niko's men saw her, it wouldn't turn out good for Gabbi.

"There is the Loveland police station right up ahead, let's park and get this over with." Eric broke the silence of his thoughts with this good news. Michael and Anthony got out of the car and headed into the station behind Eric. He was eager to find out information about this area and if there were any leads into the illegal operations here.

PJ had pulled into the police station a few minutes ago and was a little curious as to why they had called a mandatory meeting in the middle of the day. His boss had called in all the rangers and, from what he heard, most of the Loveland police force. Something had to be happening, and he had hoped it was something good. They did not need any more bad news after finding the body of the young girl yesterday.

He had walked into the briefing room at the police station and was surprised at what he saw. There were about twenty people in the smaller room. Most he recognized, but some he did not. There was the police chief and most of his police force. Surprisingly many of the park rangers were also here. But to his surprise, there were also about five FBI agents. He knew all of them but one. They had all worked together over the years to try to bring down the human trafficking ring here in Colorado and for various other high-profile crimes in this area. The gentleman he didn't recognize was a tall built man in a suit. Which was a sure fact that he worked for the FBI. PJ acknowledged a few of the guys as he passed by them and sat down with a friend of his, Layla. Layla was a park ranger that had been working here in Loveland for about a year or so.

"Do you know what is going on?" PJ asked Layla.

Layla replied, "I have no idea, but I can guarantee you it is a little bit bigger than a lost hiker!"

PJ didn't have time to reply because at that moment, in walked three very important-looking men that he did not recognize at all. They were all big, tall guys, but one stood out as extremely athletic and tall. In fact, PJ thought he looked familiar. The bigger guy walked in and smiled at a few of the FBI agents and even shook hands with one or two. So he assumed that this bigger guy was FBI for sure. The other two were dressed nice and had the feel of importance about them that he had seen plenty of times. They were men that you did not want to mess around with. PJ sat back and waited to see what was going on. He and Layla were very curious now.

The police chief, George, stood up and started the meeting. Everyone became silent. It wasn't surprising that his first topic of discussion was about the human trafficking operation in Loveland and surrounding areas. That was always a topic around here on most days. This time though, he was specific and mentioned Niko, who was the well-known leader of this ring from what they had found out from the various pieces of evidence over the years. George went on asking everyone here to be alert and report any type of unusual behavior. He had divided up the whole police force and the rangers and had a chart of where he wanted them to patrol.

"I know all of you are outstanding police and rangers and FBI agents in your fields, but for the next few days, I need everyone to be more alert out there." He went on to say that there is someone that showed up in Loveland that could bring Niko and these human traffickers out in the public eye. This last sentence caused a complete automatic silence. George had caught the attention of everyone in the room.

PJ thought to himself, *Who would show up here in Loveland that would possibly cause these guys to come out and be more active in public? Well, George, you definitely got my attention.*

George called up the three gentlemen that had walked in and introduced them. Eric and Michael had a law firm in Ohio, and Anthony was a retired FBI agent that still did private work. Right now he was working for Michael. George went on to mention that the governor of Colorado had requested that we do everything that we could to help these gentlemen with their visit here in Loveland. Well, PJ thought to himself, he was right on. These guys were the kind of guys you don't want to mess with. If the governor of the state was involved, then this had to be important. He wondered why they showed up here in Loveland in the first place. George gave the floor to Michael.

"Hello, everyone, and I want you to know that we all appreciate your time here today. I am looking for my daughter. There is a long story behind her visit here that I would rather not put out there at this time. My wife and I are extremely worried for her safety. She came out here to take revenge on Niko and his trafficking operation, and I do believe she has every intention of trying to bring Niko out in the open. Of course, as we all know, she does not understand what she is trying to take on." Michael went on to say that they had just arrived in town, and they believe that their daughter has been around town or a surrounding town for the last few days. "This is a picture of my daughter. Her name is Gabbi, and she is nineteen years old."

PJ almost fell out of his chair when he saw Gabbi's picture on the screen above. He had a million emotions going through him, and he felt like he needed some fresh air now. What the hell? Gabbi had lied to him? The girl he was falling in love with was not the girl he thought she was. He took a deep breath and focused on Michael's presentation.

139

"If anyone has seen Gabbi or if you see her, please let us know. We are staying in town here, and George will be giving you the number you can reach Anthony at. I have hired Anthony, who is a family friend, to help us with this case. Like I said, there is a background to this story, and my daughter is determined to take down this human trafficking ring herself, and we all know how that could end. So please help us by being alert and reporting any information to us as soon as possible."

They were passing out pictures of Gabbi, and one ended on PJ's lap, and he picked it up and stared at the girl he had started to fall in love with. He was starting to feel angry. Was she just using me to find information? PJ knew he had to talk to Michael, but he wasn't looking forward to telling him that he and his daughter had become a little more than friends. He knew he had to do what he could to help, no matter what Gabbi's intentions were toward him. He didn't want to see her get hurt or kidnapped.

The meeting had just ended, and PJ was trying to figure out the best way to give Michael the information he knew, when he realized that all three of them, Michael, Eric, and Anthony, were headed right over to him. And leading the pack was George. George must have told them that he was seen with Gabbi throughout the town. He knew just by the look in Michael's eye as he walked over toward him that this wasn't going to be a good outcome for him. PJ wasn't one to hide, not that he could anyway, so he stood up and held out his hand.

Anthony walked up first, and he could see the hesitation in his handshake. George introduced PJ to Michael and Eric and told them all to follow him as he led them all into a private room. Michael looked at PJ and told him to have a seat.

"So, PJ, we have some information from a few of the guys that you and my daughter have been seeing quite a bit of each other."

PJ shifted in his seat. It didn't help matters that these three big guys were all standing around him, and he was sitting in a chair. PJ knew he wasn't a little guy himself, and he stood up to prove it. "Yes, Gabbi and I have become quite good friends over the last few days." PJ went on to tell them about how he met Gabbi and how she hated him at first, but he had won her over when she found out he was working with the police in trying to take down this human trafficking problem here.

Michael looked over at Anthony and Eric when PJ told them about this. Michael understood completely now. Gabbi had no interest in this guy. He was just a source of information for her cause. Anthony almost felt sorry for this kid. He had known Gabbi since Michael and Alysse adopted her. She calls him Uncle Anthony even to this day. Anthony thought how protective he was when he was around Gabbi, and now she was here in this town, and this kid had fallen for her. Anthony could tell from the first sentence out of PJ's mouth that he had feelings for her. Part of him wanted to push the guy back in the chair and drill him on every little detail, but now the other part of him was feeling sorry for the guy because his heart was about to be broken when he found out the whole story.

"Okay, PJ, we need to know every single detail from the few days you spent with Gabbi," Michael had said in a little sterner tone.

PJ pushed his hair back on his head. He really had no idea what was going on here, but he knew he had to tell them everything. Well, maybe not everything. PJ started with the whole story about how he got Gabbi a place to stay that was owned by his brother. Eric had glanced at Michael at this bit of information. PJ was quick to say that he thought Gabbi was a young pretty girl, and he felt she would be safer back at the house that his brother owned. After he gave them the address of the place Gabbi was staying outside of town, he went on to tell them the rest. The story about the gunshot he heard while in the park and finding the guy Jeff ready to kidnap Gabbi.

Michael grabbed PJ's arm at this news and interrupted him, asking if she was hurt at all. PJ assured him that he came at the right time, before anything could happen, and called for backup, and they were able to arrest Jeff. Michael was quick to take a deep breath, and he put his hand on PJ's shoulder and thanked him. Eric and Anthony also changed their opinion of this young park ranger. He was obviously a guy who can take care of things, and more importantly, he had the good instincts to know when something was wrong. If that wasn't the case, Gabbi could be gone right now and maybe for good.

PJ shook his head and said he couldn't be happier that he was able to get a guy like Jeff off the street and into jail. He also told them about the baby wolf and how Jeff was going to sell it and that was why Gabbi had made herself known to Jeff. PJ said he wasn't there in the beginning, but Gabbi had told him that when she saw Jeff capture that baby wolf and put him in a cage and try to shoot the other wolves that were hanging around trying to get the baby back, that she had just barged into his camp and started demanding that he let the baby go.

Anthony just shook his head, and Eric glanced over at Michael. Worry filled Eric's eyes. He knew Michael was about to lose it with all this information. Michael sat down now and said, "Of course Gabbi would forget about her safety to protect a wolf."

Eric stepped up to question PJ next. "PJ, when was the last time you saw Gabbi?"

PJ swallowed hard and told them how they had breakfast together early this morning and how she said she had a busy day planned and was headed over to the park for a hike first thing. Michael got up and wanted to move now, but Anthony stopped him and told him to stay put for a second. He walked out and brought George in.

"George, would you mind if we take PJ with us today on our search for Gabbi? He seems to have been in contact with her the most, and we can use his help around this area."

George, of course, agreed to this and told PJ to help them out around the area. PJ wasn't sure how he felt about this, but he followed them as Eric told them to move the rest of the conversation to the car. When they were all in the car, Anthony got in to drive and asked PJ for directions to the house. That would be their first stop. PJ told them how to get there, and as they started out toward his brother's house, Michael asked him to give any other information that could help them. Michael knew that they were not going to like the next conversation, but he had to tell them. As PJ told them about how Gabbi was always asking for information about Niko and the human trafficking crime in this area, Michael went white. PJ quickly added that Gabbi had said she was doing a research project on the state of

Colorado's human trafficking statistics and operations. He looked up at Michael in the front seat and apologized.

"I honestly thought she was doing a project for college, but now with all this information, I should have seen that the questions she was asking were specific to Niko. I will never forgive myself if something happens to her."

Eric reassured PJ that it wasn't his fault. Gabbi was a smart girl, and she had this planned out from the beginning, How was he supposed to know that she was coming out here for revenge on her mom. That last word got PJ's attention.

"Mom?'" he said.

He looked at Michael and said he was sorry for his loss, and Michael told PJ to sit back in his seat because he was going to tell him a story that not too many people know. He asked PJ to keep it to himself for the safety of his daughter, and PJ agreed. Gabbi's safety was his top priority. Michael started from the very beginning about how they found Gabbi in the forest living with wolves. At that point in the story, Eric and Anthony made it a point to look over at PJ.

PJ did not disappoint with his expression. He moved forward in his seat and started to talk, but Michael put a stop to that and told him to let him finish the story, and then PJ could ask any questions he felt that he needed to. Michael talked for about fifteen minutes, leaving out some details but getting the whole story out. He explained about Jesse being the real mother of Gabbi, one she did not even know about until her nineteenth birthday just recently. PJ caught the just recently part and thought back to when Gabbi had said she would be twenty in a few months. It looked like Gabbi had not been honest with quite a bit of information. This thought made PJ sad. He really was starting to fall for that girl, and now he didn't even know who the real Gabbi was. PJ decided not to waste his thoughts on that right now; after all, they had to find Gabbi and make sure she was safe. He understood why she wanted revenge. That poor girl had her mother taken from her without even spending any time with her or even getting to know her. That was a terrible thing to have to live with, and on top of that, Gabbi was the wolf girl. She didn't even blink when he had told her that story when they first met. She was good at keeping secrets, that was for sure.

He turned his attention back to Michael just as Michael was asking if he had any questions. PJ did not even know where to begin. The first question he blurted out was about Gabbi's past growing up. Was she a normal child? Did she have issues to overcome? Michael answered PJ's questions without telling him too much. Michael still wasn't sure what kind of relationship, if any, this young ranger and his daughter had together. Michael could sense that PJ wanted more than friendship from his daughter. Let's be honest, Gabbi was a tall, beautiful girl. Michael was sure many guys were interested in her, but what kind of interest was it? Eric and Anthony had picked up on that right away too. Michael did not want to think about any of that right now. The only thing he cared about was getting his daughter back before something terrible happened to her. She did not know who she was dealing with. And if Niko still ran this trafficking ring and got a glimpse of Gabbi, who knows what would happen.

There was no proof to tie Gabbi to Jesse, except of course her looks. But there was no actual proof, and he didn't think that Gabbi would say anything to confirm that piece of information. Ever since this happened, Michael had been feeling guilty. Maybe Alysse had been right. He should have kept the story of Jesse a secret, but he had made a promise to Jesse, and he wasn't the sort of man who broke his promises. That reminded him that he needed to check in with Alysse. He called her to find out if she had any luck with the posters. The information that PJ had given him was not going to be shared with Alysse right now. She would worry, and that could put her over the edge. When they had Gabbi safe and sound at home, then he would fill in the blanks of this ongoing story.

Michael reported back to Anthony and Eric that Alysse was showing Gabbi's picture around town, and quite a few town people had recognized her. Some had even said that she was with the young park ranger one night. PJ squirmed a little in his seat at that comment. He glanced at Anthony to see if he was looking at him, and he was. PJ told them that he had taken Gabbi out to dinner and to a festival. Trying to make it sound like it was more of a business date than personal, he told them that she had wanted more information about her research.

Maybe I should say her revenge plot.

The timing was perfect, as Anthony asked PJ if this was the house, when he pulled up to the driveway. PJ nodded his head yes. They pulled in, and PJ got the key from his brother. Gabbi's jeep was not in the driveway, and that really didn't surprise any of them. That would have been way too easy. They all exited the jeep and headed into the cabin. Anthony and Eric spread out and started searching the rooms. Michael had PJ with him, and he went into the bedroom Gabbi was using. Everything looked in order, and there were really no clues anywhere to be found. There was a notepad on the table but nothing written on it. Anthony showed up with Gabbi's computer. Michael didn't know what she had packed for her trip, so he didn't know what was missing, if anything at all. He noticed the blue dress on the chair and some make up by the mirror. He picked up the dress and looked at PJ.

PJ backed up a few steps and slowly admitted that Gabbi had worn the dress when they went out to dinner. Eric, who just walked in the room at this moment, raised his eyebrows at this and stole a glance in Michael's direction. Eric really wanted to see Michael's reaction to this bit of news. Michael looked at PJ and told him how he had never seen his daughter wear a dress when she wasn't being forced to. Not ever. PJ assured Michael he did not force her to wear a dress and that he had picked her up and she had it on. Michael set the dress down and double-checked for any other piece of information to show where Gabbi may have gone that day. Anthony told Michael that he was going to access Gabbi's computer.

He added, "Of course, if you don't mind?"

Michael said of course he didn't mind. The only thing he cared about right now was finding Gabbi safe and sound. They gave the apartment one quick sweep and headed back to the car. PJ dropped off the keys to his brother, who was standing by the door looking very curious.

"Hey, PJ, what is going on?"

PJ told John that he would fill him in later. He introduced Eric, Anthony, and Michael to John. And added that Michael was Gabbi's father. John looked worried at the comment.

"She just asked for a place to stay, I didn't realize she was a runaway."

Michael assured John that Gabbi was of age to do what she wanted and that he appreciated him giving her a room. "At least here she was safe," he added. He looked at John and said, "Did you happen to see Gabbi today?"

John told him that when he left this morning around nine fifteen, her jeep was already gone. Anthony gave John his business card and instructed him to call if he saw Gabbi come back to the room at all. John said he would. They all got in the car and headed out to the street.

"Okay, PJ, give us directions to the park that Gabbi mentioned she would be at today."

PJ gave the directions, and they all sat in the car silently as they sped off. Eric got into the driver's side so he could drive while Anthony worked on getting the laptop's information. Anthony had pulled up Gabbi's computer, and it wasn't long before he was pulling up her searches. He was frowning at what he found.

"Okay, it looks like Gabbi had been searching for information on Niko and any information she could find on the sex trafficking ring up in these parts. Her recent searches also pulled up information about the body that was found here the other day and past cases of kidnappings. It looks like she was trying to find out in what area would be best to visit if she wanted to find Niko and his gang."

Anthony could tell Michael did not like any of this information, but he also stated that the chances were going to be slim for Gabbi to find any hideout. It was not likely that the hideout for these guys would be in the open with a sign saying, "Come on in." He also reassured Michael that Niko and his men aren't going to be out shopping or hiking during the day, especially after a body was just found. Whether they had anything to do with killing that little girl, they knew that something like that would bring out more police and bring in the FBI. This bit of news did put Michael and PJ at ease a little. PJ broke the silence by telling them that the entrance that Gabbi usually went to was right up the street on the left, just after the curve in the road. They were all eager to see if Gabbi was up here or if anyone had seen her in the past few hours. PJ let himself think that maybe they all overreacted and Gabbi was just hiking up here in the forest. Somehow he knew that wasn't the case.

Chapter 12

Gabbi sat in her jeep and just stared out the window. She was exhausted. She was trying to catch her breath and think about the next plan. This day did not turn out how she had hoped for when she started out this morning. Her feelings were between agitation and desperation. Plus, besides feeling very agitated, she was hungry. If she was being honest with herself, she knew this whole revenge plan was a long shot. But she was determined, and she had felt like she would be able to get some piece of information to help bring down this organization. Even if she wasn't involved herself, she at least wanted to be able to walk into the police station and give some clue that would help catch Niko. Her hope was that she would be able to help save some young girls' lives in the process. Nothing was what she had found so far. Absolutely nothing. This was not what she was hoping for when she started out today.

She had stopped at a couple of the parks and literally ran up the trails, praying that she would see someone suspicious. Or anything out of the ordinary. But she had seen nothing. At one point, she saw the wolf family run in and out of her path, and at one point they had stopped, and she had just sat with them for a while. The mother wolf even let her pet her fur as the little baby pup ran around Gabbi's legs. That had been the highlight of her day so far. More than anything, she would have loved to stay there all day and spend time with these magnificent creatures. Her spirit animals, according to the old Indian lady. But Gabbi was on a mission today, and she was going to do everything in her power to find some sort of hint or clue or anything to lead her to the lowlife traffickers. She had driven down to Boulder, which was about forty-five minutes away. She had

148

walked around Boulder with her backpack and just sort of hung out in places she thought she may be able to see something unusual or even hear Niko's name.

Her sweatshirt off and some pink lipstick on, she was hoping to attract attention. A few guys had passed her and tried to strike up a conversation, but she didn't feel like they were related to any criminal activity, so she brushed them off. Nothing was unusual as she drove around some back roads to see if she could see any hideouts. Hell, she didn't even know what a hideout looked like. She even asked store owners or random people if they knew where she could find Niko. And most of them said "Niko who?" She even parked her car and walked onto the berm of Highway 87 to see if anyone would take notice or stop or if she could see any suspicious cars. But nothing. Nothing! She didn't have one single clue to show for her day of investigative work.

Her parents were probably back in town right now with half of the US military. They may not have found where she was staying, but they had to be in Loveland by now. That would limit her ability to continue with her plan. Michael, her father, would never let her stay here in the city where Jesse was kept. She was near tears. This was not the way it was supposed to end. She pulled out the picture of Jesse again, and she just couldn't help it. She started crying nonstop. Failure was what she was feeling. She had failed her mother. This one thing she wanted to do for her mother, to help stop Niko and put an end to all these innocent children getting used and enslaved. If she could save one little girl from that kind of life, then her mother's death wasn't for nothing.

After a few moments, she dried her eyes. What was wrong with her. She was better than this. She was stronger than this. Sitting in her car and feeling sorry for herself wasn't going to help anything. Glancing at the clock, she saw that it was seven o' clock. No wonder she was starving. The last time she had eaten was at breakfast. And that seemed like it was years ago. Her mission kept her searching for clues for hours, and she really hadn't stopped for anything except bathroom breaks and to hydrate with water. She thought about PJ. Gabbi realized she was going to have to tell him the truth about everything. How would he react? Would he hate her and never want to see her again? That thought made her very sad, and she realized she would probably be heading back to Ohio.

Her future suddenly felt hopeless. She didn't want to go back to Ohio. She wanted to stay here. Gabbi wondered if she would be able to stay here in Loveland and go to school in Denver. If she could convince her parents to let her stay, then she could have more time. But she knew they would not let her stay here with Niko being close-by. Well, she was an adult now, and this was something she would have to work out with her parents. Realizing now that it probably wasn't the best idea for her to have run away like she did, she would explain and apologize. Her love for Michael and Alysse was genuine, and she wanted them to be able to trust her, and she would show them that she could be trusted. Gabbi realized she was feeling so emotional because she was so exhausted and hungry.

Not wanting to admit defeat, but realizing she was out of time, she decided that she would go back and face her parents. And probably half of the United States Army that would be there by now hired by her father. She smiled at that. Her dad sure did know how to do things big when he was in charge. She started up the jeep and passed a little convenient store off to the side. Looking in the mirror to make sure she had dried all her tears, she grabbed her backpack that had some money in it. She may as well stop and grab something to snack on while she was driving back. Coffee sounded really good about now too. She told herself that she did the best she could, and it was time to head home.

Gabbi ran into the store and picked out a turkey sandwich to hold her over until later. Turning around, she noticed a big burly guy with a beard staring at her. Feeling uneasy, she quickly grabbed her sandwich and went to get the coffee. Glancing behind her, she saw the big guy walking down the other aisle. Maybe she was imagining things. Her mind was playing tricks on her. Suddenly she froze in place. Her heart was beating so loud she wouldn't be surprised if the whole store heard it. Gripping her coffee cup hard because the coffee almost slipped from her hands at what she had heard.

The big guy was making a phone call, and she swore she heard him say, "Hey, Niko." Was she just hearing what she wanted to hear? Gabbi felt excited, but she also felt sick to her stomach. She looked back again and saw the man on the phone facing the back. Inching closer, she decided to eavesdrop. Trying to look like a girl shopping for some snacks, her hand reached for a candy bar on the aisle next to the one the man was on. He didn't see her come back, and she was close enough to overhear him talking.

"I know it's crazy, Niko, but I am telling you that this girl looks just like Jesse. She is a little taller, but she could pass for her twin."

That was all Gabbi needed to hear. She ran back up to the front of the store. Well, this was her lucky day after all. She realized she wasn't sure what she should do. Her plan wasn't lost at all, but was it worth the risk? Maybe she could follow him and see where he goes, and maybe he would lead her to the hideout. Gabbi felt that this guy was too smart to let this happen. Would getting his license plate number help? What if it was a rental or a stolen car? She wouldn't let him disappear after finally having him fall in her lap. Her hand reached for her bracelet automatically. This was fate, and she had to act on it. Her mother was with her; she just knew it. There was only one thing she could do to guarantee that she would find Niko.

Gabbi's exhaustion seemed to disappear as she was playing out in her mind how to make this work. She would have to strike up a conversation, and she decided she would play the part of the back-packing teen just wanting to see the world before she gets old and gray. Gabbi saw the man coming up to the register so she jumped in line, and when the boy at the counter started to ring her up, she smiled at him. The boy had to be about eighteen, and he was having a hard time keeping his eyes off Gabbi. Blushing, he rang her up, and Gabbi asked loudly, "So do you know of any good campgrounds around here or cheap motels that I could stay at?"

Surprised that Gabbi was talking to him, the boy couldn't seem to get any words out, and he ended up just shaking his head no. So Gabbi turned around to James and asked him, "How about you, sir, do you know of any cheap camp areas I could stay at for a night or two?"

James laid his items on the counter and rubbed his beard with his hand. "Well, I sure do know of a few good places you could stay for cheap. Are you out here camping with your friends?"

Gabbi told James that she was traveling the world solo, and Colorado had always been on her list of places she needed to see. James couldn't believe his good fortune. This girl was practically begging to be kidnapped. And, boy, was she a looker. She would make them lots of money. Niko had commanded them to lay low for a while. All because they had found the girl they had left in the woods. That little girl from Boulder had managed to jump out of the moving car when they were transporting her, and they had no choice but to scoop her up and kill her. Her leg was pretty bad from jumping out of the car, and they couldn't afford to mess around trying to fix her injuries. So James had put her out of her misery. Stupid girl, trying to escape like that, she deserved what she got.

They had to shoot her and dump her body in the forest. They didn't think that the body would be found so quickly and that had put Niko in a terrible mood. His mood always seemed to be bad lately. James knew the feds were making it harder and harder to get new girls for their clients. And ironically, their client list was growing. They had the best operation out in the west. And with the body of the Boulder girl being found, they both knew it meant that they would have to either leave the state to get girls or take a little break.

Niko had his whole operation set up here in Colorado, just outside of Loveland. He didn't like change, but it was part of keeping the cops one step behind them. The whole operation had been going great for over twenty years. Of course there had been a few close calls, like Jesse and then that baby being found being raised by wolves. James always wondered if it was the baby girl he brought out to the cave that rainy day years and years ago. Niko had lost it when the story came out. He had said that the timing matched up perfectly with Jesse's baby, but James had held onto his story that he had killed the baby. But still, he always wondered, even though he didn't really believe that anyone could have survived that fateful night, especially not a newborn baby.

Shit, he was the best man that Niko had working for him. He deserved a break. Now all of a sudden today he was given a gift. A gift of a beautiful blond girl that seemed so innocent and definitely naive. You don't go running around trusting people when you look the way this girl looks. This girl was practically begging to get kidnapped. Niko was going to flip when he saw her. She looked just like Jesse. He had to play this smart though because the store clerk had witnessed the conversation. But then again she was a girl traveling by herself. Who would even know she was gone? And that store clerk was a young kid that probably didn't know what day it was.

This was like being handed a pot of gold. James could not believe it. Gabbi had smiled at him when he answered her question, and she asked him if he could tell her the names of the places to stay that he knew of.

"I'll tell you what, young lady, do you want to walk outside, and I can write down the names of the campsites, and I will even throw in the directions for you so you won't get lost."

Gabbi thanked him even though she felt a knot grow in her stomach. Following him out of the store, she passed by her jeep. If things went bad and her dad couldn't find her, at least they would find her jeep here, and that could give them an idea of the location. Gabbi decided to make small talk as they were walking out the store.

"So do you know of any cool sites to see here? I really don't want to miss anything while I am exploring this area."

James told her of course he did. He said he had a map in his car that she could have, and he could circle the places for her. Gabbi felt that feeling of unease again. She just knew he was going to try and take her, and even though that was what she had been hoping for, she wondered if it was the best way. She kept up the grateful tourist act as she debated in her head if she should let him. After all, she wanted to know where the elusive hideout was, and what better way to see it then to be taken there. But she had seen how big of a guy Niko's helper was. There were some doubts starting to arise. It would destroy her parents if she disappeared forever. On the other hand, if she could escape from the inside and get the police over there, then this whole trafficking thing would be ended. That was her goal, what she needed to do.

The answer was clear now. She knew what she had to do. Gabbi trailed behind James as he approached his car. She stayed back a little from the car. James just smiled at her and said, "Let me put these groceries in the back seat and I'll grab your map for you." He opened the back door of the car on the opposite side of the driver's seat. He told Gabbi to come on over to that side and he would show her on the map which way to go. Gabbi hesitated. She knew all of a sudden that this was going to happen unless she ran for it. She could still give them a description of this man. She just wasn't sure. She looked down at her wrist all of a sudden and saw the bracelet and knew without any doubts that this was fate for sure. It was meant to happen. The wolf bracelet. She touched it for a moment, and all of a sudden she felt stronger and ready. How do you prepare yourself to be kidnapped?

This whole day was spent finding a clue with no luck at all, and then all of a sudden she was given a clue. Not even a clue, it was more than a clue. It was a guaranteed way to see Niko and come face-to-face with the son of a bitch that had her mom killed. Was she really going to back down now? What if this guy gets rid of this car and stays hidden for a while? They would never be able to track him down. For the past twenty years they avoided being caught, and did she really think that he was stupid enough to be caught now? Besides, she reminded herself that she had the advantage of surprise on her side. She knew exactly what she was getting into They would think she was some young stupid girl, and she could act that part. They would never expect her to try and fight back.

Her hand brushed against the secret compartment she had made just in case she was taken. Her phone was still hidden there. She had brought another phone that she never used. They would think that was her cell phone, and if things worked out the right way, she could drop her real phone outside the hideout, and it could signal help. All right, she had made up her mind. She was going to get herself kidnapped.

As she walked over by James, he leaned the map against the window. He started showing her directions. He pointed to a dot on the map, and she moved in to see what he was pointing at, and she felt the cloth up against her mouth and smelled the chemicals. Her reactions kicked in, and she held her breath to try and keep from breathing too much in. She let herself go limp. The next thing she knew, she was being thrown into the back seat of the car. She pretended to be passed out, and in all honesty, she was feeling a little sick. Stars were floating above her eyes, and she was going in and out of consciousness as James sped out of the store parking lot. Closing her eyes, she just lay there. She tried taking little breaths to try and see if she could get the chemicals out of her system. His hand was quick as he had put it against her mouth and she had inhaled some of it. Actually more than some of it. She put her head back and saw nothing but black.

James glanced back and saw her passed out on the seat. He laughed a big hearty laugh. Man, was Niko going to be happy about this. He couldn't help but look at her again. Boy, he almost wished he could just keep this one. He licked his lips. Yes, he could keep her for just a night. But that thought quickly left his mind. This job was about the money, and there was good money to be made for a girl like this. He wondered how old she was. If he had to guess, he would guess about seventeen. He put his foot on the gas a little harder. He was anxious to show Niko his prize catch. Yes, she was going to bring in lots of money for them. James thought again about quitting this business. He was getting older, and he had enough money saved up from years of being in this business. Money enough to live anywhere he wanted. Niko said it again and again; they had been very lucky! They had had a few close calls, but they were smart, and they hadn't been caught yet. Things were starting to get tougher though with the FBI closing in, and he thought it was about time he got out. The thought of him spending the next twenty years in federal prison did not sit well with him.

Driving along the road, he couldn't help but smile. This was one of his easiest kidnappings, and he ended up with a great prize! Yes, he thought, this might be his last girl that he ever took, but wow, she was a good one to go out with. James turned up the radio. He was dancing to the music. After all, he had just won the best lottery ever.

Chapter 13

PJ was feeling exhausted, both mentally and physically. They had driven all over the town. Actually, quite a few towns. Any place that had shown up as a potential search on Gabbi's computer they had gone there. For the last six hours, they had been rushing from place to place. It was starting to get dark, and he was feeling more guilty now than ever for giving Gabbi information that had helped send her on this hunt for the human traffickers. He glanced at Anthony, who was sitting next to him now, trying to track down any information from his computer and other equipment he had brought. PJ thought he was up on all the latest technology, but he didn't even know what some of these electronic pieces were. They were so hi-tech.

I *guess that is the difference between FBI and local law enforcement,* he thought to himself.

Michael turned around to ask PJ if there were any other places that he could remember. Places that he may have told Gabbi about in their conversations. PJ could hear the frustration in Michael's voice. Frustration and worry. Michael had called his wife, Alysse, a few times, and he had to give the guy credit. When he wanted to, he could hide the fear in his voice and sound so positive. Overhearing the last call to his wife, he had told her that Gabbi was probably headed back to her rented house for the evening. PJ knew that wasn't the case. No one had been able to reach Gabbi at all. And Anthony had not picked up a signal from her phone all day. PJ had checked in with his brother at least four times to see if there was any sign of Gabbi. He knew that John would have called him right away if Gabbi had been home, but he felt like he needed to reach out. Hell, he felt like he needed to be doing something!

His nerves were on edge here with all these big shot men in the car with him all day. It didn't help that they were all related or close to Gabbi. He felt empathy for them all. They all had a connection to Gabbi, and they were all doing their best to find her. PJ still wasn't sure if she was actually missing. He thought to himself, he had talked to her this morning, and she was fine. But it was unusual that no one had heard from her or seen her around town. They had driven to outlying towns that were close to the parks, checked in with the ranger station in Loveland and even in Denver. They had driven roads and even hiked up the trail that Gabbi usually took. The one where she had met PJ. But there was no sign of her, and they had asked many people, even showing her picture around. PJ just didn't know where else they should check, but he knew that Michael wouldn't stop searching until he heard from Gabbi or they found some kind of clue. PJ was hoping that John would call and say Gabbi just pulled into the driveway. They could all go back and sort this out with Gabbi. He realized that they wouldn't be having their date tonight, and that thought made him feel lost.

Even if she did show up soon, they would have to make her realize that they would catch Niko and the rest, but it could take time. There were so many men working on this case. This whole human trafficking ring had been worked on for years. And they were getting closer. After all, they had found the body of the young girl, and they were almost positive that she had been taken by Niko's gang. The image of the body of the girl that had been found haunted PJ from the beginning, but now he was even more upset. He didn't want to find any other girls dead in the forest, but he especially didn't want to find Gabbi that way.

Today had been a day full of many emotions for PJ, but one thing was for sure: he realized that he wanted Gabbi found safe and sound, of course he did, but he also didn't want Gabbi to go back to Ohio. There was something about this girl. He could even overlook the dishonesty. Yes, she was beautiful, but she was also strong and a fighter. She also loved the outdoors and animals, which was a plus in PJ's book. He realized that he just loved being with her, and he wanted to spend more time with her. He was so lost in his thoughts about Gabbi that he didn't realize that Anthony was nudging him.

"Hey, PJ, isn't that your phone going off?"

PJ grabbed his phone as he sort of nodded at Anthony. The car was silent as PJ answered the phone and continued on with a couple yes words, and then his voice changed.

"Are you sure? Okay, what did she look like? All right, let me have the address, we are heading there right now." PJ put his phone down and told Eric they had a change of plans and to get onto Highway 287. Eric did not waste a moment following directions, but Michael and Anthony waited for PJ to let them know about his phone call. PJ glanced at Michael and then at Anthony.

"That was police dispatch, and they had a call come in from a convenience store employee in Boulder. The call was about a possible kidnapping."

As soon as the word *kidnapping* was out of PJ's mouth, Michael leaned toward the back seat and demanded the rest of the information. Eric put his hand on Michael's shoulder and told him to give the kid a chance to speak. It was evident that PJ was uncomfortable giving the information from the call, but he had to do it.

"The kid working at the counter said that a blond-haired girl was talking to a man about directions and followed him outside. He said he looked out and saw the girl being thrown into the back seat and the car speeding away."

PJ told Eric directions on where to go and then told the rest of them that it was about a thirty-minute drive. Anthony pulled out his laptop and started working on something related, while Michael asked PJ again if there was any other information about the girls looks, her weight, her age. PJ told Michael that they would question the employee when they got there and that the Boulder police were already headed there and would beat them to the destination. Anthony said there was still no signal from Gabbi's phone since this morning. Michael started talking. His tone was filled with worry.

"Gabbi is a smart girl, she couldn't just walk outside with a guy she didn't know. That is not her style at all. She took years of self-defense. She knows better than that, it probably isn't her."

Eric agreed with Michael. "Michael, come on, you know there is no use in worrying until we have all the facts."

Anthony and PJ agreed. The rest of the drive up to Boulder was mostly made in silence. PJ could feel the tension and the worry coming from everyone in that car. He had learned long ago not to draw any conclusions until the facts were made. Besides, the report had stated a probable kidnapping. This kid could be wrong completely about what had happened. But PJ wanted to get to that location just as fast as they could. Every minute thinking about Gabbi being kidnapped was a minute too long. PJ finally broke the silence and told Eric where to get off the freeway and how to get to the store.

When they pulled into the parking lot, PJ's heart sank. Gabbi's jeep was in the parking lot, or a jeep that looked just like hers. He did not miss the look Eric gave Michael when they ran up to the jeep. It was definitely Gabbi's jeep. The doors were locked, and there were no signs of a struggle anywhere near the jeep. They headed into the store. The place was filled with police from the Boulder Police Department. PJ knew most of these guys from working with them before on other cases. He quickly introduced Anthony, Eric, and Michael. Michael asked to talk to the employee. PJ quickly explained the situation to the Boulder chief, Robert. He wasted no time walking over to the employee, who looked like he was going to go into shock.

The employee was a young kid and was definitely intimidated by everything going on. Fear was written all over his face as he was looking around and talking fast. Michael walked up to him first, with the rest coming up behind him. Eric held out his hand and introduced himself to the young kid, trying to make him feel less intimidated. The employee, Sam, nervously shook his hand and got his name out. Eric knew Michael was going to push the kid for information, so he put his hand on Michael's shoulder to pull him back and said, "Let me handle this, you're too upset, and you're going to scare the kid."

Michael knew Eric was right, so he let Eric do the talking.

"Okay, Sam, I need you to tell me exactly what you saw again, and don't leave out any details."

Sam looked nervous with all these big men around him. He slowly started to tell what he saw. Sam told the story of the pretty girl who was asking for directions to a hotel or a camp area. He said the big guy, who was behind the girl in line, started a conversation with the girl. Sam went on to say how the girl checked out and then the big guy had told her that he could write the directions out for her to some of the campsites if she wanted to wait for him and walk outside to his car so he could get a pen and the map.

Sam stopped for a minute and said, "I wanted to tell the girl that she shouldn't trust the man, I have seen him one or two times in the store, and I get a bad feeling about him. He is the kind of man you don't want to mess with."

Michael couldn't wait another minute, so he pulled out the picture of Gabbi he had in his pocket. He held the picture up to the store employee and asked him if this was the girl that was in the store. Sam looked up at the picture and said that she was definitely the girl in the store. Michael went white. He asked Sam again, "Are you one hundred percent sure this was the girl, Sam?"

Sam nodded his head yes. "I could never forget what the girl looked like, she was so pretty."

PJ stepped up and asked Sam if the girl had pulled in with the red jeep that was parked outside. Sam glanced out the window and said he honestly wasn't sure. He just saw her when she walked into the store. Anthony asked where the store cameras were, and the clerk pointed above to the three cameras they had placed in the store. After he got the name of the owner and his phone number, he quickly walked away. Michael knew that Anthony was going to try and pull the camera footage from the store. Maybe they would be lucky and get a picture of the guy that kidnapped Gabbi. Eric went back to the questioning.

"Now, Sam, tell me what happened after the girl left the store."

Sam let out a sigh and then went on to tell how he watched the girl walk outside, and she seemed to be talking to the big man. He said he saw her walk over to his car, and he pulled something out of the front seat. Everything had happened so fast, Sam had explained, and he couldn't save her. He was near tears. The next thing he saw was the man pushing something into the back seat of his car and then jumping into the driver's side and driving away. Both Michael and PJ knew at that moment that Gabbi had been kidnapped. PJ asked Sam for information on the make of the car, and Sam did not know. He just said it was a red four-door car. Eric asked for a description of the man that had walked out of the store with the girl, and Sam had described him as a big guy. Over six feet in height and at least 230 pounds. Sam was able to say that the man was middle-aged, he wasn't sure, somewhere between thirty-five and fifty, with brown hair and a big beard. That was all the information they could get from Sam.

Eric thanked Sam, and he pulled Michael aside.

"We will find her, Michael, I promise you."

Michael looked like he aged ten years in the past few minutes. Eric suggested that he go back to Alysse and let them handle it from here. Michael exploded with rage at Eric.

"I am not going anywhere until we have Gabbi back safe and sound and I have this guy put in jail for the rest of his life."

Eric and Michael were interrupted by Anthony calling them from the back of the store. They headed back to the office, and PJ joined them. The Boulder police were back there too. They had gotten permission to play back the camera from the store. They all sat back and watched the screen. They saw Gabbi picking out some snacks and then looking at the big guy. The look in her eyes showed she was uncomfortable as she walked away. They saw the guy take his phone out and walk over a couple aisles. Gabbi seemed to jerk her head back at the guy who was facing away from her. Gabbi walked over closer to the man and seemed to be glancing at him but pretending to be shopping. Anthony stopped it there for a minute.

"She obviously decided that this guy was someone she needed to talk to. She was trying to get away from his glances at first, but then look how all of a sudden she looks like she is trying to eavesdrop on his phone conversation. Dammit! This camera has no sound, only visuals."

Anthony started it back up again, and they could see Gabbi slowly go up to the clerk and smile at him. Sam, the employee, looked like he was taken with Gabbi. Then the big guy walks up, and Gabbi starts talking to him. She smiles at the big guy, and they seem to have a conversation. She waits for him to walk out and follows him out. Then Anthony pulled up the outside camera footage and said, "The store has one camera for the outside. So this is the footage from that." They all continued to watch the screen. They see Gabbi and the man walk over to the car, and Gabbi stands back at first, but the man pulls out something from the front seat.

"It looks like a pen and paper," one of the Boulder police stated.

But Anthony shook his head and told them to look closer. Anthony tried to slow down the speed, and then they saw it.

"Son of a bitch," PJ said loudly. "He has some kind of drug on a what? Napkin?"

Anthony jumped in. "Yes, look, he is fast, but he gets Gabbi to come over to the passenger side, and in one swift move, his hand puts the cloth on her mouth, and he pushes her in the back seat."

Michael walked out of the room. It was just too much to see. Eric and PJ followed, and Anthony got a still shot of the big man and sent it to his phone. PJ and the Boulder police took the photo of the guy that took Gabbi and sent it back to headquarters to run it through the system. They were hoping for a record on this guy. The police already ran prints from the areas of the store. They were running those through now. Michael went outside and tried to get into Gabbi's jeep. The doors were all locked. Anthony came over and was able to break the lock on the driver's side. They searched the jeep for any type of clue, but there was nothing to be found. The only thing they found was a picture of Jesse in the glove department. Michael took the picture and put it in his coat pocket. Eric had called to get the jeep towed back to the house that Gabbi was staying at. When that was taken care of, he walked over to Michael and the rest. Michael was pacing.

"We have to move now, before it's too late. Two hours have already passed since he pulled out of the store with my daughter."

They all felt that Michael should step back from this. This was personal for him, and it wasn't the best situation when your family was involved, but they also knew he wouldn't. PJ couldn't blame him. Nobody would be able to change his mind about going on this search for Gabbi. He was full of worry right now too but also rage. His anger overwhelmed him when he saw what had happened, and he wanted to kill that guy for taking Gabbi. He was also angry that Gabbi put herself in this situation.

Robert, the police chief, walked over to them and told them they had a hit on the guy who was on the camera. The guy that had taken Gabbi. His name was James Roland, and he had a long criminal record. He had been arrested in the past for robbery and assault. There were also some other smaller charges attached to his name. He stopped for a minute and looked directly at Michael.

"He is also connected to Niko Faro, the leader of this trafficking ring that we have been trying to end for many years now."

Michael slammed his fist on the wall. "Damn this guy, we need to find her now, right now!"

PJ told Michael that they were alerting all police and rangers in all the cities surrounding Denver. "We have the plates on the car, and we have every unit available out looking for them."

Robert looked at Michael with pity. He couldn't imagine having his daughter kidnapped and especially if he knew she was kidnapped by men known for working in the sex trafficking business. The next twenty-four hours were critical. They all knew that. If she was not found by then, the chances diminished by the hour that she would be found alive. PJ felt helpless. He needed to do something or to come up with a plan. They couldn't just drive around and hope they find Gabbi. They needed some kind of clue or at least a direction that James had gone. They were trying to pull cameras up and down the streets and highways, but that could take a while, and it may not show anything at all. And if James had not gone far, then the car could be parked or hidden, and there was no chance of finding it. He knew they had to find Gabbi tonight or risk never finding her. They were all thinking the same thing. Every minute she was with these men meant that she could be hurt or a fate worse than death.

The thought of any of these lowlife criminals putting their hands on Gabbi made PJ's blood run cold. He looked over to the store entrance where he heard arguing. He saw that Michael and Eric were having a disagreement. Anthony had his laptop up, trying to find any clue at all. Michael and Eric walked up to PJ.

"PJ, you're from this area and have helped with these trafficking cases, so what area do you think we should attempt first?"

PJ shook his head and said he honestly didn't know. He told them he didn't even want to guess. They needed something solid, no use driving around the whole city and wasting time. PJ was hoping that some kind of sighting of the car would come in soon. Someone had to see something. The car didn't just disappear. It had to have gone somewhere, so there had to be a camera that picked it up. PJ told them that they had a police helicopter up, and hopefully that would help with the search. The Boulder police left the store. They were all helping in the search too.

Michael saw that Alysse was calling, so he hit the End Call button on his phone. He couldn't talk to her right now. The last thing that he wanted to tell her was that the same thing that happened to Jesse was now happening to their daughter. Gabbi's sweet face popped into his thoughts, and he put his hands to his head. He texted her back that he was in the middle of something and he would call her soon. He put the phone in his pocket and walked away. Never in his life did he feel so helpless. He didn't want the rest of them to see him break down and cry. Michael was a strong man, but his daughter, his sweet Gabbi, was in the hands of his worst nightmare.

Every minute counts in these kinds of cases were the words that were running through his mind.

He didn't want to think about what his daughter was going through right now. Bending his head, he prayed to God that they would not touch her. The tears just started falling, and they wouldn't stop. He was not the type of man that cried, and now he couldn't stop the tears. He wiped them with his hand and turned in the opposite direction so Eric and the rest of the men couldn't see him like this. He wished he had never told Gabbi about Jesse. If he had known that she would run to Colorado and try to avenge her mom, he would have broken the promise to Jesse. Without a doubt, Jesse would have understood. The last thing she would ever want was for her daughter to suffer the same fate as herself.

Michael had failed them both. Even though they had tried to protect her, Jesse had been found dead, and now his daughter was kidnapped by the same men that killed her mother. Michael felt an arm go around his shoulder, and he knew it was Eric. Eric didn't say anything. He just stood by him. Michael turned to Eric and said, "We have to find her tonight, Eric, you know what could happen to her, and I can't live with that."

Eric told Michael that they would all work together and find these guys and get Gabbi back. He said they just had to hold tight and wait for a break. Someone had to have seen the car. A camera had to pick something up. They just had to wait. Eric didn't say it out loud, but he was thinking that they needed a miracle, and they needed it fast. Usually he wasn't really a religious man, but he said a silent prayer for his best friend and his daughter. This world could be such a cruel place, and it made him crazy that innocent young girls and boys could get plucked off the street and have their lives changed forever and for the worst. Just then, God provided that miracle that they needed. PJ came running over to them with excitement on his face.

"I just got a call from Gabbi. I mean, she didn't say anything, but she dialed my number. That means we have a trace!"

Michael and Eric grabbed Anthony and had him trace the call. The trace showed that she had dialed PJ. Whether it was by mistake or on purpose, this was the break they needed. Michael thought that Gabbi may have risked this call in order to give them a clue. Or could she have escaped somehow? If she had, she would have said so on the phone call. That thought gave him hope anyway. God knew he needed all the hope he could get. His daughter was small, but she knew how to fight. They all looked over at Anthony pulling the call. Michael had gotten himself together and in fighting mode now. They were all ready and waiting. They just needed the location, and they would go find Gabbi. They would get these sons of bitches and put them away for good. Michael and PJ were both thinking that they would like to have a minute alone with Niko and James. That thought put a smile on both of their faces as they jumped in the car and waited for the direction.

Chapter 14

James looked in the rearview mirror to make sure he wasn't being followed. The routine he knew like the back of his hand, and he was damn good at it. Their hideout here in the low-lying mountains of Loveland Pass was one of the best hideouts to date. Situated by the mountains and hidden in the forest. Niko and himself had packed up everything they needed and the girls they had at the time and just moved into a new place. They did this every year or so. This was why they hadn't been caught so far. The feds had gotten close a few times, but he and Niko were just a little smarter than those FBI fellows. James chuckled at that. You would think those federal agents and the local police would be a little bit better at their job. James was feeling invincible! *Yes,* he thought to himself, *this may be a good time to get out of the game.*

His eyes glanced at the back seat and settled on his prize. His captive in the back seat was still out. He looked at her lean body and those long legs. His body reacted at the sight of her. This girl was going to bring in some good money. Maybe more money than any other girl that they had sold in the past. As he reached the long driveway that was partially hidden from the road, he stopped the car and looked back again at the girl in the back seat. Man, he couldn't get over his luck. She was a looker for sure. She had that blond hair that almost appeared silver in the sunlight, and it was hanging down almost to her waist. It really didn't matter how old she actually was; they could sell her easily as sixteen. He hoped she wasn't much older than that. The high-end clients that they dealt with were willing to pay good money for a prize like this. But they liked their girls young.

He smiled again. Again his mind wandered to the thought of possibly approaching Niko about maybe purchasing her for himself. He had the money, and he would love to have her tied to his bed for the next year or so. That thought was very appealing indeed. He knew that Niko would probably say no to that plan. James wished he would have just sampled some of the prize before he brought her in. James put his hand on the door handle to exit the car and glanced at the front door of the hideout. He got that feeling in the pit of his stomach whenever he thought about getting Niko mad. Niko was one scary bastard when he was crossed. James knew this from years past. He had witnessed this himself.

He thought back to the time when one of the men brought in a cute little brown-haired girl. According to the media, her name was Gina, and she was only fifteen years old. A petite and a very shy girl. She was not James's type of girl at all. He liked a little challenge with his girls. If the girl would fight back and scream, then that was the perfect girl for him. It just so happened that Thomas, the guy that Niko had hired on earlier in the year, had decided to rape the girl before he brought her in. The girl was a mess by the time Niko saw her. Niko had found out when he overheard Thomas bragging to the other men. This particular girl had been a virgin, and Thomas had ruined that. Niko had lost it completely.

Nowadays bringing in a virgin was like bringing in gold! Niko didn't even question Thomas about it. He walked right up to him when he was talking to the other men and pulled out his knife and came right up behind him and slit his throat. The men definitely got the message, and since then there had been no other cases of the girls being touched or raped before they were brought in. James knew he was Niko's right-hand man, but he also knew that it wouldn't stop him from killing him in an instant if he thought for a second that James had betrayed him or broken the rules. No, James valued his life over having some fun with this girl. But still, he couldn't help but wish. At least he would be praised for bringing in the best prize ever.

Wow! He still couldn't believe the way this day played out. He wasn't even looking to grab any girls for a while, after Niko told them to lay low. At least until the dead body of the last girl was buried and forgotten in a couple weeks. Niko was going to be so happy with him. James got out of the car and waved to the armed guard by the door. The house was watched twenty-four hours a day. No one could come in or out without Niko's permission, if they didn't already work for him.

James yelled over to the guy, "How is everything going, any excitement?" Patrick was the guy on duty, and he just shrugged his shoulders and reported that nothing exciting was going on at all. Well, thought James, that was definitely going to change. He opened the back door and pulled out the girl, grabbing her backpack as he did. She had opened her eyes and was just staring at him.

In the back seat of the car, Gabbi had remained calm. She knew that what happened in the next few minutes would be the difference between getting rescued or becoming another statistic in the trafficking market. She had taken in enough of the chloroform to put her in and out of consciousness for a while. But she did her best to breathe out the poison instead of breathing it in when it was held up to her mouth. She had pretended to faint right away, so her captor had pulled it away quickly. He probably thought she was a tiny thing, and it didn't take much to drug her. Gabbi recalled all the self-defense classes that her mom and dad made her take. She knew what to expect, and she knew the best way to react. A calm head was the key, and she had a plan.

Her dead old phone that she had hid in her backpack would be the one her captors would check and just assume she hadn't been able to charge it for a while. They wouldn't be able to check it because it had no power. Her phone that she used daily she had hid in the side of her bra. Then as she was walking over to James's car, before the kidnapping, she had taken it out and made sure it was on mute. She couldn't risk the phone going off because that would be the end to all her plans. The phone had been opened to PJ's contact info. She put the phone in her pocket of her shorts while James was driving, and she took a deep breath.

The first thing they taught you in self-defense class was to clear your head. Put emotion aside. It was important that she played the helpless, scared little girl so they wouldn't think that she had a plan to fight back. This way they would not worry about her escaping. The plan was to get inside and see if there were any other girls being held captive. Not only was this going to be a revenge mission, it was also going to be a rescue mission for herself and hopefully a few other girls. That was, if things played out right. Payback time for Niko and everyone involved in this business. Gabbi thought about how important it was to her to put a stop to human trafficking here, at least in this area. The thought of visiting her mom's grave and telling her all about it was a hope she had. This had to be done right. No mistakes. This was for her mother. If she messed up, then she would cross that bridge when she got there.

Right now she knew she had the advantage. She knew what she was walking into. Well, sort of, and this guy would think he kidnapped her right off the street with no issues. Gabbi opened her eyes and pretended to groan when she heard the car stop. The last thing she wanted was this big idiot carrying her in. Her plan would only work if she walked in. Watching James open her door, she saw the evil in James's eyes as he opened her door and stared at her far longer than he should have. His dark eyes roaming over her body. Then all of a sudden, his arms reached in and pulled her out of the car. Gabbi tried to stand up and quickly put her hand by her pocket. James was holding her with two hands, and she mumbled that she was fine to walk, even though she was still a little drowsy.

All of a sudden, she knew she wasn't alone. She looked around, sensing the wolves. Were they here? She felt their presence; she was sure of it. They were out there in the forest somewhere. Had they followed her? She lifted her head when James started pulling her along. She thought she saw something move in the forest, an animal, right beyond the driveway. This was a perfect distraction! Her hand lifted, and she pointed to an area beyond the driveway and pretended to scream in terror, "A wolf, I see a big wolf!"

James dropped her arm and looked quickly. He hated the wolves and couldn't help but shudder. These damn animals were everywhere up in the forest. The quick flash of gray confirmed that something was out there. As he was looking to make sure they did not come any closer, Gabbi got loose from his grip and fell onto the side of the driveway. Her head landed in a pile of leaves. James swore, "Dammit, girl!" He realized she must still be too weak to walk. He glanced again into the forest and mumbled "Damn wolves" under his breath. His dark gaze turned to Gabbi, and he warned her that if she decided to be stupid and escape, then she would end up as a midafternoon snack for the wolves that were out there.

As he was warning her, he lifted her up like she weighed nothing. She squirmed to get down, but he told her he didn't want her falling again. Gabbi decided to let him carry her. After all, her plan had worked. The wolves had been a perfect distraction for her to stumble and fall. James never noticed her hand take the phone out and hit the call button for PJs number and throw it under the leaves where she fell. The call would go through. Hopefully, they would be able to trace it when they found out she was missing. They had to know by now that she was missing. Gabbi hoped and prayed that they already found her jeep. There was no doubt that her dad was in town by now and searching everywhere for her. Gabbi was sure that her dad had brought everyone to Colorado for the search. She envisioned him coming in like the army. It made her feel guilty again for putting her parents through this. But if this ended the way she had hoped and planned, then it would all be worth it.

James had opened the door and walked in still carrying Gabbi on his shoulder. When he got in, he put her down but held her arm in case she fell again. The last thing he wanted was a bruise on that pretty little body of hers. Niko hated bringing in anyone from the outside. So if a doctor was needed, they either had to pay one for his secrecy, which was always risky, or fix things themselves. Most of the time, Niko decided to handle things his own way. And that usually meant shooting any girl that was injured too badly. Yep, Niko would not be happy if this prize he brought in today was bruised. He turned to Gabbi and asked her what her name was.

Gabbi decided she wanted them to know her name. So she told them. James took her backpack and poured the contents on the table. Her fake phone and a few other items fell out. James took the phone and opened it and saw it wasn't charged, so he threw it on the table. He told Gabbi to spread her arms, and she did. He searched her from top to bottom but found nothing. He grabbed Gabbi's shoulder and pushed her forward. Gabbi took mental notes on everything she saw. There were two men sitting in the living room. They both had guns in front of them on the table. They stood up when James walked in the room with Gabbi. James gave them a nod and asked where Niko was. Before the words fell from James's mouth, in walked Niko. Gabbi knew by looking over at the two men in the room that they were just hired men. She could tell right away that the man that had kidnapped her was someone of more importance than these hired men. Both men had looked at him with respect.

The man that had just walked into the room was definitely the man in charge. This man had to be Niko, without a doubt. Gabbi knew the moment Niko walked in the room that he was the man that had ruined her mother's life. Rage filled her body, but she tried not to show her emotions. That was the hardest thing she ever had to do. What she really wanted to do was to scream at him and ask him if he cared that he had cut his mom's life short. That he had taken her own mom from her before she ever got to meet her. But she didn't. Her success at getting out alive was dependent on playing the part of the helpless little kidnapped girl. She had to keep to the plan.

No matter what she felt on the inside, she had to keep her outside emotions hidden. Gabbi stood up straight and looked this man right in the eyes. She could tell right away that this man that walked into the room demanded the attention of everyone in the room. His aura evoked fear. Niko was tall, maybe about six foot one or so, with an athletic body, and looked to be about forty to forty-five. He was not a bad-looking man for a criminal. His wavy black hair matched the little bit of stubble on his face. There were a few tattoos on his arm. But the thing that caught Gabbi's attention and made her blood run cold was his eyes. Niko had dark brown eyes that almost looked black. Looking into those eyes, she saw the devil. This was not someone you messed around with. Gabbi would have to be very careful around him.

Niko looked mean and unapproachable, but it didn't sway her from her plan of seeing him locked up forever. Looking in person at the man that had torn her life apart, she realized she wanted nothing

171

more than to see him in jail. She wanted him dead. This feeling of hate was new to her. She had never felt anger like this. This man had taught her how to hate for the first time in her life. And now he had also made her want to kill for the first time in her life. Gabbi blinked back tears. These new emotions were coming at her all at once. She needed to get her act together now to make her plan work. Her hand went up to her face, and she wiped the tears from her eyes. Niko slowly walked over to her and put his fingers on her chin and pulled her face up to his level. She felt his hot breath on her face, and it made her want to gag.

"Hey, beautiful, don't cry, I am not going to let anything bad happen to you."

Niko stepped back from Gabbi and took her all in. James had been right. She was gorgeous. As near to perfect as they come. And as he walked around her to look at every detail, he felt something stir in him. Something that he had not felt for a long, long time. Those feelings that he had buried deep inside when he had Jesse killed. This girl was a spitting image of Jesse. Niko had put her out of his mind a long time ago, and just like that, all the feelings he had felt for Jesse came flooding back. That was over twenty years ago that he had fallen for his captive who had been pregnant. And because of that pregnancy, Jesse had stayed with them at the hideout much longer than any other girl had. Niko just couldn't kill her because of the pregnancy. He remembered feeling that it was a weakness keeping this girl, but he did keep her for a long time.

The girls that were captured were usually in and out within two weeks, a month at the most. It was vital that he needed to keep the girls moving. That was how he made money for one, and that was how he kept one step ahead of the police and the FBI. But this girl, standing in front of him was bringing back all the feelings that he had buried away. In his line of work, he couldn't afford to have a girlfriend or a family. It wouldn't be fair to them, and it would be a liability to his business. Niko never let himself or the other men enjoy the girls he had brought in to sell. That was the golden rule. He had to run a tight ship, and he did. The men that worked for him knew that all girls were off-limits. That was the reason he had to sell

Jesse. It had killed him to do it. He had really fallen for her over the months she was here. She was so beautiful but also a fighter. She had been so strong, and he had admired that trait. But if he made laws for his men to follow, then he needed to follow them too.

This whole business was based on loyalty. Only men that he could trust were hired. Of course, he had to prove to them once or twice that it was not a good idea to disobey his orders. Remembering what happened made him smile. It only took one time for the men to know that he meant what he said. But Jesse had worked her way into his heart right from the beginning. She was so beautiful, just like this girl standing before him. Niko pushed his hair back with one hand. It was a nervous habit he had. He just couldn't believe that fate had brought this girl to him. It had to be fate. He stood in front of Gabbi. He was so close to her that Niko felt her breath on his cheek.

Those beautiful blue eyes of hers were still damp with tears. At first he thought that they were tears of fear, but could he be mistaken? Looking into this girl's eyes, he swore he saw something else. Something darker. Was it hate? Whatever it was, it made him feel uneasy. And he never felt uneasy about anything. It unnerved him a little, but then he knew he had to be wrong. This girl was his captive, and she was obviously afraid of him. He backed away from her and asked her what her name was. The girl said that her name was Gabbi. She said it very quietly, almost a whisper.

"Gabbi, such a pretty name for such a pretty girl," Niko said. He walked up to her again and took a strand of her blond hair in his fingers. "Well, Gabbi, I am so glad you were able to drop in today for a visit. I want you to shower, and I will get you some new clothes, and then we are going to take some pictures. Almost like a photo shoot! After all, you definitely could be a model, so you should feel very comfortable with this."

The other men laughed at Niko's comment. They all knew what the pictures were for. Niko wasn't wasting any time getting this one on their secret site for high-paying customers. They all knew that this girl was going to bring them in some good money. And that made them all happy.

"James, take her into the room with Lizzie, and make sure she showers and changes into the clothes I bring for her."

James smiled at his directions. "Sure, boss, anything you say!" James pushed Gabbi slightly with his hand on her back. Gabbi started inching forward. Her mind was taking all this in. So Niko was planning on selling her to the highest bidder.

This is how things worked? Gabbi's thoughts turned sad. *Was my mom sold to the highest bidder?*

It took every ounce of self-control not to try and kill Niko right now. The plan was to sell her, like she was an object, not a human being. Well, she would have to make her escape before that ever happens, she thought to herself. In the back of her mind she was praying that PJ had gotten her phone call and was tracing the number now. She didn't want to count on that, just in case something went wrong. She had to have a backup plan.

In her mind, she decided she would play their game for now. She would shower and change and take her time doing it. It was important that they thought she was scared and helpless. So as they walked away, she started pleading loudly, "Please don't hurt me, please let me go back to my family!"

Her fake cries echoed throughout the room as Gabbi tried to seem hysterical. She wanted them to believe that she was no threat at all, just a scared little girl. This seemed to aggravate James.

"Stop crying! You're not going home, so get that out of your mind. You are going to follow directions and do what I say."

Niko realized quickly that this new girl was nothing like Jesse. Jesse had been a fighter. For some reason, this made him mad. He needed some fresh air. As Niko walked out of the room, James pushed her into a room off the hall, as he opened the door. Gabbi noticed there was another girl in the room, and she jumped up when the door opened. She ran to the back of the room. You could tell she was scared. Gabbi walked in with James behind her.

"All right, I am going to give you exactly ten minutes to shower. And if you're not out by that time, I will be coming in to help you finish." He pushed her through the bathroom door that was connected to the room and turned on the shower for her. James said, "I will be bringing you in some new clothes, so take those off." Gabbi looked at him, waiting for him to walk out the door. James stood his ground. "I said take those clothes off now, or I will do it for you."

Gabbi could tell by his evil grin that appeared suddenly that he wasn't kidding. She turned her back toward him and started removing her clothing and jumped quickly into the shower. She heard James walk back out and shut the door behind him. Gabbi showered quickly. The last thing she wanted was James coming back in here. The thought of his big grubby hands touching her body made her sick to her stomach. She would make sure he was locked up for life just like Niko. These two guys deserved no mercy. Gabbi showered and grabbed the towel that was thrown on the floor and wrapped it around her. The new clothes were thrown over a chair, so she picked them up.

The clothes consisted of a jean skirt that was pretty short on her with her long legs, but it fit pretty good. It was a little big around the waist. And the shirt they gave her was a very fitted black T-shirt with Minnie Mouse on it. Gabbi was thankful she had clothes to put on at the moment, so she didn't really care what they were. A comb was placed by the sink, and next to it was a brand-new toothbrush and toothpaste. As Gabbi was brushing her teeth, James walked in and stopped to take a good look at her. He seemed pleased. The directions he yelled at her were surprising. He told her to brush out her hair and put them in two pigtails. Then he handed her a bag full of makeup.

"I want you to put some makeup on, but not too much. We are going for a young look here. Do you understand?"

Gabbi nodded her head at him. She really just wanted him to leave her alone. The sight of him disgusted her. After another look at her, James walked out the door but left the bathroom door open. Gabbi quickly brushed out her hair and applied some of the makeup. She hurried out of the bathroom and walked into the bedroom, where the other girl was sitting with her arms wrapped around her knees. This poor girl was rocking back and forth, and there were tears in her eyes. Walking up slowly toward the younger girl, Gabbi smiled at her. She was of medium build and had medium-length blond hair.

The girl didn't smile back, and she didn't say a word. Gabbi thought that the girl was maybe sixteen at most. Sitting down next to the girl, she reached out and put her arm around her. The girl pulled away. She was so scared, and Gabbi felt so sorry for her.

"What is your name, sweetie?" Gabbi asked the girl. Glancing up, the girl looked at Gabbi but still wouldn't say anything. "Listen, I am not here to hurt you. I was captured by these men, and I need you to help me so I could get both of us out of here and get you home to your family."

This seemed to make the girl come alive, with the mention of the word *family*. She looked at Gabbi and said her name was Lizzie.

"Well, Lizzie, it is so nice to meet you." Gabbi held out her hand when she said that, and to her surprise, Lizzie shook it. Gabbi wanted to ask Lizzie so many questions, but she didn't want to scare her. She smiled again at Lizzie and asked her how old she was. Lizzie whispered that she was fifteen. Gabbi felt sick to her stomach. This poor girl was only fifteen years old and was being held by these men. No wonder she was scared to death.

"Listen, Lizzie, I need you to tell me how long you have been here and where are you from."

Lizzie looked at the door. She wasn't sure if she should be talking to this new girl.

Gabbi reassured her, "I am going to try and get us out of here as soon as possible."

Lizzie took one more glance at the door and started rocking back and forth. "I am from Colorado Springs, and I was kidnapped on my way home from school. That was a few days ago. I am not even sure what day it is. Can you really get us out of here?" Her eyes were full of hope. Gabbi told Lizzie that she was counting on some help but would do everything she could to save her and get her home to her mom and dad. This seemed to make Lizzie relax a little. Gabbi asked Lizzie if there were any other girls held captive here. Lizzie said, "I saw one other girl when I came in. She had red hair, and she was crying, but after they put me in this room, I didn't see anyone else. They took me out one time to get pictures, and that was yesterday."

Gabbi noticed that the girl had on a tight T-shirt with balloons on it and a pair of shorts. They were obviously trying to make them all look young, and for some reason this made Gabbi even more determined. Putting her hand softly on Lizzie's shoulder, she asked her, "Did they hurt you?"

Lizzie shook her head no. Her voice sounded so young when she told Gabbi that they made her shower and do her hair, but they didn't want any makeup on her. She went on to tell Gabbi that they brought her food two times a day and checked in on her every few hours. Lizzie started to cry again. "I just want to go home." Gabbi held her tight and tried to reassure her.

"Listen carefully, Lizzie, if you hear any unusual noises or gunshots, promise me you will hide under the bed with the blanket and stay there until I come and get you."

This seemed to terrify Lizzie even more, but she nodded her head yes. Together they sat there for about a half an hour and just talked. Well, mostly Gabbi talked, and Lizzie just listened. Lizzie kept her head on Gabbi's shoulder. Gabbi knew that Lizzie was feeling less scared, and that made her happy. There was no way she was going to let any of these guys touch this little girl. She would die fighting them first if she had to. Niko and his men deserved to go to jail and rot there for the remainder of their lives. They deserved to rot in hell! The thought of them sitting in a cold jail cell with no one else around gave her some pleasure. Just then the door slammed open, and James walked in.

"Well, isn't this just precious, you two seem to have become good friends." He walked over, and Lizzie closed her eyes. She was terrified of him. Gabbi stood up and blocked Lizzie from James. James seemed to get a laugh out of this. He pulled Gabbi by the elbow and said, "Lucky you, girlie, the boss wants to see you." Gabbi shook her arm free from James and walked in front of him out the door. She glanced back at Lizzie, who had her head down and was just rocking back and forth. James laughed again and told Gabbi, "Don't worry, your little friend there is being sold to the highest bidder as we speak. She is going to bring in some decent money because she is so young and innocent."

Gabbi stopped and looked back at James. "Does it make you happy to sell little girls to perverts?" she said.

James laughed at that and told her that it always makes him happy when he gets big money, even if it comes from selling little girls. Gabbi wanted to kick him right now, but she held her course. If they knew she could fight, then they wouldn't be so free with her, and that could stop her from finding a way to get her and Lizzie out of here. So she walked through the living room and ignored the two hired men's eyes on her. They were nothing to even think about right now. Her goal was James and Niko taken down, and she wanted that so badly. James took her to the back of the house.

The room they entered was guarded by one man, and he stood in front of a big wooden door. She didn't notice any other girls being held, but they did pass one locked door, and she wondered if there were one or two girls being held captive in there. The guard opened the door for James and Gabbi. Gabbi walked in, and James just stood there. Niko got up from his desk and walked over to Gabbi.

"You even look more beautiful than when I left you. How old are you, Gabbi?"

Gabbi decided not to say anything, and that made Niko mad. He walked right up to Gabbi and pushed her up against the wall. He pressed his body up against hers and whispered in her ear, "I don't like to be ignored, Gabbi. I am the kind of man that gets what he wants, do you understand me? If you can't answer my questions nicely, then I will find a way to make you answer."

Gabbi knew she could push Niko off easily, but James was still in the room, and she knew that she could not fight them both. Especially with an armed guard at the door. So Gabbi decided to look really scared.

"I am seventeen," she lied softly. She wasn't sure why she didn't want them to know her real age right now. Would they remember that nineteen years ago they left a newborn baby in the cold forest to die? For a brief second, she wanted them to know who she was and why she let them kidnap her, but after meeting Lizzie, she knew she had to save her need for revenge right now. It was more important that she get that poor girl out of here before she was gone for good. Niko seemed happy about her answer.

"Good girl," he said. He backed away from her and turned around and told James to leave. James seemed a little upset that he was being dismissed, but then again, now he could go try and get in a few hands of poker with the guys. He walked out without a word. Niko stared at Gabbi for what seemed an eternity. "You know, Gabbi, part of me wants to keep you for myself. I have a few more years in this industry, and then I want to get out. I have played the game well and have never been caught. I would love to settle down in a cabin up in the mountains with a girl for some company. Some pretty young girl. Would you like that, Gabbi?"

He walked back over to her and put his hand on her cheek. He ran his fingers down to her mouth and put his two fingers inside of her mouth. Gabbi turned her face, trying to get the fingers out. Niko seemed to like that she was fighting a little bit.

"I once fell in love with a girl that looked so much like you, but she was a fighter, she had spirit. You, on the other hand, are the opposite. I like a girl with some spirit. So I think I am going to go with my original plan and sell you off." He looked at Gabbi to see if there was a reaction and seemed disappointed that there wasn't any. Slowly he moved his hand down to her neck, where he took one finger and slowly traced an invisible line across her neck. "See, let me tell you the plans I have for you. I am going to sell you to one of my elite clients. A million dollars is nothing for them to pay for the best I have. They want only the most beautiful girls, and they like them young and innocent." His hand went to the top of her shirt. "Are you innocent, Gabbi?" He moved his hand all the way down her body slowly, very slowly.

Gabbi started to squirm. She wasn't afraid, but the thought of having the man that killed her mother's hand touching her body made her want to throw up. Niko laughed and walked away.

"Oh, Gabbi, I would love nothing more than to throw you down right here and see if you are innocent or not, but you see, I have to follow my own rules. And that means that you are safe from any of us until you are sold."

He turned quickly though and walked back up to her. He grabbed the back of her neck and kissed her hard while pressing his body against hers. Gabbi couldn't stand his mouth on hers, and she lost control and started fighting back. Her knee went up to hit Niko in the groin. As he was bent over in pain, he screamed. Gabbi took a punch to his back and had him lying on the ground in one minute. Quickly she looked around the room to see if there was a window so she could escape. She started running toward the window when a hand reached out and grabbed her around the neck. Niko held her body tight to his, and he wrapped his leg around hers so she couldn't kick or move. Gabbi thought that Niko was going to kill her. His big hand tightened around her neck, and she couldn't breathe. Her arms were trapped under Niko's body, and just when she started seeing black dots growing in front of her eyes, he let go of her, and she fell to the floor, gasping for air.

"Ha, it looks like our little captive is a fighter after all. Well, I won't make that mistake again," Niko said. He reached inside his desk drawer and pulled out handcuffs. Gabbi was instantly sorry that she had fought back. She couldn't let him handcuff her. If that happened, then she would not be able to get out of this room at all. She wanted to go back to Lizzie to make sure she was all right. Gabbi started pleading with Niko.

"Please don't handcuff me, I promise I will be good."

Niko took the handcuff and put it on her wrist and took the other one and handcuffed it to the pole he had next to a couch in his office. Wriggling her hands, she tried to get out, but she couldn't. Niko was mad, but it had intrigued him that she had fought back like that. He ran his hand through his hair again. This one was going to bring in even more money if he let his clients know that she was a fighter. One or two of his best clients loved a challenge. The thought of teaching a girl that was misbehaving how to behave made these guys dish out the big money. He was torn. This new Gabbi that liked to fight made him want her for himself; he definitely couldn't deny that. Her fighting like that when he tried to kiss her really turned him on. But if he took her for himself, his men would lose respect for him. And without respect, he was nothing. Niko knew he was a big name in this business.

Sitting down on his big chair behind his desk, he just stared at her. Looking at her made him think of Jesse, and he realized that it was Jesse he wanted. It was the resemblance to Jesse that made Niko want this girl. His mistake was selling Jesse. When he found out she had escaped from his client, his client was furious. He did not want his identity to be known. This client that had bought Jesse was losing interest in her anyway, he had told Niko. Niko was there to see what he could do about the situation. And then Jesse had escaped. He had no choice in the matter. He had to have her killed. She knew too much, and that was his policy. The girls escape and the girls get killed. There was too much at stake. She had known too much about their base camp and the men. It had broken his heart to issue the orders to have Jesse found and killed. He didn't want to know any of the details of her death. It saddened him even after all these years. What a waste of a great girl.

His thoughts went back to Gabbi. Yes, he would have to continue with the sale. He had a customer in mind already. This was his best client, and he was a high official in Egypt. His passion was for tall blondes, and he had told him he would send pictures within the next twenty-four hours. This was one of his best customers, and he couldn't back down now. He would get the pictures of Gabbi and then see what the customer would offer. If the amount wasn't high enough, then maybe he would change his mind. Niko knew that the longer Gabbi was with them, the greater the risk of him caving in and keeping her. Either way, he would have to keep a better eye on her. She was not as scared and helpless like he originally thought she was.

Sticking his head out the door, he called in James and told him to get the pictures of her but to leave her handcuffed. James was a little surprised by the request, but like usual, he never argued with the boss. James went to get the camera and came back and gave Gabbi orders on how to pose. Gabbi didn't feel like cooperating at first, but after James started to threaten her, she gave in. She already messed up by letting her temper get the best of her and lost some of her edge.

He took about twenty photos of her, posing in various positions. Niko had walked out halfway during the photo shoot.

When he was done, he left her handcuffed to the wall by herself. She sat there alone wondering what was taking PJ and her father so long to rescue her. Maybe she was in over her head a little. If they didn't get the trace and find her, then how would she get out of here? She would have to fight them all if she had to. They wouldn't leave her tied up forever. When the opportunity arose, she would make her move. She had to do this. She had to succeed. Now this succeeding with the plan wasn't only for her mother; it was also for Lizzie and other girls past and present who were kidnapped and used for trafficking.

Chapter 15

Michael, Eric, and PJ all stood perfectly still, looking at Anthony. Anthony had his laptop out and his equipment and was trying to trace the phone call from Gabbi. PJ had left the call on even though Gabbi was not talking. He had hoped to hear something, any kind of clue, but was met with complete silence. But Anthony was confident that it was enough to trace it. They were all ready to jump in the car and go. Michael prayed they weren't too late to help Gabbi. He knew it hadn't been that long, but the thought of his daughter in the hands of Niko and this James guy was something he didn't want to think about. He would kill them both with his bare hands if he got a chance.

Anthony jumped up and shouted, "I got it! I was able to trace the destination. It looks like it is up in the higher elevations, a place called Loveland Pass." Anthony started picking up his equipment and running to the car, so the others followed. Eric got into the driver's seat, but PJ pushed him away.

"Let me drive, I am familiar with that area, and it could be difficult to navigate."

Eric agreed and jumped in the back seat with Anthony. While Michael was sitting in the front, PJ started the engine and called his captain. After reporting the details, he confirmed that they would meet them there. PJ informed everyone that it was a little over an hour, but he would drive fast, and he knew some shortcuts. Michael swore.

"Dammit! An hour is too long, anything can happen by then."

Anthony assured Michael that they were getting the FBI and local law enforcement to act on this too. He told them that this could be the moment they take down this operation, but they had to be careful. This was up in the mountain, and the element of surprise was in their favor. The forest offered some cover, so they all were grateful for this. The plan was to meet about ten minutes away from the general area of the address so they could go by foot. Michael wasn't feeling good about this plan at all. He wanted to storm the place and take them all down at once. PJ reminded Michael that this operation had been top notch from the beginning.

The FBI and local police had been trying to take down this particular operation for years. Niko and his men were not just going to stand by and allow them to storm the place. They had to stake out the cabin or house that Gabbi was held up in. Maybe if they were lucky, there wouldn't be that many men guarding the outside. By the time they would get there, it would be about forty-five minutes before sunset. That could work in their favor, but it could also work against them. The FBI wanted them to meet up on the road, and they would all go together. They were requesting civilians to stand back and stay on the road.

"Hell no," Michael said. "I am not staying away from this. My only goal is to rescue Gabbi and keep her safe and sound."

No one said too much during the hour drive up into the foot-hills of Loveland Pass. It was beautiful scenery in that area, especially with the sun starting to go down against the mountains and the forest. The thought that this world had such beautiful places but some of the people were pure evil left Michael feeling very disheartened. Watching the trees pass by, Michael couldn't help but remember the start of all this. Remembering the day like it was yesterday. Alysse and himself hiking up in the mountains that fateful day they found Gabbi. It was all coming full circle.

After about an hour or so of driving, they pulled up to an indent off the road. There were already two cars and a van there. FBI agents and local police were waiting for them. Anthony exited the vehicle and went right over to the other agents and was showing him the location of the trace.

"Wow! That little girl is a smart one if she made that call to get a trace," said Mario, the head FBI agent. "Remember, right now we have the element of surprise, and let's try and keep it that way until we can get the cabin surrounded." He started issuing orders to everyone to start heading down and locating themselves at various locations around the area of the cabin. Anthony had pulled up blue-prints of the cabin, and it looked like it had a wraparound porch with at least three doors they would have to cover. Mario went on to tell that they had the disadvantage of not knowing how many bad guys there were total inside the building. Also how many hostages, if any.

When that came out of Mario's mouth, Michael began to say his daughter was in there, but Anthony stopped him. He knew as well as the rest that almost two hours had passed since the call, and if this was Niko's hideout, then he could have shipped Gabbi or any other girl out already. They had not avoided getting caught for the last twenty years because they held onto the girls or stayed in one location. They all knew what they were dealing with. These were the worst kind of criminals, and every single man and woman there was hoping for an end to Niko and his operations. More than that, they were hoping they could rescue at least Gabbi and hopefully other girls that might be held captive there.

"Remember, any man that would sell young kids for money to the highest bidder is the kind of man that will shoot to kill you first, so be careful."

Mario tried to get Michael and Eric to stay back, but they were not having it, so he told them to stay low and stay behind them and not to go out in the open. They agreed. Slowly they all started to move and take their positions surrounding the cabin. As they walked through the forest going downhill, they saw the cabin about a half a mile down. They all took their positions and waited. Michael was going crazy. He didn't want to wait, but Anthony was keeping him grounded.

PJ came up behind Michael and Anthony and sat low. He took out his binoculars and said, "As far as I can see, it looks like one guard at the door, but he had a rifle in hand."

They waited less than a minute before Mario gave the signal to be ready to move. PJ and Anthony saw the movement next to the man guarding the cabin. It happened so fast. Two FBI agents came up behind the guard and grabbed him from behind. The guard, who was totally surprised by these intruders, tried to react and fight back, but he was overpowered. During the struggle, the guard's rifle went off. They saw two men come out the door with their rifles raised and ready to shoot. They were met with FBI agents, and they retreated back into the house shooting off a few shots before slamming the door shut. PJ and Anthony ran forward, telling Michael to stay back. Michael ran forward, refusing to listen to them. There was gunfire coming from the windows, so the men pulled back. PJ and Anthony snuck around to the side of the house to see if they could check out the windows and see if Gabbi was in any of the rooms.

It was hard to tell how many men were in that house. Mario ordered everyone to stay put and wait it out a minute. He didn't want any of his men killed or injured. They needed to assess the situation. Michael started to move along the side of the trees. Eric jumped behind him and stopped him.

"You are going to get yourself killed, and how is that going to help Gabbi? You know she will live with guilt the rest of her life if something were to happen to you."

That last sentence stopped Michael in his tracks. Eric was right. He couldn't risk Gabbi having to live with guilt because he wanted to play the hero. Slowly they retreated and went back to PJ and Anthony, and they all moved slowly to the back of the house. Anthony felt this was a good position to be able to sneak in. And he thought that if Niko tried to escape, it would be from the back. That was his best bet. As they started moving in that direction, Mario gave the motion for everyone to move forward with caution. They had a few sharpshooters aimed at the windows, as the rest of the men tried to reach the cabin.

In the midst of the shooting back and forth, some of the men made it to the porch of the cabin. They were going to get ready to storm in with guns loaded. Michael was thinking that this was a scene from an action adventure movie, and he was watching it play out live. Nothing would have made him happier than to realize that this was just a movie, and he was sitting there with Gabbi and popcorn watching it together. His focus was to find Gabbi, and he was scared of the shots being fired. He did not want them to accidentally hit his daughter. All of a sudden, the back door slammed open. The shooting stopped as Gabbi walked out onto the back porch. Michael jumped up to run and get her, but Anthony pushed him down and held him down.

"What the hell, Anthony, I have to get her!" screamed Michael. Anthony told Michael to look closely. Michael paled at the sight before him. Gabbi was at the door, but a guy had his arm around Gabbi's shoulder with his body pressed up to hers. The man had a gun pointed right at Gabbi's head.

Gabbi tried not to show her fear. She had heard the shooting in Niko's office and was relieved. She knew that help had arrived, and they would be rescued. Not even a minute after the shooting started, Niko ran into the room and uncuffed her.

"So, my pretty, you are going to help me get out of here, and when you do, I have a nice gentleman waiting to purchase you for almost a million dollars." Gabbi tried to fight back, but Niko was ready for her this time. He put the gun to her head and cocked it. "I am sure you don't want your brains spilled across the floor, do you?" Niko whispered in her ear. Gabbi felt fear, real fear for the first time. Niko was crazy! She had no doubt that he would kill her if he had to. His hand went around her waist and pulled her body close to hers. She felt repulsed at this and made a sound of disgust. This made Niko put his lips to the side of her neck and kiss her up and down her neck. "I may even break my own rule after we get out of here. It may be your lucky day and you and I can get to know each other so much better."

Gabbi tried to kick away from him. Niko wasn't as big and burly as James, but he was solid. She could feel his muscles through his shirt. They started walking toward the door when he heard the shooting stop and wasn't sure if his men were dead or holding off the cops. Realizing that there was no time to find James or get the other girls, he decided his best bet was to grab Gabbi and use her as a shield. After all, with her helping him escape, he could lay low for a while and start up again with the business. The money he would sell Gabbi for was enough to go forward and set up a new hideout.

Niko knew that the police wouldn't shoot at him with Gabbi out in front of him. "Start walking," he told Gabbi as he pushed her body forward. He told her to open the door and step outside. She prayed that she was not shot by mistake when she walked out. Closing her eyes, she started thinking of her parents and how they would never be able to bounce back from her being killed. The guilt overwhelmed her. It was her fault for putting herself in this position and not realizing how it would destroy her parents. Her mom would never be able to come back from her death. She wished now that she wasn't so stubborn and had not taken this matter into her own hands. This could be the end. That thought made her think about PJ too. Gabbi had no doubt she was falling in love with him. It was ironic. After all these years, she was falling in love with a guy, and the timing couldn't be worse. A wonderful, good-looking guy that she loved to spend time with. A guy she hoped she could continue to get to know better. She closed her eyes again as they walked outside.

To her relief there was no shooting when she walked out the door. From the distance, she saw PJ stand up when he saw her and try to run forward with his gun raised by his side. Niko didn't waste a second firing a warning shot very close to him. Gabbi yelled, "PJ, stop, please! Don't try to help me, I'll be fine."

Niko jerked her closer to him and said, "So this is your doing? You know these people?" He was angry and demanded to know how she got the word out about where the hideout was. Gabbi decided to tell him. She wanted to distract him from PJ and the others. Maybe if he was focused on her, then he would make a mistake. In the distance, she saw her dad, and her heart jumped a beat. Her mind started planning. She couldn't let them get shot because of her. Her words flowed out of her mouth as she started talking to Niko. With a very calm, slow voice, she told Niko how she pretended to fall and had made a call to her friend, who was a ranger and policeman. She felt Niko tense up, and she laughed.

"I guess your men are not so smart. For the first time in twenty years, the police found you because one of your captives was smarter." Feeling Niko tense up even more, she knew she was getting him angry. This was her plan, his focus was more on her words than on the men hiding behind the trees. "Niko, I let myself be taken. I wanted to find you. I had actually been searching for you for a while, and your man James fell right into my lap." Niko didn't believe what he was hearing.

"Why? Why would you want to find me?"

Just then, before she could answer, she heard a man yelling from the trees. "Niko, let her go and we will let you run. You will have your freedom. We just want the girl released unharmed." Gabbi didn't recognize the voice speaking, but she was hoping that Niko would listen to him, whoever he was. Niko ignored the man and started pushing Gabbi forward.

"Don't think for one second I won't put a bullet in this pretty little head, just give me a reason!" he yelled out to the men. And to prove his point, he pulled Gabbi's head back by her hair and took the gun and put it in her mouth. Gabbi shut her eyes. She was going to die in front of her father and PJ. She felt like she was going to choke with the cold hard steel sitting in her mouth. Imagining what it would be like with the gun going off in her mouth, she silently prayed to God to watch over her parents. Would she feel anything? One minute she would be here, and the next she wouldn't. Life would just be over. So many thoughts racing through her mind. Everything that she hadn't accomplished or experienced yet. She realized she would never have the opportunity to make love with a guy, with PJ. There would never be a wedding or children in her future. She also thought about her wolves. Yes, they were her wolves. They had become a part of her life, and she realized she would miss them terribly.

Niko heard the doors opening behind him, so he took the gun out of Gabbi's mouth and moved her forward with his body right behind hers. His back was to the forest. Out of the house emerged three FBI agents, with their guns raised straight at Niko.

"Put the guns down gentleman, now, unless you want to see this beauty shot and have it on your conscience the rest of your lives."

The men did not hesitate, and they all lowered their weapons. They were not going to take a chance on Gabbi getting killed. They all realized real fast that this guy was a psychopath. PJ whispered to Michael and Anthony and Eric that this had to be Niko. The man that had started all this years ago. He fit the vague description that they had gotten in the past. This was the man in charge of kidnapping little girls and selling them for money. The man that had Jesse killed and left Gabbi out to die in the middle of the Colorado mountains when she was just hours old.

As the sun started to set, Niko had started to move off the trail into the woods. Michael was going crazy. He couldn't let this psycho take his daughter. Mario met up with the rest of the agents that had burst through the door of the house. They reported to him that they had taken care of the rest of Niko's men. They stopped right away when they saw Niko and Gabbi heading into the forest. Niko was backing up quickly now. He had Gabbi in front of him like a shield. The forest was to his back. Niko was keeping an eye on the FBI agents and trying to glance behind him as he walked. As Niko moved farther up the trail toward the mountains, PJ started moving forward too, and the rest were right behind him. He wasn't sure of his plan, but he couldn't let this son of a bitch take Gabbi. Just seeing her in this man's grips made his blood boil.

Niko was getting away from them, but worse, he was taking Gabbi with him. They couldn't just try and shoot him because he was way too close to Gabbi. They would never risk the missed shot. Some of the men started heading up the mountain from the road. Mario had ordered them to try to surprise Niko from the top of the incline. They were not sure where Niko was heading. Mario told his men to be ready. The only way this would work was to plan a surprise attack from behind and to ensure that Gabbi stayed safe. Michael and PJ and Anthony started following Niko and Gabbi. Eric followed along too, but he headed more to the right. Niko was almost fully into the forest now. And with the sun going down fast, it was getting harder to keep him in their vision.

The mountains were coming up behind him, and they realized this was where he was headed. It would be more difficult to follow him once he hit the foothills. Niko knew he had the advantage, and he smiled to himself. There was a cave up a little higher up with food and supplies. Niko thought to himself, *I think ahead and plan for the worst, and this is why these agents will not be arresting me today.* He knew he was better than these young hotshots. He hadn't made it in this business for over twenty years by being stupid. The plan was to take cover up there for a day or two and walk out at night under-cover. Niko moved his arm up higher until it was around Gabbi's neck and whispered, "It looks like you and I are going to be spending a few nights together." Gabbi knew she had to escape and quickly.

PJ moved quickly and decided to try and come up from behind them, but before he could get to the area behind some trees, Niko fired a shot at him and warned him to stay back. They all just watched as he took Gabbi farther and farther into the forest. The daylight was going fast, and they all knew that it would be almost impossible to track Niko in the dark. PJ and Michael stopped suddenly. They saw movement. Something was out there a little past Niko. Michael blinked his eye. Was it a dog?

PJ yelled out, "Did you guys see something?"

Most of the men agreed there was some kind of animal up there in the forest behind Niko. This made Michael panic. He did not want Gabbi being attacked by some animal up there. It could be a mountain lion or a wolf or even a bear. They all had their guns ready but were told not to shoot until given the order.

Gabbi was trying to look for a way to escape. She knew it was getting dark and that would make it harder for her to be rescued. All of a sudden, she smiled to herself and felt her body relax. Gabbi felt the presence of the wolves before she heard them. Did they follow her? She had always felt a connection, and it must be the same for them. She felt at ease with them here in the forest with her. Her eyes kept scanning the forest for any kind of wolf sighting. Gabbi knew everything was going to be okay now. She heard the low growls behind her, and so did Niko. Niko tensed as he turned his head to look behind him and saw the five gray wolves. They were standing still as statues, but their golden eyes seemed to follow his every move. He blinked his eyes and looked again. They were right behind him now, and they looked like they were ready to attack. Niko panicked and pulled the gun away from Gabbi to fire at the wolves.

That was all Gabbi needed. She bent down and twisted Niko's arm back and was ready to try and throw him down to the ground when the wolves took advantage of the commotion and jumped on him. Two of the bigger wolves pushed him to the ground and started biting at his arms and clothing. His gun went off, and Gabbi jerked back. Did the bullet hit her? She looked over her body and did not see anything, no blood and no holes. She sighed in relief and turned around to see the wolves on top of Niko. He was screaming and trying to fight them off. Gabbi stood over him. Niko deserved to suffer. She wanted him dead.

Just then, PJ and Anthony and the rest of the agents ran up. They had never seen anything like this, ever. None of them wanted to try and grab Niko away from the wolves. As much as she wanted to see Niko suffer like her mother had, Gabbi knew she couldn't let Niko die. He could have information on more human trafficking operations. Girls could be saved. Reluctantly Gabbi stepped up to Niko and told the wolves to stop, waving her hand to the side. They all looked up at her while still growling and baring their sharp teeth toward Niko. Gabbi bent down to the ground, and the wolves stopped and came to her as she hugged them. Burying her head in their fur, she held the wolves close. They had saved her, and right now, they were her comfort as she realized that she was saved and Niko was going to be arrested. Standing up, she looked back at Niko lying on the ground, trying to stand up. He was bloody and torn up, but Gabbi thought he would live.

As she stood over his body, she said, "This is for my mother Jesse and all the girls you have taken over the years."

Niko's eyes widened at those words, and his shock turned to anger as he tried to grab Gabbi's foot. Just then the men came running up. They weren't sure what was going on, but they were not going to miss this opportunity to arrest the man they had been searching for. Mario and the agents grabbed Niko and put the cuffs on. Even though they didn't think he was in any position to fight back, they were not going to take any chances. PJ ran toward Gabbi but stopped shy of getting too close with the wolves there. The large male wolf growled low at PJ, stopping him in his tracks. Gabbi hugged the wolves one last time, and they went off into the woods. The male wolf looked back one last time as if to make sure Gabbi was not in any more harm. Gabbi turned and looked at PJ. She ran into his arms, and he hugged her hard. Suddenly she pulled back when she saw her father coming up the trail. He was holding his arm. It was all bloody.

"Oh, what happened?" She ran into his arms and started crying.

"I am fine, Gabbi, Niko's gun went off, and the bullet hit my arm, but it is just a flesh wound."

When Gabbi felt reassured that her father was going to be fine, she also walked over to hug Anthony and Eric. "I am so glad you all showed up when you did." But then Gabbi suddenly stopped. "We need to go back to the house! There is another girl in there, Lizzie. She is only fifteen." They all headed back down toward the cabin, with Gabbi running ahead. All of a sudden, she saw the little girl she had met earlier sitting on the steps with a female agent talking to her. Gabbi ran over and hugged Lizzie.

"I am so glad you're okay, Lizzie."

Lizzie smiled, and she seemed even younger than fifteen when she did. Gabbi also noticed two other girls sitting on the porch. She looked at the agents.

"These girls were in the house too?" Gabbi asked. They told her yes. Just then PJ was at her side, and he grabbed her hand and pulled her close.

Mario, the head FBI agent, pushed through the men surrounding her and said, "Gabbi, you are a brave lady. You helped save these three girls and took down the biggest trafficking ring around this area. Let me be the first to shake your hand. And if you ever want a job with the police force or even possibly the FBI, you just let me know." Gabbi thanked him and smiled. Michael came over and put his arm around his little girl.

"You and I are going to have a few conversations, my dear, but we can save that for later. I just want you to know how proud I am of you. But if you ever do anything like this again, then you will be grounded for life!" Michael tried to sound harsh, but Gabbi just smiled at him and nodded her head and thanked him. Michael took Gabbi and led her to the driveway, and PJ followed. Eric was already bringing up the car for them. Gabbi wanted to see if she could find her backpack, but the house was now a crime scene, and Michael told her they would find it for her. PJ also assured her she would get it back soon. Before she could get in the car, PJ pulled Gabbi aside.

"Listen, Gabbi, I need to stay and help with all the evidence in this house. You are probably exhausted anyway. Go back to the house with your parents and get some much needed rest. I will come by tomorrow and see you."

Gabbi felt some disappointment that PJ wasn't going to ride back with them. She wasn't going to let this guy slip away from her, but he was right, she was exhausted. She stepped closer to him, and he grabbed her and kissed her full on the lips. Gabbi did not want this to end, but Michael cleared his throat, and PJ looked up to see Anthony, Eric, and Michael all looking at him and not necessarily with happy faces. PJ stepped back from Gabbi and said he had to go. Gabbi looked at Michael and could see he had questions in his eyes. Questions she did not want to answer right now. So she grabbed her father's hand and said, "Let's go see Mom."

As they were getting ready to get in the car, Gabbi stopped as she saw the agents bringing Niko toward their car. Gabbi started walking toward them. Michael and Anthony tried to stop her, but she shrugged them off. She stood right in front of Niko.

"Niko, remember the little baby that was born to Jesse nineteen years ago? Guess what, that is me. My mom was Jesse, and I hope you rot in jail and then in hell for taking her away from me!" With those words said, Gabbi couldn't help herself, and she slapped him across his bloody face. The look of shock and then anger on Niko's face as this played out was worth every second to Gabbi.

The agents pulled Niko back and took him away. Gabbi had a million emotions going through her head. The emotions from everything that had happened over the last few days. The tears started falling from her eyes. She couldn't help it. The tears falling were a representation of her first three years, and they were for her mother, who had died at such a young age after years of being held hostage and trafficked. But most of all, these endless tears were for herself. The missed life and memories she could have had with her mother. All the holidays and birthdays and talks she could have shared but had never been given a chance to. Michael ran to her side and hugged her closely.

"I love you, Gabbi," he whispered. He practically carried her to the car and helped her get in. His arm was around her as soon as the car took off. They all drove back into town, and Gabbi was asleep on Michael's shoulder before they even drove five miles, her tears still wet on her cheek.

Chapter 16

Eric pulled into the hotel parking lot and saw Alysse sitting outside. The minute she saw them pull in, she ran toward the car. Gabbi had just opened her eyes and saw her mother waiting for her to get out of the car. The guilt overwhelmed Gabbi as she saw the expression on her mom's pale face and the look of relief at seeing her daughter safe. As soon as Gabbi was out on the sidewalk, she was in Alysse's arms. She hugged her mom tightly and whispered that she was sorry. Alysse just kept crying and wouldn't let her go.

"Did they hurt you, Gabbi?"

Gabbi assured her mom she was fine. Eric and Michael walked up, and Alysse saw the bloodstained shirt on Michael. Before she could say anything, Michael told Alysse he was fine, just a flesh wound. Alysse insisted he go to the hospital right away. Eric volunteered to take Michael to the hospital to get his arm looked at so Alysse could stay with Gabbi. Michael agreed but pulled Anthony aside to talk to him first.

"Hey, buddy, I need one last favor from you. Could you take Gabbi and Alysse to the house Gabbi is renting and keep an eye on them until I get back?"

Anthony had of course agreed, and he thought it was a better idea they all stayed there anyway. It was more private. Once this story broke, Gabbi would be hounded by reporters, and she had already been through so much. Michael hugged his two favorite women and made sure they were in the car with Anthony safe and sound before he got into the passenger side of the car, as Eric took off to the hospital. Michael sat back in the car and closed his eyes. He thanked God that everything had worked out and Gabbi had not been injured.

He wasn't sure what else she had been through in that house, but he wanted to give her time to rest before he tried to get the whole story from her. Right now he was just happy that this was finally over. Twenty years and Niko's operation was done. This nightmare was finally over. With his arm throbbing from the pain, he let himself just sit back in silence and let the thoughts of Gabbi being found safe sink in.

The next morning, Gabbi opened her eyes and felt confused. Her body felt sore and especially her arms. She looked around and realized she was back at the rental home in Loveland. It all started coming back to her as she sat up in bed. She recalled the last twenty-four hours and felt happy. It was finally over. By some miracle, she had done what she had set out to do.

As much as she thought she would be happy about the revenge, she realized that she had played a part in ending the human trafficking operations here in Loveland. That accomplishment filled her with more joy and happiness than the revenge itself. Her thought went to Lizzie and realized that the best part of this was those three girls that had been kidnapped were now free from a life of slavery. They had their lives back. She realized that her need for revenge had been replaced by her need for action. Gabbi knew the next few days were going to be full of explanations and apologies, but she also realized that she needed to decide what her next steps were. This trip to Colorado had made her want more than her normal life back home. With that thought still in her mind, Gabbi saw Alysse burst through the door, and she was smiling from ear to ear.

"Hey, sweetie, it's almost noon, and I just wanted to make sure you are doing all right."

Gabbi jumped out of bed and realized that her body was feeling a little sore. She rubbed her arms and saw that the smile on her mom's face suddenly turned to one of worry. Gabbi assured Alysse she was fine and told her she was getting up now because she was starving. That made Alysse relax, and she sat down beside her daughter.

"Gabbi, I know this has been a rough time for you, and I want you to know that your father and I are here for you if you need to talk about what happened or about anything that may have happened while you were being held captive."

Gabbi knew what her mom was thinking, and she wanted to put her mind at ease. "Mom, I promise you that nothing happened to me. They did not lay a finger on me at all." The relief that showed on her mom's face caused the guilt to bubble up inside of Gabbi again. She had put her mom through so much. Gabbi walked over, and she put her arms around her mom and hugged her. "I love you, Mom, and I am so sorry that I made you and Dad worry about me. This was something that I had to do."

Alysse hugged her daughter and told her it was all over now. They walked downstairs together, and Gabbi was surprised to see Eric and Anthony there with her father. They were all sitting around the table. There were plates of pancakes and sausage, and Gabbi's stomach started growling at the smell of all these wonderful flavors. They all stopped talking when Gabbi came down. Michael got up and kissed his daughter on the cheek and said good morning. Gabbi greeted everyone with a hug and poured herself a cup of coffee. Gabbi could tell they were all trying to assess how she was doing. She decided to just get it all out so everyone could get back to normal and relax. Gabbi started talking.

"I just want you all to know how much I appreciate you all coming here to find me. I am really sorry that I put all of you through all this worry, but this was something I felt I had to do. I realize now that it could have turned out much worse than it did. And before any of you can give me that speech about thinking things through and how I could have ended up dead or much worse, I want you to know that I do understand all of that. But I do understand that even worse than that is that I could have put all of your lives in danger, and I want you to know I will stop and think before I react in the future. And when I feel I have to go on an adventure and possibly risk my life, I will talk it over with all of you first."

They all nodded their heads in agreement, but every single one of them told her they understood. She walked back over to Eric and Anthony and hugged them again.

"I love both of you, and I will never forget how you dropped everything to help me."

Eric said, "You're family, Gabbi, and we both love you too."

After they all finished their brunch, Eric said his goodbyes as he headed to the airport. He was flying back home to take care of the law firm. Plus he missed his wife, Nikki, and his son. While the police were wrapping up the case against Niko and his men, he knew Michael would be out here in Colorado for a couple more days. But he needed to check in on his clients. Anthony stood up minutes later to leave for town, telling them all that he was going to see what was happening with the investigation, but he would be back later this evening.

While her mom and dad finished their coffee out on the deck, Gabbi went upstairs and showered and got dressed. Michael had told her this morning that the FBI and police would need her down at the police station to get her complete story. She was eager to find out about Niko and James and everything that had happened after they had left. Of course, Alysse and Michael had insisted on going into town with her. Michael had gotten the heads-up from PJ this morning that the news stations were crawling all over the place. Reporters were taking over downtown Loveland. They all wanted to interview the girl that helped take down one of the biggest human trafficking operations around.

The story of the wolves and Gabbi had also leaked out to the press, and that brought even more interest to the story. News channels were reporting the wolf girl had grown up, and she and the wolves had been the ones to take down Niko. When Michael told her this news, Gabbi burst out laughing. After all, the story sounded like something out of a movie. Michael did not want Gabbi to have to go through the media circus like they had years before. PJ had come up with a plan, and Michael had agreed. They decided to keep Gabbi safe and start a rumor that the girl that was friendly with the wolves had left town, and no one was sure where she was headed. The police chief had agreed to this. He was so happy to have shut down this operation that he would agree to anything.

Michael, Alysse, and Gabbi drove into town, and right away you could see all the news trucks parked. There were reporters interviewing people and many just waiting to see who showed up. Michael decided to park at the shopping mall instead of at the police station. This way they could look like regular townspeople walking around. Hopefully it would throw off the newspeople. They walked up the street casually, and Michael had Gabbi and Alysse hurried into the police station through the back door. He waited back a few minutes and followed them in.

Inside there were a few FBI agents and Mario, the one in charge. Gabbi was led into a conference room, and she sat down. Mario asked her to "just start from the beginning, and please don't leave out any detail." So Gabbi told her story. Once she started talking, she couldn't stop. The words just started coming and coming, and she found herself telling everything about her adventure. She realized it felt good to get her story out.

Michael and Alysse listened to the whole story, and at times Gabbi would glance at them and see different emotions displayed on their faces. They sat quietly through it all, and when Gabbi was done, Alysse came up behind her and hugged her. The park ranger that was in charge asked Gabbi about the wolves. She had looked at Michael to see how much she should tell them. Michael just nodded at her. Gabbi ended up telling them a shortened version of how she had always had a connection with animals. Smiling, she told them how she had saved the baby wolf from the poacher and how the wolf pack had seemed to accept her as a friend. She also went on to tell them that she had a few other interactions with them.

Everyone was silent for a minute when she told this story. The silence was interrupted by PJ walking through the door. Everyone in the room saw the connection between Gabbi and PJ. His eyes were locked on Gabbi, and he smiled. Walking over to Alysse, he introduced himself and then shook hands with Michael. After Gabbi gave her statement, Mario, the FBI chief, asked her if she would be staying around town for a while in case they needed any other information. Gabbi told him that she wasn't sure of her immediate plans, but she would always come back to help if they needed her. Mario also asked her if she would be able to come back for the trial. Gabbi said she wouldn't miss it for the world.

As they were leaving the station, PJ stopped Gabbi. "Hey, Gabbi, I know you have been through a lot the last few days, but I was really hoping we could talk."

Gabbi took PJ by the elbow and led him a few steps away from everyone. "PJ, how about dinner tonight?" she asked him. PJ smiled at this and said he would pick her up at seven. Gabbi felt the excitement fill her body with the thought of seeing PJ tonight. Now with her plan completed and successful, she could concentrate on PJ. Just the two of them. She knew she owed him an apology, but she felt confident that he would understand why she had used him for information. Gabbi knew what she wanted to do with her life now. There was no doubt; she was sure of it.

Knowing that, she needed to have a talk with her parents and persuade them. She had been thinking about everything that happened, and she felt like it had happened for a reason. Nineteen years ago she was a victim of circumstance, and she believed that this was all part of her destiny. Gabbi had always been a strong believer in "everything happens for a reason." Interrupting her thoughts, Michael walked over to them and asked if she was ready to go back to the house. Gabbi nodded her head yes and said her goodbye to PJ. On the way back to the cabin, Gabbi was consumed in her thoughts of her future. The car ride was quiet. It seemed everyone had something on their mind.

Gabbi spent the rest of the day with her mom. They went for lunch at a local restaurant, and Gabbi took her on a little hike up to her favorite off-trail path. Michael had gone into town with Anthony to take care of some details. Alysse had enjoyed the day with her daughter and was so thankful that she still had a daughter to spend time with. She had seen her daughter's interaction with that young policeman PJ. Not wanting to interfere, but being very curious, she had asked Gabbi about him, and Gabbi just said that he was a friend. Not wanting to tell her mom too much right now, she added that he had found her the cabin to stay at. Knowing her mom wanted more,

Gabbi turned and smiled and told her that they had hung out a few times.

Alysse had jumped up and down with joy as she asked, "Gabbi, did you go on a date? Where did you go? What did you wear?"

Gabbi started laughing so hard. "Mom, please, I will admit that I like spending time with PJ."

Alysse felt there was more, but she knew Gabbi enough to know that it wouldn't do any good to push her. She would go into more details about him when she felt ready. Alysse was thrilled that Gabbi had a boy that she was interested in. She was starting to think that Gabbi would never want to date and possibly never get married and have children. Alysse wanted to hope that there would be grandchildren in her future. But she couldn't help but worry because this boy that held her interest was in Colorado, and her daughter lived in Ohio. A long-distance romance would not be the right way for a girl as young as Gabbi. Alysse decided to put her worries on hold and enjoy this day with her daughter.

As they finished the hike and returned to the car, Alysse told Gabbi that this area of Colorado was so beautiful. Gabbi had agreed and said that she felt like this was home for her. Alysse had been a little upset about that comment, but after all that Gabbi had been through her young life, maybe she was right. This was where it had all started for her daughter. When they arrived back at the house, Gabbi had said she needed to take care of a few things and retreated to her bedroom. Michael and Anthony had returned to the house a few hours after they had arrived from the hike. When he walked into the front door, Michael saw the sparkle back in his wife's eyes and knew she was happy. He was eager to get back home and have a normal life with Gabbi and Alysse.

Anthony had decided that he was flying out tonight and would still be involved in the investigation and trial of Niko and his men. Knowing that they all had an interest in this trial, Anthony assured Michael that he would update him and keep him posted. He was trying to rally the prosecutor to get Niko life in prison at the very least. Anthony asked Michael when they would head back to Ohio. He knew that Michael and Alysse would want to drive back to Ohio with Gabbi instead of flying back with him. They wouldn't want to let her out of their sight after everything that had happened these past few days. Michael had looked at his beautiful wife and daughter and smiled.

"As pretty as this state of Colorado is, I am eager to get back home as soon as possible."

Anthony walked out onto the deck where Michael was busy grilling out the steaks. Pulling out a chair, he sat down and admired the view from the deck. His plan had been to fly out earlier in the day, but Alysse had invited him to stay for dinner, and when she told him she was grilling out some steaks, he knew he had to stay. This worked out even better for him, not only would he get a great home-cooked meal, but he could say his goodbyes to Gabbi anyway.

Michael was getting Anthony another beer when he almost dropped it to the ground. There was Gabbi walking into the room looking like a supermodel. Trying to hide the shocked look on his face, Michael couldn't believe what he was seeing. This was not the way Gabbi usually looked. Gabbi had always looked like, well, just Gabbi. He exchanged glances with Alysse, and he could tell she was feeling the same way.

"Gabbi, you look beautiful!" Alysse cried out. Alysse looked at her little girl. She was all grown up now. She had her hair curled with wavy big curls falling halfway down her back, and she was wearing makeup, complete with pink lipstick. Gabbi had on her jeans but had a nice black blouse tucked in and she had on a pair of nicer boots. Smiling, she saw that her daughter was glowing.

Anthony stood up and hugged Gabbi. As he pulled her over to hug her, he whispered in her ear, "I think that you put your parents into shock!"

Gabbi chuckled and grabbed her jacket. "I am going to go out to dinner with PJ tonight. We really need to talk, but I won't be late."

Before either of them had a chance to say anything, the doorbell rang. Michael got up to answer it and ushered PJ in.

"So, PJ. you came by to update us on the case?" Michael couldn't resist getting PJ a little nervous. Gabbi gave her dad a look and rolled her eyes. PJ wasn't sure what to say and just looked at Gabbi. Gabbi took his hand and said her goodbyes to her parents and thanked Anthony again for everything he did to help her. PJ opened the door for Gabbi, and they stepped outside.

PJ and Gabbi made small talk while they drove. A couple blocks away, PJ pulled into a driveway of a small cabin that was nestled back in the woods. Through the moonlight, Gabbi could see the outline of the mountains behind the cabin. Curious, she looked at PJ, and he just smiled at her, not saying a word. After parking the car, he walked around and opened her car door and took her hand.

"Welcome to my humble abode," PJ said. Gabbi smiled. So this was where PJ lived. PJ turned to Gabbi and said, "I hope you don't mind if we don't go out to a restaurant tonight. Instead I made you dinner, and I thought it would be nice if we could sit and eat under the moonlight."

Gabbi was ecstatic. She had really wanted to talk to PJ in private, not in a public place. It was going to be hard telling him that her parents were planning on leaving Colorado in a day or two, and they were driving back with her. She wanted to be able to tell PJ goodbye in person. Tears were threatening to fall even thinking about leaving PJ. Gabbi wasn't going to let anything ruin tonight, so she put the sad thoughts out of her head. PJ unlocked the door and stepped back to let her walk in first. She walked inside, and the cabin was just how she would picture PJ's house. It was decorated with just the basics, but the furniture was rustic looking. It was small, but there was a big fireplace in the middle of the great room, and there were large windows along the back.

"This is amazing," Gabbi told PJ. She was even more impressed when he took her hand and led her out back on the deck. There were candles lit on the table that was set for two, and the moonlight was shining down, making it seem like they were in a spotlight. A magical spotlight for two. He had even put a little vase on the table with some flowers, and there were two wineglasses set out. The solar lights that were set up around the deck sparkled with light. Even more lights danced in the slight breeze along the path that led to the forest. Gabbi felt the familiar feeling of peace when she glanced beyond the path and saw the forest with the mountains behind it. How could she ever leave Colorado? It felt all wrong. She had to stay. She took a deep breath and smiled. Hearing the country music playing softly, she looked at PJ and said, "This is so much nicer than any romantic restaurant!"

He pulled out Gabbi's seat for her and she sat down. "I am glad you like it here, Gabbi," PJ replied. He poured her a glass of wine, and she looked at him in mock surprise. PJ laughed and pretended to pour it back. She stopped him instantly.

"PJ I may not be twenty-one yet, but I assure you I can drink a glass of wine."

They both laughed, and PJ went in to bring out dinner. Gabbi was impressed again. He had made chicken piccata and rice with a big green salad. They laughed and ate dinner, and when they were done, PJ went in and brought out two plates of fresh strawberries with whipped cream on top. Gabbi held her stomach and said, "If I didn't know better, I would think you are trying to get me fat with all this delicious food." PJ just smiled at her and put his hand on top of her hand. Gabbi felt herself blush at the touch of his hand. She knew they needed to talk, and she wanted to do it now so they could put it behind them.

As she stood up and walked over to the deck, she could hear a wolf howl in the distance. The familiar sound made her feel relaxed. She leaned against the railing. As she did that, she felt PJ come up behind her and put his arms around her waist and pull her close. She turned around and faced him. Before she could start explaining why she had lied to him, he kissed her. Gabbi couldn't help the moan that came out of her mouth. Wrapping her arms tightly around PJ's neck, she kissed him back.

After a few minutes, she pulled back from his body, and said, "PJ, I am sorry that I used you to get information about Niko. And I am really sorry that I didn't tell you the whole truth about why I came to Colorado. I don't want you to think I don't care about you at all, because I do. You're the first guy that I ever had an interest in." Gabbi paused and smiled at PJ. "I have to admit, at first when I met you, I didn't want anything to do with you. I was on a mission, and that mission did not include a handsome young guy." She laughed.

"But when I found out that you were working on the human trafficking case, I couldn't help it. I needed as much information as I could get and as quickly as possible. I knew my parents would be flying in with the whole US Army."

PJ took his hand and traced the side of her face. "I know, Gabbi. I know your whole story, and I am not blaming you. You're very passionate about what you want, and thank God that it all worked out for the best. I have to admit, though, when I first found out that you were on this mission to take down the whole trafficking operation from the start, I did feel used. I really like you, Gabbi, and I don't know how or when, but I am going to have a relationship with you. It is not my wish to leave Colorado. My heart is in this state and of course my brother and his family too. But dammit, Gabbi, if I have to follow you to Ohio and become a midwestern farmer, then I will."

Gabbi burst out laughing and couldn't stop. PJ was a little offended by this, until she said she could not picture him as a farmer and that he needed to do a little more research about Ohio because not everyone there was a farmer. PJ smiled at that and kissed her again.

"Am I really the first guy you have been interested in?" he asked, pulling her closer. She nodded her head yes and put her arms around him. All these feelings she was experiencing were new to her. It was a feeling of complete happiness and belonging. This was fate, she thought to herself. Her body was telling her that she wanted more. She wanted something more than kisses. Even though she had never been with any guy before and she had no experience, she knew she wanted more. The butterflies were dancing in her stomach. She leaned into PJ until their bodies were as close as they could possibly be. This time PJ groaned. And before she knew what had happened, he picked her up in his arms and carried her into the house and up the stairs to his bedroom. Gabbi knew that it was finally going to happen, and as she was put on the bed, she closed her eyes and pulled PJ down with her.

Gabbi woke up a few hours later to her phone ringing. She went to reach for it and realized where she was. She was curled up against PJ, and she smiled. This was where she belonged. Their night together was everything she could have dreamed. Moving very slowly, she got up and put her clothes back on, remembering how it felt when PJ was slowly taking them off. Every brush of his fingers against her bare skin had felt like electricity. Interrupting her thoughts, the phone rang again, so she ran into the other room to answer. The phone stopped ringing before she could answer it. She looked at the missed call and realized it was her mom. Looking at the time, she saw it was well after midnight and knew that her parents were probably worried about her. She texted her mom that she would be home soon.

When she turned around to get PJ, he was standing in front of her with just his boxers on. She smiled at him, and he came over and kissed her. There was worry in his eyes as he said softly, "I am sorry, Gabbi, if things went too fast for you. I had no intention of us sleeping together when I planned this evening." She hugged PJ and told him that it was fine. More than fine. PJ whispered in her ear, "I wish you could spend the night and wake up in my arms in the morning."

Gabbi felt a wave of sadness come over her. She would be leaving soon, and that meant leaving PJ. She didn't want to go, but she realized she had put her parents through enough right now, and it wouldn't be fair to them if she stayed here permanently. At least not right now. PJ went to go get dressed and came back with his keys.

"Let's get you back to your place before your dad and his friends hunt me down," PJ said. He was kidding but only partially. They drove the short way to the cabin where Gabbi was staying. The whole drive back, PJ had his hand on Gabbi's knee. As they pulled into the driveway and parked, PJ came around and opened the door for her and stopped her before she could walk up to the door. "I meant what I said, Gabbi. I don't want to lose you." He kissed her and took her hand to walk her up to the door. Gabbi didn't want this night to end, so she stood at the door for a minute. They stood there hugging under the moonlight, and in the distance Gabbi could hear the far-away howling of the wolves.

Michael and Alysse were sitting at the table eating breakfast when Gabbi came down. She was expecting questions, but surprisingly none came her way. Alysse smiled and said good morning and asked her how her date was. Gabbi said it was nice and noticed her dad look up at her for a brief second, but he just smiled and said good morning. Gabbi knew that it had to be hard for her parents to keep from asking questions about PJ. But she was glad she didn't have to try and explain what she was feeling. She wasn't even sure what she was feeling. Michael got up and kissed Gabbi on the cheek.

"Today we have to go downtown and finish up the paperwork, and they have some additional questions for you before we leave. Are you up for it?"

Gabbi stopped at the words "before we leave to go home." She felt pure terror at those words but managed to get out, "Yes, of course I am up for it, but when are we leaving to go home?"

Michael told her that he wanted to start the drive back tomorrow morning. He went on to tell her that he needed to get back to work, and he wanted Gabbi back home before the media figured out who she was. So far, the media was only speculating about the wolf girl that helped stop the longest-standing human trafficking operation in this state. Michael had met with authorities, and they were all under the same conclusion that it would be best for Gabbi if she didn't have to be pulled into the media circus. She had been through enough.

Michael noticed the look on Gabbi's face as she blurted out, "Why do we have to leave so soon? I was hoping to have at least another week here."

Alysse came over and put her arm around her daughter and said, "You have been through a lot, and trust me, sweetie, you will feel better when you're back at home and can continue on with your life."

Gabbi went upstairs to get dressed without saying a word. The whole car ride to the police station was quiet. Alysse tried to make some small talk, but Gabbi just wasn't in the mood for it. When they arrived in town, they parked the car like last time and walked to the back of the police station. Michael noticed that the news crews were still hanging around, and he didn't want them guessing Gabbi's identity. They walked into the station, and Gabbi was totally surprised at what was waiting for her. The policemen and a few FBI agents were all standing and clapping for her as she walked into the room.

She noticed PJ in the back of the room, and he was clapping with a big smile on his face. The police chief came forward and presented Gabbi with a plaque and a handshake.

"Gabbi, you are one brave girl!" he started saying. "Human trafficking has unfortunately been increasing every year. Every state in the US has seen numbers increase. In the United States alone 3.8 million adults and 1.0 million children are trafficked for commercial sexual exploitation, changing the life of that child or adult forever and tearing apart the families of these victims. This particular operation, with Niko being the head man, had been eluding both the FBI and police force for years. Gabbi, you have helped to bring down this organization with your fearless actions, and we all owe you a debt of gratitude."

Gabbi was speechless but felt honored and proud. Holding the plaque up, she thanked everyone and said that no one was happier to see Niko behind bars along with the rest of his men than her. All of a sudden a girl walked up to Gabbi with her parents following behind. Gabbi almost didn't recognize the girl. A smile broke out on her face as she realized who it was. It was Lizzie, the little girl who was rescued from Niko's hideout. With tears in her eyes, she ran up to Gabbi and hugged her tightly. The tears were streaming from her eyes as she was thanking Gabbi. The emotions from seeing this little girl being able to live her life again instead of being held captive made Gabbi start crying too. Just the thought of this young girl being captured and sold like she was nothing more than merchandise made her blood boil.

The whole room was silent. Everyone was touched by this little girl who could have had a much different life if Gabbi hadn't helped them arrest Niko and the rest of them. The whole room started clapping again, and the police chief brought Lizzie's parents over to Gabbi to introduce them. They hugged her and thanked her for saving their little girl. Gabbi posed for a few pictures with them and promised to keep in touch with Lizzie. Michael and Alysse came up and hugged their daughter.

"We are so proud of you, Gabbi. We wish you hadn't put your life in danger, but still so proud of you."

Gabbi wiped her tears, and the chief came over with PJ. He told Gabbi that they would need her to come back to Colorado and testify, and she agreed, of course. He told them they had arrested three men, including James and Niko. The captain was gleaming with satisfaction when he told them that they also confiscated two computers and were sure that they would be able to make some arrests and hopefully shut down some of the scumbags that think it was okay to buy people for their own pleasure. Gabbi was even more happy to hear that information. After all these years, this operation would be shut down. Gabbi let herself think of Jesse and how happy she would be to hear this.

PJ waited patiently with Gabbi until they were alone and hugged her close and also congratulated her. "I am so proud of you. Right from the beginning you told me you could take care of yourself, and you were right." Gabbi smiled and thanked him. She then looked PJ in the eyes and took his hands and held them as she told him that they were leaving tomorrow, driving back to Ohio. PJ took Gabbi's hand and pulled her out back. His voice was low and sounded sad when he replied, "I didn't think you would leave so soon. I know you will be back for the trial, but I don't want to wait that long. Gabbi, stay, please."

Gabbi felt her eyes tear up again. "I can't stay right now, PJ. My parents would be devastated. But I promise you I will be back. Just give me some time to figure things out. I need to think things through."

PJ looked devastated, but he told Gabbi he understood. "Let me see you tonight then, one last date."

Gabbi wanted to say yes, but she knew that one more date would make it so much harder to leave him. She shook her head no. "I think it is better for both of us if we say goodbye now. It will make it harder for both of us to say goodbye if we spend more time together. Besides, I need to pack and thank your brother for lending me the house."

She saw her parents walk out of the police station. They walked over, and they said goodbye to PJ and told Gabbi they would meet her by the car. Before they left, Michael thanked PJ for all his help and patted him on the shoulder, telling him if he ever needed anything to let him know. As they walked away, Gabbi leaned in to kiss PJ, and she felt the tears start to fall uncontrollably. Her voice was soft as she tried to get the words out.

"Goodbye, PJ, thank you for everything. I promise that I will keep in touch."

Before he could respond, Gabbi turned and ran to the car that her parents had pulled up in. PJ stood there feeling helpless. He felt that he had just lost the only girl that had ever mattered to him. The girl that he was falling in love with. He watched them drive off in the car until it was out of sight, and he turned around and walked back into the police station.

Chapter 17

The sun was shining into the bedroom, and PJ turned over onto his side and pulled the covers up to his eyes. It was Saturday, the day Gabbi was leaving for Ohio. He normally would be up and doing a shift as a park ranger, but he had called in sick today. He told his boss that he just wasn't feeling that well, but he promised him that he would be in tomorrow. PJ wanted nothing more than to erase the pain he felt when he thought of what he lost. One day of rest was what he needed. A day to try to forget the girl that had come into his life like a whirlwind and turning it upside down. PJ didn't feel like getting up today, but he wasn't the type of guy that would waste a whole day feeling sorry for himself either.

Reaching his hand over to the other side of the bed, remembering Gabbi lying beside him with her body curled up against him. Closing his eyes tight, he told himself he needed to snap out of it. If it was meant to be, then they would reconnect. Maybe after a few days, he would call her. Gabbi had been through a lifetime of grief, and she was only nineteen. As hard as it would be to wait, he would have to give her time. Glancing at the clock, PJ saw it was almost noon. He never slept this late. Just when he was about to make the decision to go back to sleep, he heard the pounding on his front door. Deciding to ignore the door, he rolled over. After all, it was probably his brother checking in with him, wanting to know about Gabbi and what happened. This was a conversation he couldn't do right now. Sighing with relief when the pounding stopped, he tried not to feel guilty about ignoring his brother.

All of a sudden, PJ jumped out of bed when he heard the back patio door open. Did he leave it open? What the hell, was someone breaking in? Grabbing his gun, he quietly ran down the steps and saw the patio door partially open. Looking around, he didn't see anyone. Carefully, he went over to the door and closed it, and when he turned back around, Gabbi was standing in his living room in front of him.

"Gabbi what are you doing here?" PJ was startled to see her. Not wanting to waste the time to answer his question, she ran over to him and jumped into his arms. She started kissing him, and he lifted her up in his arms and held her close. Was he dreaming? If this was a dream, he didn't want it to end. He stopped and put Gabbi down on her feet. PJ asked her, "What is going on, I thought you were well on your way to Ohio by now?"

Gabbi took PJ's hand and led him to the couch. After they both sat down, she went on to explain how they were all ready to go when she realized that she couldn't. She told PJ how she had turned around and told her parents that she needed to talk to them. Startled and worried, her parents sat down with her, and she had carefully explained how she needed to stay here right now. Telling her parents that this was her destiny. So much had happened, and the arrest of Niko and his operation was finally closure for her. PJ sat quietly and listened to Gabbi explain what happened.

"So your parents were fine with you staying here in Colorado?"

Gabbi took PJ's hands in hers and said, "No, they were not. But I told my parents that I was going to stay and go to school here. This is where I needed to be. I have been thinking about everything that had happened and realized that I needed to do more to help stop human trafficking. After explaining all this to my parents, I told them of my plan of getting my degree in criminal justice at the University of Northern Colorado, right here in Loveland. That I realized I would like to eventually work for the FBI. I also told them that I wanted to start a support group for victims of human trafficking. It took them a while to agree to this, but I had a plan, and they saw how much this means to me. They also know that I need to be close to the area where the wolf pack lives. My wolf pack." Gabbi stopped talking and put her hand on PJ's leg and started smiling as she continued, "Oh, and by the way, I assured my father that you would be watching out for me. He had raised his eyebrows at that, but I gave him your number, and I am pretty sure you can expect a call. Probably a call every week."

PJ made a face at that comment. Pulling Gabbi into his arms and holding her tight, he told her in between kisses that he couldn't be happier and that he would help her achieve her plans. Looking into Gabbi's beautiful blue eyes, he asked, "So are you staying in my brother's house?"

Gabbi smiled and shrugged her shoulders as she told him that she was homeless. She had checked out of the house with her parents. "Do you think I could rent it long-term from him? I will have to get a job here in town. There is college money that I have, but I don't want my parents paying for everything."

PJ pulled her onto his lap and told her that his brother will not rent it long-term to her because she will be moving in with him. "Someone has to keep you out of trouble, and I guess there is no better person than myself to do that." He laughed. Gabbi kissed him again and promised to help out with the cleaning and cooking. "So, roomie," PJ said, "what would you like to do today besides move you in?"

Gabbi replied, "I really was hoping you would go with me for a hike up the trails. I want to see if the wolves are doing okay." PJ agreed and asked her if she wanted to go right now. Gabbi winked at PJ and said that she was hoping they could have a nap before they go. After all, they needed to rest up for all that hiking. As Gabbi faked a yawn, PJ grabbed her and threw her over his shoulder before she could even finish the sentence.

"Your wish is my command, beautiful," PJ told her. Feeling like his world was suddenly complete, he carried her upstairs to the bedroom. As he set Gabbi gently down on the bed and started showering her with kisses, he whispered softly in her ear, "What is meant to be will always find a way."

The End

About the Author

TJ Ritossa has always known that when you read a book, you leave your old life behind and journey to a new one. With her debut novel, *Fate of the Stolen*, she brings her readers to a new world of romance and excitement. She has been a longtime advocate against human trafficking, which has inspired her to write *Fate of the Stolen*. TJ Ritossa resides in Ohio with her husband and her chubby puggle, Rocky. She is the mother of four wonderful children. She would love to hear from her readers. Visit her website at tjritossa.com.

CPSIA information can be obtained
at www.ICGtesting.com
Printed in the USA
BVHW031306010921
615831BV00009B/47